Jane Marlow studied French before going on to drama school and working as an actress. Now a journalist and writer, she has an MA in Women's Studies from the University of Westminster and has also exhibited her photography. Born in Hertfordshire in 1966, she grew up in Dorset and lives in London.

Maddie & Anna's Big Picture

JANE MARLOW

First published 2002 by Diva Books,
an imprint of Millivres Prowler Limited, part of the Millivres Prowler Group,
Worldwide House, 116-134 Bayham Street, London NW1 0BA
www.divamag.co.uk

A catalogue record for this book is available from the British Library

ISBN 1 873741 71 5

Printed and bound in Finland by WS Bookwell

Distributed in the UK and Europe by Airlift Book Company,
8 The Arena, Mollison Avenue,
Enfield, Middlesex EN3 7NJ
Telephone: 020 8804 0400
Distributed in North America by Consortium,
1045 Westgate Drive, St Paul, MN 55114-1065
Telephone: 1 800 283 3572
Distributed in Australia by Bulldog Books,
PO Box 300, Beaconsfield, NSW 2014

To Louise

25 DECEMBER 1998

When night is falling

"Do you think Morecambe & Wise are the ultimate in Christmas entertainment?"

Anna didn't bother to heave her turkey-stuffed carcass round to make eye contact. "You what?"

"You know," said Maddie, swinging her legs over the side of the armchair to face her partner. "Do you think *The Morecambe & Wise Christmas Special* is Christmas TV's defining moment? The climax, the apex, the ultimate festive televisual experience?"

Anna glanced at the clock on the mantelpiece. It was only just gone eight but it had been a long day and, although she admired Maddie's effort to make conversation, a grunt was all she could muster. Once she had an idea in her mind, however, Maddie was nothing if not tenacious. Especially when the 'ideas' were being fuelled by half a bottle of Dubonnet and an armoury of Snowballs.

There was a pause. The two women contemplated the comedy duo performing in front of them before Anna replied: "No." Another pause was filled with another round of cheek slapping and spectacle wiggling from the box in the corner.

"It's got to be *The Sound of Music*, hasn't it really? Or *The Wizard of Oz*. Red shoes and wimples – that's when you really know Christmas has arrived," concluded Maddie.

"Mmmm. Wanna watch something else then?" Anna was beginning to find the overall beigeness of the show rather challenging but it wasn't quite irritating enough to make her hoist herself off the sofa to do anything about it. She knew if she could whip up enough enthusiasm in Maddie, she might even get her to make a fresh round of drinks while she was on her feet. "I think French & Saunders are on at nine-thirty..." Anna threw this piece of information into the arena as bait. She suspected Maddie wouldn't be able to resist checking the facts.

"Chuck me over the TV guide then." She was right.

Trying to put off the awful moment when movement became inevitable, Anna's swivel-eye radar located the magazine – which had handily doubled as a coaster, a tray, a mat and a dishcloth over the past couple of days – right at the edge of her field of vision. Her plan hadn't taken into account the possibility or her being nearer to the guide; she certainly hadn't banked on having to move. Anna weighed up the amount of effort she would expend reeling it in with her foot as opposed to fighting her lethargy, moving her whole body and retrieving it manually.

"Come on," urged Maddie.

Anna groaned with the effort of it all. She knew Maddie would accuse her of being lazy next, so, to head off any un-Christmas-like accusations, she tried to distract her with a cute but helpless smile.

"Pulling stupid faces isn't going to work!"

Anna tried even harder to look pathetic.

"Stop it! You look like the bleedin' TV Hound!" Maddie laughed, arranged the remote controls carefully in the Hound's pouches and ran her hand lovingly over its needlecorded body, which anchored it to the arm of the chair.

Anna's early evening torpor didn't prevent her from laughing at the monstrousness of this item. Their friend Andy had made them promise it would remain in use for the duration of the holiday season. At least.

"I can't believe we only bought Andy and Phil a book of pictures of people with mullets, and they gave us this beautiful thing," said Anna. "I feel shamed and humbled."

They laughed wearily and sank back into their chairs. Anna waited for Maddie to remember the issue of the TV. She hadn't banked on it being this hard to goad her into action.

"Do you know what I fancy?" Anna punted the question high into the air – having spent at least half an hour without food or drink, she was beginning to feel peckish. "Some Stilton and a drop of that port your mum gave us." She glanced over at Maddie to see if the combination of French & Saunders and port would be enough to get her on her feet.

"Hmmm. Sounds tempting."

Maddie dumped the magazine and remotes on her girlfriend's lap en route to the kitchen and Anna congratulated herself on her extraordinary powers of manipulation before settling back to plan the evening's further viewing. She knew that in the safety of the kitchen Maddie would be cursing her slothfulness but, for once, it was total exhaustion that pinned her to the sofa, not what was usually described as her 'innate ability to manage the workload of others'. The pre-Christmas frenzy in the office coupled with the glut of parties she had been obliged to attend had taken their toll.

She was comforted by the familiar sounds of food preparation coming from the kitchen, followed by the draught excluder being jammed back into place as Maddie came down the hallway with a tray of cheese and port. She put it down next to the sofa and went over to poke the fire. The flickering flames in the grate made the fairy lights on the tree look even more fairy-like and Anna shivered as the warmth from the revitalised flames made her realise just how cold she had become.

"Should have got more logs," Anna observed as Maddie wedged the last of their stock in the grate.

"Why don't I bring the duvet in?" suggested Maddie, foregoing her usual tirade about the folly of renting a place that the previous tenants had referred to simply as 'The Fridge'.

"That's a brilliant idea."

Until that moment, everything had followed the Christmas Day routine that Anna knew would be going on at her parents' house: up around ten o'clock, cocktails at half past eleven, presents at eleven-thirty-five, more cocktails at quarter to twelve, family phone calls at three, turkey at four, TV intermittently throughout. That pattern was great but it was the 'lying with your girlfriend on the sofa at eight-thirty' that she had always felt was lacking.

Maddie pulled on another pair of socks, transferred the TV Hound to the arm of the sofa and assumed her usual place in Anna's arms.

"Have you found out what's on at the pictures tomorrow?" asked Maddie, as she wiped a blob of pickle off the duvet and sucked her finger noisily.

"It's a toss-up between *The Mighty* and *Enemy of the State*. What do you reckon?"

"The Sharon Stone thing sounds good…"

"Umm." Anna knew she was meant to agree so she kept quiet about her own choice. When it came to it, she'd just tell Maddie that *The Mighty* was sold out. Maddie would believe her. She always did.

"I don't think I've ever been to the cinema on Boxing Day before…"

When the cheese had been discarded and Maddie's fidgeting had stopped, it occurred to Anna that they fitted together as snugly as the crisp wrapped around the peanut of the Shanghai nut she was biting into. She smiled at her own ability to liken her relationship to a savoury snack. But it was apt. Their names were associated in their friends' minds like the best collocations: 'bunch of flowers', 'stick of celery', 'heinous crime', 'Maddie and Anna'. They had become inextricably linked. Anna breathed in the aroma of her partner's shampoo-fresh fair hair. The short, idealistic blonde and the tall, easy-going brunette. Perfect counter-balancers. That's how Anna thought other people categorised them and it was how she liked to see them.

They both slurped their port.

"No Advocat left?" asked Anna, surprised that Maddie had abandoned her favourite Christmas tipple.

"Yes. I just didn't fancy it."

"No?"

"To tell the truth, I don't like it that much."

"You're telling me that now, after we schlepped round six different supermarkets to get some!" exclaimed Anna.

"Yeah. I know. It's mad, isn't it?"

"Mad? Bleedin' typical, I'd say!"

"No, it's a tradition, that's all. Christmas morning we open our presents and have a Snowball."

"You're not wishing you'd gone to your mum's, are you, Mads?" Anna pulled her lover in tighter to her chest.

"God no! I'm having the best Christmas ever."

"Yes, me too. Tell me again why we haven't done this before?" They had been having the 'shall we stay in London for Christmas' conversation ever since they met, but she couldn't resist one final dig. "I suppose we have only been together the six years..."

"Come on, Anna. Don't start all that again. You saw how disappointed Mum was when I told her I wasn't going home for Christmas this year."

"I know, sweetheart. But I'm pleased you've made the break."

"Yeah. I know what you mean. It's great being just the two of us."

"It's romantic, isn't it?" Anna's eyes were welling up with happy tears. "I really feel like we're turning a corner, don't you?" she said as she stroked her lover's hair.

Maddie smiled and for once agreed with her. Anna snuggled down, comforted, her eyelids beginning to droop, then she felt Maddie stir.

"This is perfect," Anna murmured contentedly. "I feel all warm and glowing inside."

"Yeah, me too."

Anna jumped as Maddie suddenly levered herself off the sofa.

"Where are you going now?"

"To get the Gaviscon."

Topsy turvy

"I can't remember the last time I didn't have to do any food preparation on Christmas Day," said Sheila, as she relaxed into the corner of the settee.

The way her arm swung sideways so that her hand hovered over the chocolate box on the occasional table, seemingly independent from the rest of her body, put her husband in mind of a crane on a construction site. He watched as the hand was lowered and allowed to pluck another chocolate from the box. Unfortunately, the effort of such detailed observation made his eyelids droop with fresh tiredness. He felt his chin disappear into the folds of skin that were meant to be his neck. Through slit eyes, he saw the crumbs from shop-bought mince pies nestling on his new lambswool V-neck, and his folded arms rising and falling with the rhythm of his full to bursting belly. Leaving the question unanswered, he fell into a deep and immediate sleep.

"Malcolm!" Sheila barked. His wife had had years to perfect the precise tone of voice that was guaranteed to rouse him when conversation was required: urgent and piercing, with a hint of Sybil Fawlty.

"Yes, dear." A disorientated Malcolm snuffled into consciousness.

"I was just saying I can't remember the last time I didn't have to prepare a meal on Christmas Day."

"Oh, yes. Wonderful, isn't it." He sat up in his chair and pinched the bridge of his nose in an effort to wake himself up. "I think we did the right thing going out for a meal, don't you?" Malcolm had become an expert 'hedger' over the years. He rarely committed himself to an opinion before it had been approved by his wife. This way he avoided confrontation and an easy life was had by all.

"Absolutely," said Sheila enthusiastically (though he recalled her having said that the roast spuds weren't up to much and the stuffing was unimaginative).

"Shame Maddie and Tom couldn't come though, eh?" Malcolm was sure he couldn't go wrong with this comment. Family was even more important to Sheila than her Marks & Spencer charge card.

"I suppose it was a shame, but, to be honest, I couldn't have been more relieved when Maddie said she was staying in London."

Malcolm turned to look at his wife as she dipped into the chocolates once again. He watched in amazement as she peeled off a squeaky, cellophane wrapper and tossed it back into the box. She missed. It fell on the carpet. "Whoopsie!" she said flippantly. Malcolm's eyes were wide as she continued: "Maddie's thirty-one now and she's come home for Christmas every single year since she went off to art college..." Sheila popped the chocolate into her mouth and stored it in her cheek while she spoke, sucking occasionally to draw off excess saliva "... so it's about time she did her own thing."

Malcolm looked at his wife's brandy glass and then at the bottle on the coffee table in front of them. She hadn't been drinking excessively. He felt confused. He had to do some quick thinking to adapt to the new path their well-worn conversation had taken.

"And I suppose Tom will come home when he runs out of clean Y-fronts!" Malcolm laughed and waited nervously for his wife's response.

"Exactly. It's not as if we never see them and I think it's nice for Maddie and her gir... that... her partn–"

"Anna."

"Yes, Anna, to be together over Christmas."

"Just like it has been for us," enthused Malcolm, who was entering new conversational territory, willy-nilly.

"Yes. Just like us," agreed Sheila, although the words seemed to stick in her throat. She reached for her glass and chugged back the remaining brandy. "A little splash more, darling?" she asked as her fingers closed round the neck of the bottle. Malcolm nodded and held out his glass. He stared at the hefty measure lapping at the side.

"Shall I put the television on, She?" he asked. He wasn't sure how long he could keep up with Sheila's unexpected behaviour and he knew her televisual likes and dislikes inside out. "I think that comedy duo you like are on at half past nine." Malcolm consulted the *Radio Times*. "Yes. Here we are. French & –"

Sheila groaned. "Ugh! Not them!"

"But we always watch them…" Malcolm was feeling more insecure by the minute.

"They're Maddie's favourite, not mine. To tell you the truth, I can't stand them."

Malcolm found a documentary about the making of *River Dance* and hoped Truth and Honesty would not rear their ugly heads in his house again that evening. He held his breath. The idea of finding out that his wife's love of Irish dancing had also been a sham made his right eyelid twitch with fear.

Stranger than paradise

Kat was transfixed by the sight of her own eyelashes hanging off her sleep-heavy lids. This phenomenon was so diverting that it took her several minutes to realise she had woken up in a room that was totally unfamiliar. The duvet drawn up round her body smelt nice – clean, which was good – but it wasn't the smell of her own favoured blend of Ariel liquid and Comfort Silk. She opened her eyes more fully and sized up the room. *Open plan apartment; main living space 30′ x 25′; galley kitchen with en suite dining area…* her eyes fell on a door. It didn't look like the front door and she could see no shower tucked in a corner... *Separate bathroom/shower room; this is an exceptionally spacious apartment...* She looked at the cracked paintwork on the ceiling and the flaking gloss on the frames of the large windows... *the interior of which needs a little attention, but boasts excellent views of...* she'd have to fill in that gap when she finally got out of bed, for she had no idea where the cab had taken her after the party. The taste of stale cigarettes and too many Jack Daniels lurking in her mouth reminded her that the night had been intense. Kat pulled at the duvet. There was a warm feeling growing inside her as she pieced together the events and she didn't want to let it escape. As she yanked on the cover, she felt some resistance and heard a half-hearted groan of protest. Then she remembered Miro.

The warmth turned into a tingle of excitement in her stomach as Miro wriggled closer to her. An arm slipped round Kat's waist and thighs nudged the back of her own. Miroslava – Kat tossed the name around in her head, smothering it in a thick Eastern European accent – but most people called her Joan. Why call someone common-or-garden Joan when you could have a lover called 'Miro'? It struck Kat as an extraordinary coincidence that her new lover should have the same name as her favourite artist.

Hard nipples brushed against Kat's back, pubes tickled her buttocks and images of the Spanish painter's Constellations series were pushed from her mind, for the memory of Miro, the woman, was complete. How could Kat have failed to remember she was at the apartment of the gorgeous Miro? The gorgeous, sexy, creative and perfectly named Miro.

Kat turned over and kissed her sensuously on the mouth. "Happy Boxing Day," she said shyly.

In one swift movement, Miro was sitting bolt upright. "Boxing Day?" she yelled. "Oh, Jesus fuck! What time is it?"

The moving target

Although the window panes and seats seemed to be held together by gaffer tape, The Emerald Isle was about the best pub on offer in Kilburn. Maddie and Anna had intended to go for a walk round Queen's Park before heading off to the pictures, but the smell of ashtrays and beer-soaked carpets that wafted out of the Emerald's open doors lured them in like dysfunctional Bisto Kids. They settled onto their usual banquette in the corner by the window – the fact that it was furthest from the swing door into the men's toilets was reason enough for their choice – and sipped on their Guinness.

"Happy Christmas to you, girls!" said the young barman as he came over to clean their table. "Now, did Santa Claus fulfil your every desire?" Patrick managed to inject sexual innuendo into everything he said. On this occasion he managed it with a leer and a gurn. Who replied depended on how tolerant each was feeling. It was Anna this time.

"Patrick, I can honestly say that I can't remember the last time Christmas has left me feeling so satisfied," she said, turning to her girlfriend for confirmation. Maddie blushed slightly as she muttered her agreement and turned her attention to recreating the shamrock on the head of her pint.

"And what about you, Patrick? Are you having a good Christmas?" asked Anna. Patrick chuntered on about his festive exploits as he cleaned their table. Having passed a cloth over the sticky surface which had been thickened by year-old layers of spilt alcohol, he whipped out the dreaded paintbrush and bucket. Picking up Maddie's cigarette, which was resting on the side, he passed it carefully to her.

"If you'll just hold on to that for a minute, darlin', I'll clean out your ashtray for you," he said politely. He completed the job with a flourish as the filthy tool sent clouds of detritus billowing into the air. "There you go, ladies. That's better. Now if you need anything, you just come and tip me a wink, all right?" Both women forced a smile and Maddie put her fag out with a grimace.

"Why does he always do that?" she asked. "We've been coming in here for years. I can't believe he hasn't twigged that we're not interested in what he's got in his pants."

"Do you remember that night when I was practically mounting you on the pool table?" Anna laughed. "If he was going to put two and two together, I think he would have done it then."

"You do realise I was only pretending not to be able to play so you would show me how to hold the cue," teased Maddie.

"That was the night when you gave me your identity bracelet, wasn't it?" Anna's laughing tapered off into a smile.

"Oh yeah," chuckled Maddie. "And I think I remember pledging my undying love as well."

"Yep. You did."

Maddie couldn't believe how impetuous she'd been – but then she also recalled how drunk she'd been. The only other person she'd said that kind of thing to was a youth she'd met on an educational trip to California (east coast UK, not west coast USA) when she was fifteen. She shuddered at both memories. Maddie now realised that was the moment when Anna seriously started to hope they would be together for ever.

"I love you," Anna said softly and pressed her thigh up against her partner's.

"I love you, too." Maddie smiled back and felt pleased that she was now so comfortable with the idea of being in a relationship that she was able to say the words without hesitation.

They called it a day after two pints and continued on their way to the park. Maddie would have been happy to stay in the pub until the film started, but Anna seemed to be in need of some fresh air and led them back onto the High Road. Maddie was kicking her way through the litter that still lined the street when Anna called her over.

"Look at this, Mads." There was something strange about her tone of voice that made Maddie suspicious. It was as if she was trying to sound spontaneous.

"What?" Maddie made her way over to Anna, tensing up when she realised she was heading towards an estate agent. So that was it.

"You don't see many around for that price."

Maddie found herself looking at the details of a one-bedroom flat in West Hampstead, and sighed.

"Yeah. That would be a real bargain for someone who's looking to buy a one-bedroom flat in West Hampstead," she said coolly.

"It's got a fitted kitchen and everything," said Anna, with a forced nonchalance.

"So it has."

They stood in silence, staring at the picture of the Victorian terrace conversion.

"We could just have a look," said Anna tentatively.

"Anna, please don't push me. I've told you, we couldn't live in a one-bedroom. I can't afford it –"

"But I can!"

"– and I'm really not ready to take that step!"

Anna looked at her partner in despair.

"Please, Anna, can't we just leave it? Come on. We could slip in a round of pitch and putt if we hurry."

"It's not open on Boxing Day, you pillock."

Apparently, two could play at pissing on parades.

Wonderland

Andy held the phone away from his mouth while he bellowed a reply to his mother, who wanted him to play another hand of rummy with his Aunt Elspeth.

"I've just got a couple more calls to make and I'll be right down!" he shouted obligingly.

"You're not working on Boxing Day are you, darling?"

Andy didn't even pause for thought before telling his mother he had to discuss a very important point of law with a colleague, the outcome of which could have serious implications as far as legal precedents were concerned. He knew she loved it when he talked posh lawyer-talk and he felt duty bound to feed her desire. After all, his parents had paid enough to turn him into a lawyer, so he owed it to them to sound as important as possible at all times.

Andy turned his attention back to the phone and heard Anna chortling at his ludicrous claim. Anna was one of the few people in their stiff City firm who understood his sense of humour and they had become what his mother would call 'bosom buddies' from the day he joined her team.

"I didn't know your mother was fluent in legalese," said Anna when Andy finally rejoined their conversation.

"She's learning, but progress is slow with me as her only teacher."

"Just as well, huh?"

"You're not kidding. I think I've gone a bit far this time though," said Andy.

"What have you done now?"

Andy heard Anna's giggles and started laughing too. "I think I might have given her the impression I'm on a fast track to junior partnerdom!"

Both mouthpieces got sprayed as they spluttered with laughter.

"Holy moly!" said Anna.

"I know. She thinks I'm some sort of Wunderkind. Anyway, enough of my tangled web. What have you been up to? Did you have a nice day yesterday?"

Anna told Andy how wonderful Christmas Day had been. How it hadn't mattered that she and Maddie shared a turkey crown instead of a whole bird because the meat was just as succulent and she always thought stuffing the cavity was a bit dodgy anyway. She told him how they'd bought a small box of crackers, played a couple of games and only drunk themselves silly rather than stupid.

"Sounds idyllic..." said Andy. "But did you manage to broach The Subject?"

"Unfortunately, yes," replied Anna.

"Oh. Didn't go down well, then?"

"No. It didn't erupt into a row or anything, but she's still absolutely against us buying a place," said Anna, allowing her frustration to filter down the line. "I can't understand why. She says it's not because she doesn't love me, so it's not like we're not committed to each other."

Andy let Anna vent her frustration about the whole scenario. He was always sympathetic about her predicament, but knew that no amount of talking was ever going to convince Maddie to take the relationship onto the next level.

"Maybe it just wasn't the right time. Keep plugging away and you're bound to catch her with her guard down sometime," Andy heard himself saying. He was mid-flow when he realised Anna was being distracted by someone else in the room. "Is she there?"

"Yes. I'm very pleased to say that the silent treatment doesn't prevent coffee from being distributed among the household."

"A normal day with the Munsters then!"

Andy heard Maddie ask who Anna was talking to and shook his head despairingly as Anna wound her up even more by refusing to tell her. "Put her on," he said into the mouthpiece as he listened to Anna milking the situation.

"No, Maddie, I'm not going to tell you," she whined. "It's just not healthy for us to live in each other's pockets..."

He heard Anna launch into a lengthy tirade about privacy, personal space and not being able to breathe and Maddie humph at having her standard battle cry regurgitated so mockingly word for word.

"For fuck's sake, Anna, you're such a child. I know it's only Andy."

There was a scuffling noise, some unfinished sentences – "give me –", "I just want to –", "what the fuck –" and a scream and then a moment of silence before Maddie came on the line.

"Andy?"

"Happy Christmas, Mads!" said Andy. He waited a moment before asking: "How are you doing?"

"Oh, you know. Not too bad." Maddie's voice was empty of Christmas cheer.

"Blimey, sounds dreadful," joked Andy.

"We had a huge row this afternoon," confided Maddie.

"Oh no. What about?" Andy never alluded to the fact that Anna talked to him about their relationship all the time, so he had become accustomed to acting dumb.

"The bloody flat thing. She keeps pushing me, Andy, and, you know, sometimes I'm that close to telling her to fuck off and stop hassling me. It's all so fucking stifling."

Andy wasn't prepared for the strength of Maddie's feeling. "She only does it because she loves you so much. Maybe you should tell her how you feel."

"Yeah, I know. I'm just afraid that it'll all come out wrong." There was a pause as she digested Andy's remarks. "I love her too, but..."

"But what?" Andy asked, even though he was afraid Maddie would actually tell him. Why couldn't she phone her mum like everyone else? Where was Kat, for Christ's sake? Pacifying Maddie was *her* job.

"Oh, nothing. So how has your Christmas been? Have you spoken to Phil?"

When Andy had finished dissecting the highs and lows of sharing his life with a mechanic, he put the phone down and sat silently in his father's study. Then, with the mother's attention diverted from the son for an instant, he took the opportunity of slipping in another phone call to Phil. It was a good seven minutes thirty-four seconds before his mother shouted up at him for a third time. He worked on the 'three strikes and you're out' rule, so was just grateful that he hadn't been out for a duck.

He trudged down the stairs and couldn't help but smile when he saw his Aunt Elspeth sitting in the armchair in the living room. The cards were ready for rummy but his elderly relative's bobbing head meant it would be a while before the game got underway. Andy drifted into the kitchen and started on the washing-up. He was searching for a new sponge in the cupboard under the sink when he heard his mother enter the room.

"What did I do to deserve a lovely boy like you?" She planted a kiss on his cheek and reached for the tea towel, but Andy plucked it from its hook before her hand could get a good grip. He secreted the faded image of collies dressed in Welsh national costume behind his back and persuaded her that he would be quicker if he worked alone. His face relaxed as she reluctantly accepted the opportunity to go and put her feet up.

Standing in front of the large, water-splattered picture window overlooking the garden, he was able to examine himself in the blackness. He was slightly fuller in the face than last year and he knew a couple of laughter lines had emerged at the corner of his eyes but he could still get away with it. Breathing in only sucked his slightly rounded belly up into his chest. He relaxed his body and the escaping air made his limp lips flap together noisily. Okay, so he'd had his thirtieth birthday that year, but he wasn't old, for heaven's sake. He could still go clubbing with the best of them. The sparkle in his eye that had helped him maintain a healthy love life over the years was still alive and glinting.

He thought about Anna and Maddie and wondered if he would ever get to the stage where he was contemplating moving in with anyone, let alone buying a place together. He worried about Anna. He loved Maddie to bits, but she didn't seem to look at the relationship in the same way Anna did. He was seeing them fast approaching Spaghetti Junction and he wondered if they were going to end up as sauce. He wondered if his new bloke, Phil, liked Italian food...

Life is sweet

Ever since their win on the Premium Bonds, Barbara had felt like a new woman. She'd felt like quite a lot of new things actually – a new house, new car, new clothes, new hairdo, new everything. And she got most of what she wanted; except a new husband, that is. In fact, she had embraced the idea of 'new' so heartily that she was delighted when she heard people whispering about them being 'nouveau riche'. Her daughter, Anna, had translated it for her from the original French.

She was disappointed that Anna hadn't made her usual Christmas pilgrimage to see them and hoped she hadn't been driven away by Graham's obnoxious behaviour. At least Mum and her friends were coming, she thought, as she dumped the cutlery and a pile of mats on the table. She was glad her mum had good friends like Vi and Betty to keep an eye on her now that Dad wasn't around.

"Graham!" called Barbara. Their guests were due to arrive any minute and she needed an extra pair of hands to set the table. She snapped off her rubber gloves, checked her nails and made a note to buy the flock-lined gloves next time. There were times when she envied her mum. At moments like these, living with friends in a large house in west London sounded very appealing indeed.

"Graham!"

No way out

Graham was on the loo. At the sound of Barbara's voice, he froze. He had managed to escape doing anything towards the Christmas preparations and, with the winning line in sight, he didn't want to blemish his untarnished record. So he sat still. So still that even the pages of his form guide stopped rustling. He heard the clatter of his wife's stiletto heels on the expensive parquet flooring and then a soft thud as she came up the stairs. Although he was expecting the knock at the door, it still made him jump.

"Mum's going to be here any minute. Come down and give me a hand will you, Grae?" she asked through the faux-panelled door.

Graham grunted as the sound of her footsteps faded. He shook out the pages of his paper and waited for his bowels to grind into action. As mothers-in-law went, Doris wasn't so bad, and Vi and Betty weren't too offensive. The old dears were quite entertaining in their own way. What he couldn't stand, however, was his daughter. Carrying on with another woman, it was disgusting. It always became an issue around Christmas time. His wife bent his ear about Anna being her only daughter, asked why couldn't he just get over it, and he ignored her. He remembered the day Anna had told them she was gay and he didn't regret saying that he never wanted to see her again. Of course, she popped up most Christmases, but at least she didn't bring her pervert 'friend' with her. The whole business made his stomach turn. He'd spent hours in his shed chewing it over and still couldn't understand how a red-blooded male like him had managed to produce a sexual deviant like his daughter.

He felt his sphincter twitch and reached for the loo paper.

The Big Picture

Maddie pulled the dust cover off the 3' x 5' canvas. It was smooth and taut and still blank.

It had always been her intention to finish it for Christmas – it was going to be a present for Anna, something that said 'this is what you mean to me'. It was a kind of swan song, one last 'big picture' as Anna liked to refer to Maddie's work. The way this term trivialised her efforts used to annoy Maddie, but the more she railed against it, the more Anna teased her by using it as often as possible, until it was subsumed into their personalised lexicon. Anna's references to Maddie wearing plastic protective clothing, using spill-proof water pots and powder paints like a primary school artist had come to mean she cared about what Maddie did even though she pre-tended not to understand. These days, Anna didn't have to ask what she was doing and Maddie didn't have to explain. But soon, 'these days' would be a thing of the past. Maddie looked around the studio, trying to log every detail in her memory. The sight of Kat's freshly fired pots lined up on the side were enough to bring a pre-menstrual tear to her eye. She hoped her friend would turn up, but it was New Year's Eve and with a new love inter-est to distract her it was unlikely she'd remember their rendezvous.

Instead Maddie focused her attention on her work and opened the sky-light in the hope that the crisp winter air would breathe life into her and her painting. It had been easy to visualise herself working on the picture but now that the time had come to put her thoughts into action, the expanse of whiteness looked daunting. Maybe she was trying too hard to come up with a composition that was poignant to her and Anna's life. It was at times like this that she would usually have turned to Kat for advice. But the studio was Kat-less, inspiration-less, kick-up-the-arse-less. She reached into the box where she'd stored the notes and objects she'd collected to help her define the essence of her relationship with Anna:

- *A sketch of a chicken done with chicken tikka sauce*
- *Three squares of emulsion – red, yellow and blue – primary colours of the kind usually reserved for bathrooms or kids' bedrooms*
- *A tangle of pink legal ribbon*
- *A feather from their duvet*
- *A piece of paper with a ring on it made by a damp coffee cup (Was that a stain or a statement? She'd come back to that.)*
- *A 'What's On' guide for the Belle-Vue cinema at Willesden*
- *A picture of Conchita Martinez winning Wimbledon*
- *A squirt of Anna's perfume – Hugo Boss (for Men)*
- *A funny shaped potato.*

Now it was just a question of blending all the elements, so the forms, colours and textures produced something meaningful, something moving, something with gravitas. Something Anna wouldn't mind hanging on the living-room wall.

The late show

Kat stuck her key in the deadlock and turned. As she felt the lock slide back, she sighed. She'd missed her. She pushed the door open and looked around. The cloth in the sink was wrung out but still wet. A fresh heap of pencil shavings lay on the floor next to the bin. Five screwed-up balls of paper were lodged on the window sill. The smell of cigarette smoke was still fresh in the air. Maddie had been there all right.

She left, double-locking the studio door.

"You idiot. You stupid fucking idiot," she muttered as she clattered down the stairs and onto the street. Now she would have to wait until after New Year to hear what Maddie had to say to her. She wondered again why Maddie couldn't just say whatever it was over the phone like a normal person.

Déjà vu

"Anna, come and help me, will you?"

"Hold on a sec," she replied with a mouth full of frothed-up toothpaste. "What's up?"

After the spitting and gurgling of the final stages of her ablutions, Anna went to investigate what was wrong in the bedroom. "What are you doing in bed? We've got to leave in a minute."

"I don't know what to wear," groaned Maddie, drawing the duvet up to her chin. "I've tried everything on and none of my clothes fit. I look like a bleedin' heifer in everything I bought before Christmas and it's really PISSING ME OFF."

The way Maddie isolated and emphasised the last three words indicated a crisis was about to occur, and this one looked like being one of the worst – a Clothes Crisis. There were several stages in a such a crisis and Anna had just heard stage three of five. If she didn't smooth the situation over, conditions could easily deteriorate into a full-blown 'I can't be seen in public' scenario. Given that it was New Year's Eve, this had to be avoided at all costs. Anna picked her way through the molehills of clothes that had sprung up all over the floor and plonked herself down on the bed next to Maddie.

"Come on, Maddie," she said soothingly. "Everybody feels like a bit of a chunker after Christmas, I thought we'd established that…"

"I know but…" Maddie held her head in her hands. "I've been through my whole wardrobe, Anna. I can't believe after all that hard work I've just piled it all back on again."

"So what are you going to achieve by sitting here fretting about it?" There was no reply. "Anyway, it's only a couple of pounds. I don't think nine and a half stone really counts as fat! Get back down the gym next week and stop your bleedin' mithering! You're such a drama queen sometimes." Anna chose to go with the aggressive, pull-yourself-together approach. It was often the fastest route to a resolution.

"It's all right for you to sit there getting annoyed with me."

"I can't help my metabolic rate. Now come on. Put on something black and floaty and no one will know the difference." There was a slight pause. "Get a wriggle on then, we're going to be late for Julia."

Maddie heaved her body off the bed, threw on something black and floaty and headed for the bathroom to apply last-minute makeup. Anna waited for the words that generally confirmed that the rescue from the ledge of despair had been successful.

"You wait," came Maddie's voice after a worryingly long thirty seconds. "I'm going to be as fit as Madonna before the month's out." Anna breathed a tentative sigh of relief. The familiar reference meant partial positivity had been restored. She waited for the signal that the process was complete.

"And I'm definitely going to stop smoking."

Mission accomplished.

Boogie nights

By the time Maddie and Anna arrived at Julia's flat in Maida Vale, she had already started cooking.

Anna buzzed up to Julia's apartment – there was no way their friend's executive pad could be described as merely 'a flat'. It was stuffed to the gunnels with essential consumer durables like electronic pepper mills, ergonomic bottle openers and inflatable wastepaper baskets. It had occurred to Anna that these things were filling the space Julia's ex-husband used to occupy, but she didn't bring it up. Even during their most intimate chats, the Ex was out of bounds. It was as if she'd blotted him out.

Julia's voice filtered down the intercom and, squeezing past Ed's bike, which was parked (illegally) in the entrance hall, they climbed the stairs to the top floor. The faded silk flowers were still fading on the window sills of each floor and the mat with the obscenely chirpy, wholesome message was still outside number five, as was the pile of interesting-looking catalogues. They could hear Julia's voice shouting down at them before they could see her.

"Happy nooo year, ladies," she bellowed in an over-eggnogged, pseudo-American drawl. Anna hooted back up at her.

"Is it still snowing?" asked Julia as her friends came into view.

"No but it's brass-fucking-monkeys out there," said Anna.

Maddie was the first to be hugged and kissed, cleverly managing to avoid the dripping wooden spoon Julia was brandishing.

"Ed got caught in it. He's thawing out in the bath at the moment."

"He didn't cycle over here, did he?" asked Maddie.

"No – I just sent him out to the shops."

"So he's been staying over?"

"Just for a couple of nights." Julia winked and grimaced. "I'll tell you later." Maddie shot Anna a 'what the fuck's she up to this time' look and they both laughed as they were bundled into the steaming kitchen.

Julia went over to the stove and began stirring the bubbling substance.

"So what are we having?" asked Anna, venturing nearer the hob in an effort to guess.

"Well, I thought we'd start off with some soup." Julia drizzled the liquid off the wooden spoon and back into the pan, thus demonstrating the soup. "A blend of squash and spinach complemented by a delicate pinch of marjoram."

"Sounds great," said Maddie enthusiastically, but Anna couldn't muster the words and went looking for other sources of sustenance.

"Did you get any bread in?" asked Anna.

"I told Ed to get ciabatta but he came home with frigging baguettes!"

Anna pulled the bread out of a bag. "Any dips, Jules?"

"In the fridge. Why don't you get them out? ... Is Kat coming, by the way?"

"No," said Maddie. "Some chick called at the last minute, you know what it's like. Someone she met on Christmas Eve, or something."

"It was a party on Christmas Day, actually –" interjected Anna.

"Whatever," replied Maddie.

"Tough choice, I suppose," said Julia. "Hot date with new bird or Pictionary with old mates..." She laughed but Anna thought she looked disappointed. When Kat was there, things were guaranteed to get way out of hand. Not that Julia would mention anything, of course. "Well, good on her, that's what I say!"

"Yeah – chance would be a fine thing!" said Anna, squeezing her girlfriend's hand to let her know she didn't mean it.

"She didn't even turn up at the studio today, so I couldn't tell her the news. She's going to think I'm such a wuss for chucking in my painting after all this time," said Maddie.

"It's not like you're 'chucking it in' –" piped up Anna.

"– It's more like 'repositioning it in terms of my priorities'. I know." Maddie was well equipped with the words to finish the sentence.

"What's all this?" asked Julia.

"Maddie's making a New Year's resolution," replied Anna, before waiting for her to pick up the baton. The changeover was clumsy, however, and Maddie needed prompting. "Tell her then, Mads."

"I was just thinking that maybe it's time for me to consider my future and think about where I'm going in life."

"Nothing like a little light conversation on New Year's Eve…" replied Julia, as she rooted around in the fridge for the vegetables, kindly washed and prepared by the good people at Sainsbury's. "So what have you decided?"

"I've been really lucky to have been able to support myself through doing bits and bobs along with my painting –"

If the intention had been sarcasm, Anna's cough couldn't have been better timed. Maddie glared at her partner. Anna pointed to her throat to indicate the interruption had been involuntary.

"I've been really lucky to have been able to *get by* for so long," repeated Maddie pointedly, "but I've got to start thinking about earning a real wage, and I've decided I should resurrect my photography."

There was a pause while Maddie collected her thoughts. Julia exchanged glances with Anna, who smiled and nodded to confirm that this was not a wind-up.

"I've been working alongside Kat either at college or in the studio for most of my adult life," continued Maddie. "I'm really going to miss her and I don't know how to tell her that I'm going to have to give up my share of the studio, but I think it's the right decision. I need to concentrate on one thing and try and make a go of it. If I were to keep the studio on, I think it would be too easy to slip back into my old routine."

Anna suddenly realised the magnitude of the change Maddie was about to undergo. Not wanting to draw attention to this, she resorted to platitudes instead. "Kat's not going to disappear, you know, hon," she soothed. "She'll understand."

"Well, I think it's dead exciting." Julia was forever the optimist. "I'm not saying your paintings aren't great, Madge, but just think about the possibilities that lie ahead of you as a photographer. As well as the cash you could make..."

"It's not like it's going to be just weddings and photographing overly made-up make-over women in off-the-shoulder flying jackets..." added Anna, keen to feed this groundswell of encouragement.

"Anna's right, you know." Julia swung round from her place at the hob and illustrated her point with her soup-covered spatula. Anna tried to ignore the spots of liquid that were flying through the air, and the (rather ironic) fact that Julia was creating her very own Pollock-esque splatter painting on her kitchen floor. "You could do product shots for ad campaigns or books –" continued Julia.

"Arty stuff for those magazines with matt covers –" butted in Anna.

"– that feature skinny men with long fringes," finished Julia. "Oh, and there's fashion shoots."

"Celebrities in their homes –"

"Oh yes, Madge – imagine; you'd have carte blanche to go and poke around people's homes! And there's paparazzi-style tabloid stuff."

"I think I've got the idea," said Maddie, putting an end to the verbal ping-pong. "You're right. It's an exciting challenge. Adjusting to a different way of life is going to be hard, that's all."

"Yes, but all that idealistic art bollocks is for kids," said Julia, as she turned back to the cooking process.

Maddie reached for her cigarette packet and tried to line it up so it was in the absolute corner of the table.

"It's all about cash when you get to your thirties..." continued Julia.

Anna watched Maddie reach across the table for the matchbox, to align it with the exact edge of the cigarette packet which was now at the exact edge of the table.

"There's way more stuff to think about. I mean, pensions for a start," added Julia. "There's not going to be anything left in the pot by the time we get there, so it's something you've got to start thinking about sooner rather than later."

Maddie stopped her painstaking task. In one fluid movement she whipped a cigarette out of the packet, struck a match, lit up and took a long, hard draw.

"I thought you were giving up!" Anna looked at her girlfriend. If she couldn't even give up smoking, how was she ever going to make the work resolution stick?

"I am. It's not midnight yet, is it?" Maddie pulled harder on the fag.

A perfect couple

"Open another bottle of wine, will you, Madge?" said Julia, who had left the squash/spinach/marjoram concoction to infuse while she joined her friends at the table. Maybe more wine would keep Maddie off the fags and any further fights at bay. Maddie plucked a bottle of red out of her rucksack and Julia winced to see her jab the sharp tip of the screw into the cork and twist it into its flesh.

The women were absorbed in a conversation about the gross amount of pigeon shit on the pavement underneath the bridge outside Kilburn tube, when Ed emerged. He was still wet from his bath and had wrapped a towel round his waist for the benefit of the visitors.

"Good evening, ladies." He bent to give Anna and then Maddie a big, soggy kiss. "Just the four of us tonight, then?"

"'Fraid so, Eddie," said Maddie.

"You know there's nothing I like more than an evening with my three favourite women."

"Sometimes you're so slimy," said Julia, laughing.

"How else am I going to stop you getting your evil hooks into me?" A flash of the buttocks to show he meant business and Ed headed for the door.

"You know you love me, really," Julia shouted after the bare arse. He tried to muster a fart as the perfect riposte. Although, for once, he failed to deliver, he seemed satisfied with his exit. But that was Ed all over. When she'd met him, she'd thought he was impenetrable – a no-ties, self-centred bloke whose only commitment was to beer, drugs and football. That had suited her fine. Especially as he was nearly ten years younger than her. Why would a twenty-five-year-old boy be interested in settling down with her? It was perfect, a guaranteed no-pressure relationship. Once she'd discovered that, like an armadillo, he was soft on the inside, things changed slightly, but it didn't completely alter the game they were playing. Over twelve months, they'd managed to bed down together in an informal sexual and emotional Nirvana. No obligations, no promises, no expectations. It was how they liked it and it worked for them.

"Do you reckon he ever gets bored with being the only bloke all the time?" asked Maddie.

"Bored with it?" scoffed Julia. "He bloody loves it!"

"Okay, enough of this sitting around," said Anna, letting her bossy inner-child get the better of her as she got out of her chair and clapped her hands to get people going. "This is New Year's Eve for Christ's sake and we haven't even got any music on!" Kneeling down next to the leaning tower of music, she started going through the CDs.

"Jeff Buckley? Catatonia! Oasis!" Anna waved the covers at her and Julia smiled sheepishly. Anna loved to point out evidence of Ed's more permanent presence in the flat, like these additions to Julia's collection of dance music and 70s compilations. In spite of the wider choice, Anna still went for the 70s collection they all knew and loved.

"Cocktails. We need cocktails!" Anna was now directing her workers from her place at the table. "Crackers, party hats, streamers, games and a TV guide."

"You're not watching TV tonight, Anna?" said Julia incredulously.

"It's all in the preparation, Jules. You'll thank me in the morning when you're tucking into the McDonald's Maddie will have gone out to buy us and moaning that there's no cheesy TV to go with it."

"This is absolutely delicious," said Maddie as she played with the surplus dessert on her plate.

"Inter-course cocktail, anyone?" asked Julia as she stacked the plates on the side. There was plenty of soup left, which was handy as there'd be something for breakfast. She dipped her finger in the cold liquid. She was surprised Maddie and Anna hadn't had much – it was quite a triumph.

"Okay – how does this sound? One measure of Cointreau, two of gin, one of vodka, a dash of Malibu and a cup of fresh orange juice? It's called a pick 'n' mix." Anna had got hold of the book.

"Sounds great," said Julia.

The Waring was already whirring the ice into a crushed mound before a unanimous verdict could be delivered. 'Oh, What a Night' was blaring out of the speakers and Julia was up and dancing around the kitchen. She sang the words to the song louder while the blender was doing its thing. Ed threw his spoon down on his plate and slotted himself in behind Julia's writhing body, shout-singing in her ear.

Anna pulsed the blender in time to the beat and Maddie cranked up the music even louder. The glassware was rattling obediently in time to the thumping bass.

Trading places

Even though Maddie and Ed had said it was unethical to leave a game of Pictionary when being arse-whipped by the other team, Anna still followed Julia into the kitchen to make more drinks.

"Looks like Ed's getting his feet under the table," said Anna as she slumped onto the floor next to the fridge and watched Julia gather the ingredients.

"A couple of CDs is hardly moving in," hiccuped Julia.

"Life is so fucking weird, isn't it, Jules?" slurred Anna.

"What do you mean?"

"Well, you know. There you two are doing your damnedest to keep each other at arm's length and here I am! All I want is to settle down with Mads. I'd do anything to make her want to buy a place with me..."

"You showed her the flat then?" asked Julia. She picked a bottle of champagne out of the fridge, sat down next to Anna and started trying to remove the foil.

"Yeah. We went down the Emerald on Boxing Day and just happened to walk past the estate agent."

"And..."

"Same old same old," said Anna disconsolately. "I was enthusiastic, Maddie got annoyed and said she wasn't ready, that I shouldn't push her into anything, and then we went home."

"Not quite what you expected."

"No. I don't know what the fuck's wrong with her. You know, we get on so well and have such a great time together, and it's not as if we've only just met."

"Frustrating, huh?'

"Fucking infuriating!" exclaimed Anna. "I feel like something's got to give. I mean, my career is coming on fine –"

"Did you finish the report about the acquisition, by the way?"

"Yep – looks like it might happen in the spring," replied Anna, before grappling to pick up her train of thought. "I'm happy with Maddie, happy at work – I've got the cash and I want my own home." She paused. "I want my own home with Mads," she continued. "I want to buy curtains, Julia. I yearn to buy my own curtains."

"And light fittings," added Julia.

"Yes. I want to choose, buy and pay someone to fit my own light fittings in my own flat, bought with my own frigging money!"

The pair were just winding each other up nicely when Ed appeared at the door.

"Are you two coming in? We're on a roll in there," he protested with inebriated outrage.

"Anna and I are just swapping speedwriting tips," said Julia innocently. The pair first met ten years ago on a speedwriting course and this phrase had long since become code for 'piss off, we're having a private chat'.

A room with a view

"What are they up to in there?" asked Maddie impatiently.

"Speedwriting," said Ed as he slumped back into his chair.

"Oh."

Ed wondered what might have warranted such an impromptu speedwriting chat. He had asked if he could leave a toothbrush at

Julia's but you couldn't call that heavy, could you? He'd been so careful not to do anything that might suggest he was less than totally happy with the situation he had with Julia. A toothbrush was okay, though, wasn't it? It was practical.

"Anna's probably telling her what a dreadful girlfriend I am," said Maddie.

"Not the flat thing again."

"'Fraid so."

"You know, you want to steer clear of all that malarkey." The ominous beat of Queen's 'Another One Bites the Dust' filled the room. "What the fuck is this you've put on, Madge?"

She groped around on the floor trying to find the cover. As if it mattered. "Yeah, sorry. A bit shit, isn't it?"

"So, how are you two?" asked Ed as she set about updating the music.

"Okay. Yeah, you know. We have our ups and downs."

"Glad you stayed home for Christmas?"

Maddie pondered her answer. "Yeah, actually. It was really nice."

"You sound surprised."

"No, I'm not surprised. It's just... you know..."

"No..."

"Yes you do. It's like we've turned a corner but nothing's changed. You know, like the view's still the same."

He frowned. Turning corners, changing views – what the fuck was that all about? "So does that mean you're happy or you're not happy?" he asked.

"Hey, Ed – I mean, what *is* happy?"

"Cats and flats kind of happy?" That was what dykes did, wasn't it? Move in, eat vegetables and get a couple of cats.

"Let's not run before we can... errr..."

"Crawl?"

"Yeah."

"So you'll make it through another year?"

"What? In general or with Anna?"

"With Anna."

"Just when I think I've made up my mind that this is 'it', something happens to make me think it isn't or it shouldn't be. It's a big step, isn't it? Buying a flat and all that stuff. It makes things seem so final. Almost predetermined..."

"Mmmm," nodded Ed. "Don't do it, Mads. You'll be compromising everything you stand for."

Love in limbo

Kat concentrated hard on the woman who was dancing with her. She remembered some kind of physical contact occurring at midnight to celebrate the New Year, but that felt like an age ago. She looked at her watch. It was quarter past twelve. She remembered the kiss again. It had been good. Really good. Her partner for the evening moved in closer to her.

"Do you want to come home with me? I'd really like to have sex with you again," said Miro, her mouth touching Kat's ear.

Kat sobered up a little with the excitement of such an uncomplicated offer. "Sure," she said. Her memory of the time she'd spent with Miro was patchy to say the least and, although this was generally how she liked things to stay, she had an inkling that this one might be quite likeable.

Destabilised by this thought, Kat dug around in her pocket for her phone as they reached the street. She wanted to hear a familiar voice to ground her and, even though she'd made up her mind not to phone Maddie, it was impossible to resist the impulse. Her attempts at coordinating her fingers and thumbs to operate the appliance were interrupted by a text beep. That was easy – a touch of a button and the message appeared.

'Wish you were here, sweetheart. Love you loads. Hope she does too! Mxx.' She smiled at the message and kept scrolling up and down to read it over again as she swayed gently in the cold night breeze.

Even though she'd trained herself over the years not to think about Maddie 'in that way', Kat felt a short, sharp surge of regret. Then Miro slipped her arm round her waist. This was no time to be maudlin. She punched in a reply. 'I'll have 1 4 u, ok?!' Switching off her phone, she turned her attention to her new friend.

Vision quest

"What the bejesus are you doing with that phone?" asked Anna, peering over her girlfriend's shoulder.

"Nothing," said Maddie defensively.

"You're obsessed with that thing."

"I just had a message from Kat, that's all."

"Put it away, Mads, yeah?"

"Christ, Anna, you don't half go on sometimes."

"Oh, we're all right!" said Julia as she walked in on them. "Anna and Madge Bickerdyke live on in 1999 and all is right with the world!"

"We're not bickering, Jules," explained Maddie, "we're discussing the role of the mobile phone in modern –"

"Come on, let's play a game," chirped Anna. Her ability to change moods so quickly only came during periods of very heavy drinking.

Ed was lying face down on the sofa snoring lightly from time to time. His makeup bag lay on the table with its contents of dope severely depleted. Julia lowered herself tentatively onto the floor, and, once settled, introduced the subject of her new blender, again. It was late. Four-thirty in the morning, to be precise, and Anna was really keen to talk. That's how she knew she was drunk/stoned. Usually Anna was the queen of chit-chat. She could spout superficial bollocks with the best of them for hours on end, but for some reason – probably the fact that it was New Year and traditionally she did get a bit emotional at such times – she wanted to have a deep and meaningful conversation and by God she was going to get one.

"Do you realise that this time next year we will be celebrating the dawn of a new millennium?" Anna rambled on. "That is amazing when you start to think about it. Two thousand years since the birth of Christ…"

"Two thousand years since some geezers made up some story about the birth of some bloke so as to keep everyone in fear and ensure bloodshed and conflict for evermore –" Maddie could always be baited by the religion thing.

"Oh, okay! You know what I mean," continued Anna. "But it makes you feel a bit small, don't you think?"

"Yeah," agreed Julia.

"It makes you want to do something significant and life-changing, doesn't it?" blathered Anna, trying hard to provoke a response.

"You mean, like buying that Smeg?" muttered Julia. She had been talking about buying one of those enormous retro fridges for ages and they all hoped that soon she would stop talking about it, remortgage her flat and do something about it.

"Yeah. Something big like that. You know, it makes you feel like getting your house in order; putting down roots. Giving yourself some concept of permanence in this ever-changing world –"

"Anna, you've been smoking too much," Maddie said without moving her lips.

"No I haven't! It's how I feel, Maddie. I want to do it. It feels right and I want to do it with you."

"In front of Ed and Julia?" laughed Maddie.

"Maddie. I want us to buy a place together." Anna stood up as she said the words. Julia made a noise that was meant to sound like shit hitting a fan.

"No," said Maddie, firmly and finally.

7 APRIL 1999

Damascus Road

"Maddie! Maddie! We've got it! They're going to give us a mortgage!" whooped Anna as she slammed the phone down in delight. "That was Side-Of-Things on the phone."

"You what?" replied Maddie.

"They've approved our application. Isn't that incredible?"

"That's amazing," shrieked Maddie as the news finally filtered into her brain. "St John's Wood, here we come!"

"I don't know about that, but we should be able to get something around here," yelled Anna as she began leaping around the room maniacally. So maniacally that Maddie felt compelled to join in.

"Good ole Side-Of-Things!"

The poor, unsuspecting mortgage consultant who had sat on the couple's sofa, demonstrated his software and showed them his assets while sweating profusely, had had a penchant for pointing out every 'side of things' even if a side didn't exist. Their favourite example, and one that had been nominated as 'Most Inappropriate Use of a Phrase or Saying', had been: 'If you go for an endowment mortgage then you might end up with a substantial nest egg, side of things.'

A few of Maddie's birthday cards fluttered off the mantelpiece as the pair wafted round the room excitedly.

"I never thought I'd see the day! This is brilliant, Mads!"

Suddenly their screaming and shouting was accompanied by a little Nachtmusik coming from Anna's phone. It was work calling. Jubilation was put on hold as Anna answered.

"Anna Foster speaking."

Maddie marvelled at the way she was able to switch from 'home

Anna' to 'work Anna' without even changing clothes. She watched as the muscles on Anna's face tensed and transformed her expression into that of a focused and efficient businesswoman. "Tell Mr Fitzgerald to bike a copy of the contract and the affidavit to the office together with the outstanding documents and Andy will cross-reference them so that the findings can be presented to Ms Williams by noon tomorrow. Tell him there is absolutely no way we will be able to act on anything before then." There was silence as the caller responded. "Good. See you tomorrow." She turned the phone off and put it back next to Maddie's on the mantelpiece. "This calls for champagne, Mads!"

"Why, what's happened?"

"We're going to buy a flat. You haven't forgotten already?"

As Anna bounced out of the flat in search of champagne, Maddie thought about everything that had happened in the three months since Christmas. She slumped down on the chair at her desk and tried to pinpoint the key moments in her conversion from idealist with no real estate to realist with an ideal estate just round the corner. Her eyes fell on the stack of magazines with achingly trendy matt-look covers next to her desk. The moment she made up her mind to purchase that first magazine had been the kick to the back of her knees that had sent her skidding down the flume of change into the plunge pool of property ownership.

She remembered the event in detail. It had been on the way home from Julia's on New Year's Day. She'd waited until she and Anna were walking up the drive to the flat before saying nonchalantly, "Oh damn. We've forgotten to buy milk." If Anna had only given her 50p to buy it with, maybe things might have been different. But she hadn't. Maddie could still recall the feeling of the crisp fiver being pressed into her hand. A guilty flush spread up from her chest as she remembered that buying milk had never been her primary goal. The ensuing events replayed in slow motion in her mind and she saw herself, like the pram bumping down the stairs at Grand Central Station in *The Untouchables*, tumbling, out of control, to her fate...

*

Pinned to the spot by the harsh lights inside the 7-Eleven on Kilburn High Road, Maddie didn't know what to do. Finally the impulse of habit drew her towards the cold cabinet. Instinctively, she parted the heavy-duty plastic strips that covered the contents, fought hard against the compulsion to think about what they were for – stopping germs getting in, or food getting out – and reached inside for a carton of semi-skimmed. That was the easy bit. It would have been so simple to go up to the man at the counter, pay and leave, but that had never been the point of the trip. She felt the firm edges of the neatly folded fiver in her pocket and glanced over to the area marked 'newspapers and magazines'. The intensely coloured paper glinted in the glow of the striplight. Maddie licked her lips and swallowed to moisten her dry throat as she saw a parade of beautiful women with perfect teeth smiling at her. Like sirens, they chanted a million headlines, drawing her in with promises of sex, love, horoscopes, sex, skin, orgasm, romance, sex, sex sex...

Standing in front of the display, Maddie flicked her head from side to side to make sure she was alone. The motion was so fast that her hungover brain seemed to lag behind the movement of her skull. She didn't have much time to assess the situation. Titles swam before her eyes. She looked at Hello! – Ulrika Jonsson's tanned grin seemed to say: 'It's all right. Everyone feels afraid the first time. Try it. Go on. It'll make you forget everything. You know you want to...' But that was way too hardcore for a novice like Maddie. She'd heard that you only had to look at one spread and you'd be addicted for life, so the 'celebrity news' titles were out of bounds. She was looking for something to ease her in, something she could remain in control of. She was looking for something less glossy, something with great graphics, something that didn't have too many words on the cover.

"Oy! This isn't a library, sweetheart!" shouted the cashier from his podium of electronic omniscience. His voice sounded slow and distorted and Maddie panicked. She grabbed something from the shelf nearest to her, flung her fiver on the counter and fled...

*

Dogs Today might not have been quite what Anna meant when she'd referred to opportunities for cutting-edge photography commissions, but it did have some really cute pictures of Westies.

And it had opened the floodgates. In spite of her private promise that it wouldn't get out of hand, by the end of the week, Maddie was going into newsagents and buying magazines by the armful. She'd started to stuff them under the bed, in drawers and, finally, in the cupboard with the cleaning paraphernalia, in an attempt to hide them from Anna. The more involved she got, however, the more difficult it became to keep her habit a secret. In a moment of extraordinary activity, Anna had decided to wash the kitchen floor; it was then that she found bagfuls of the things. *ID*, *Wallpaper*, *The Face*, they were all hauled out and inspected...

"How long have you been doing this?" Anna asked as she reached into the carrier bag containing Maddie's booty and pulled out a *J17*. It swung guiltily between her thumb and forefinger as she looked at her partner quizzically.

"There were some free S Club 7 hair clips that week," admitted Maddie meekly, as Anna continued to turn out the bag.

"Why didn't you tell me?" persisted Anna.

"I thought you'd get the wrong idea."

"Idea about what?" Anna looked a little worried. A sudden penchant for plastic hair accessories must have seemed somewhat outlandish, let alone an enthusiasm for S Club 7.

"I was thinking about all the stuff you and Julia were saying and I thought taking some pictures for magazines *would* be quite interesting."

"Jesus, is that all?" Anna sighed. "So have you done anything about it?"

"Eve from art college put me in touch with some people, so I did some dummy jobs for them and it escalated from there. They seem really impressed with my book." Relieved that she didn't have to keep up the charade any longer, Maddie grinned at Anna.

"That's fantastic," said Anna. After a couple of seconds hugging, she pulled away slightly. "You haven't got any Mel C tattoo transfers hidden away anywhere, have you?"

Yep. It had been that darn magazine that set the whole process in motion. Once bitten by that bug, it was money which had lured Maddie further down the path to freelance photography. Twizzling around on the swivel-chair in front of the computer, her eye fell on her brand new, pristine invoice book. She couldn't deny it, money was partly responsible for her change of heart.

Even though Maddie had told herself she would just go along to meet with a couple of art editors Eve knew, for the experience, inevitably she'd got herself mixed up with the whole pecuniary thing. People had wanted to know what she charged and insisted on telling her their rates of pay for carrying out different types of shoots. The more she'd heard, however, the more she liked it. They actually paid you to go to a gig and take snaps of the bands. At first she'd just done some low-key stuff for some low-key clients to get some tearsheets, but once she'd had a whiff of the wonga that appeared in her hand at the end of a job, she'd quickly grown partial to the aroma.

The money had turned out to be as addictive as the magazines themselves. Previously, the only kind of flush Maddie had ever known was when Anna took her to her favourite Mexican and she downed a chimichanga more quickly than she ought. Anna had been really good about Maddie's financial situation and was happy to embrace the concept of 'family money', but Maddie had never been entirely comfortable about the disparity in earning power. She hadn't realised how good it felt to say to Anna: "Don't worry, I'll get this."

She picked up the bumph outlining the pros and cons of their mortgage company. Anna's mother had phoned on Maddie's birthday and done a little scaremongering over the importance of the age-to-repayment-period ratio when getting on the property ladder.

"You don't want to be coming up to sixty-five with ten years of your mortgage left to pay, do you, sweetheart?" Babs had yapped down the phone.

Maddie wondered whether Anna had primed her mother to give her this lecture, but the age factor had certainly hit a nerve.

Thus the timing of Maddie's birthday had to be acknowledged in the equation that had led to the U-turn. Having highfalutin ideas about your future, as a twenty-something, was to be expected. Sitting down on your twenty-first birthday after a lecture entitled 'Woman As A Semiotic Object' and setting out exactly what you're going to achieve, how you're going to live and what code of ethics you are going to live by was one thing. Still adhering to those same idealistic principles twelve years later seemed a little inappropriate. Everyone had moved on – except for Kat, who didn't count as she hadn't turned thirty yet. Prioritising drink and drugs over meals with vegetables had been *de rigueur* in their twenties, but time was marching on and some sort of nutritional balance had to be achieved.

Although the transformation was still in its infancy – which meant Maddie was prone to private moments of deep depression – deep down *beneath* the deep depression, she knew that saying to new acquaintances 'I'm thirty-two and building up a business as a freelance stills photographer' sounded fairly accepta–

Anna's key in the front door shocked Maddie out of her reverie.

"Can you believe it? I popped in at Alan's on the corner to buy you some fags and he had a couple of bottles out the back. Two for the price of one and a half. Bargain or what?" Anna headed for the kitchen and took two flutes out of the cupboard. Maddie followed her expectantly.

"Have you checked those for dust?" asked Maddie, even though the thought that she was turning into her mother scared her more than life itself.

"Oh, by the way. I picked up your phone by mistake on the way out and Kat called while I was at the shop," said Anna. "I hope you don't mind me answering, but I saw her name and thought –"

"Of course not. What did she want? I haven't seen her for ages."

"That's exactly what she said."

"Is she still with that Miro woman?" Maddie felt a rush of regret that she had been avoiding Kat for the past couple of months, but it was bound to take time for their relationship to get back to normal. Giving up the studio she'd found, decorated and worked in with Kat had been like cutting off a limb. Going back there and seeing Kat doing all the stuff she used to do would be like dipping the raw stump into a vat of salt.

"No. She said it never really came to anything."

Maddie would have been shocked if it had. For most of the time she'd known her, Kat had been single. She'd had many a short, sex-based encounter, but although she was happy sharing bodily fluids with relative strangers, sharing emotions with any of them never seemed to be on the cards.

"She did say you should go and visit her at the studio sometime soon. I think her exact words were, 'When is she going to haul her lazy arse round here and finish that eyesore of a painting?'"

Maddie smiled. For Kat to call something an eyesore was practically a compliment. "I guess I should get that out of her way..."

"I told her about us buying a flat together," said Anna.

"What did she say?"

"Not a lot – she seemed to take it all in her stride." Anna placed both thumbs under the bulging champagne cork and pressed until the tips of her digits turned red. "I'm not surprised it didn't work out with that woman. I mean, what kind of person has a name like 'Miro' anyway?"

Secret people

"I guess this is all a little bit downmarket for you, isn't it, Miro?" said Kat, looking at her lover's smart, tailored trousers and then at the spit 'n' sawdust surroundings of the pub.

"Don't let a trouser crease fool you. I've been around a bit, you know," replied Miro before sucking the remainder of her spritzer up through her straw. "Anyway, it's nice." She shifted in her seat to look at the old, sturdy bar and the low-beamed ceiling. "It feels solid."

"So, how was the course? Did any crazies try to leap on the life model?"

"These weekend courses are always a little..." Miro paused to find the right phrase "... different from your average evening class, but it was fine."

Kat laughed at her diplomacy. "When you say 'fine', actually you mean 'shit'."

"No..." protested Miro.

"Really shit?"

"I wouldn't say –"

"Dull as fu–"

"Oh, okay you win. It was dire."

"I knew it!"

"The heating broke in the studio, so the model kept jiggling around because she was cold, which naturally caused ructions. I asked Frank, one of the artists, to find a portable heater, and he came marching back in with a bloody industrial-sized fan heater. Given that I'd let them set up their own scenario and they'd gone for the 'Rubenesque woman on bed of rose petals' approach, with the odd feather thrown in for bulk, you can understand my concerns. Before I could point out the obvious pitfalls of the combination of fast-moving air and petals, Frank had plugged the bloody thing in, turned it up full blast, and that was that. The model looked like she'd been tarred and feathered and bits of petal had attached themselves to the great globules of oil paint Beryl had been throwing at her canvas. I'd told her she was creating problems for herself by daubing it on so thickly, but she hadn't listened. Then Mike had an allergic reaction and couldn't find his spray..."

"Sounds like a complete 'mare," said Kat, trying to visualise her calm, poised lover amid such chaos.

"Believe me, it was worse. Things just went downhill from there. The model stormed out, the others turned on Frank, and it ended up being more like a group therapy session than the relaxed Easter art course I'd been promised."

"Sounds too much like hard work to me," laughed Kat.

"Maybe I should turn my hand to something more simple, like computer design. No paint, no feathers – it'd be a joy."

The art snob in Kat made her grimace on the inside as outwardly she tried to muster a smile. Surely her nice, slightly eccentric art-teacher girlfriend wasn't going to change into a computer nerd? Kat's smile became frozen on her face while she waited for Miro to undermine the statement with a laugh or a light 'only joking' punch on the arm. She needed prompting. "You wouldn't do that. Would you?"

Kat watched her lover's face and was happy to see the corners of her mouth curl upwards.

"Of course not!" she protested.

"You had me worried there for a minute." Kat pointed at Miro's empty glass. "Same again?"

As she went to the bar, Kat turned back to look at Miro, who was oblivious to her gaze. It made her feel like a seedy voyeur but the pleasure of unadulterated looking was delicious. The way Miro held herself, her dark hair, fair skin and eyes as blue as the tiles on the bottom of the aparthotel swimming pool on her last trip to Spain, put her in mind of Pavlova. The dancer, not the meringue-based dessert.

Kat's phone started ringing as she made her way back to the table. Plonking the drinks down, she examined the display. The sight of Maddie's name made her heart leap. She knew it would be rude to take the call, but she couldn't help herself. Miro smiled serenely and picked up the newspaper lying next to her.

"Hi Maddie." Kat hated the way that caller displays had changed the whole rhythm of telephone conversations. Gone were the days when someone could be surprised by a friend, and that meant conversations now started the wrong way round. The receiver of the call opened by greeting a person by name, putting the onus on the receiver to open the conversation, instead of allowing the caller to take the initiative. It was all wrong.

"Hi Kat."

"So, how are things?" You see. Third response has to be a conversation opener, regardless of the intention of the proactive participant, the one who'd actually dialled the number.

"I'm okay. Quite busy doing one thing and another."

"Sounds intriguing."

"Oh, you know. Nothing exciting. Well, not that exciting." Maddie's voice faded to an indistinguishable mumble.

"You're well, then?" asked Kat, trying to perk up the conversation.

"Yeah. Can't complain…"

Kat cast her eyes in Miro's direction as she listened to Maddie's voice. She still had her nose in the paper but Kat couldn't talk freely while she was sitting there waiting, especially as Maddie looked like being hard work.

"You know, Mads, now's not such a good time."

"Oh right. Sorry. It's just that Anna said you'd called, so I thought I'd call back."

"Yeah." Kat squirmed in her seat. "Look, why don't you come over to the studio tomorrow? It'll be like old times."

"I can't do tomorrow. I've got a meeting." Kat's heart sank. There she was, wallowing in the notion of 'old times' while Maddie was talking about 'meetings'. It was like she didn't know her any more, and without that knowledge she was a free-form blob, random and futureless, like something trapped in a monochrome lava lamp. "How about next Friday around four o'clock?"

"Next Friday is fine."

"See you then. Maybe you could explain to me the concept behind the eye–"

"–sore. Yeah, yeah, yeah."

Kat laughed at her friend's impromptu Roland Rat impression.

Talk of the devil

Andy had missed Anna during her extended Easter break and was pleased she'd suggested going for a drink after work. His boyfriend Phil had to go and practise a weights routine for the open day at his gym, so it had worked out rather well.

"You don't mind if Jules joins us, do you, Andy?" asked Anna. She put her phone on the table and topped up his glass.

"No," he replied, although he was quite looking forward to a quiet chat with Anna after all the snippets of news he'd caught at work that day. "Where is she?"

"Just out of a meeting on the Strand."

"Okay." Andy glanced up at the station-sized clock clinging to the bare brick that lined the bar's interior and calculated the amount of time he had before Julia arrived. Strand to Chancery Lane, taking into account the roadworks at the Aldwych – twenty minutes at a push.

"So what's all this about you applying for a mortgage?" Finally he could get down to the nitty-gritty.

"We just did it over Easter. Just charged into the bank, I flopped out my pay slips, Maddie showed them her... Well, Maddie showed them her prospects and that was that."

"So Maddie's finally agreed to the whole shebang?" He was finding it a little hard to believe. Wasn't it just last Christmas that Anna had been despairing over her girlfriend's inability to take the plunge?

"Yeah. Crazy, isn't it? I think she realised she can't act like she's twenty-five forever and said yes."

"Wow!"

"Quite a turn around, I know, but who am I to reason why? I'm just happy it's happening. No. I don't think 'happy' quite does the job. Ecstatic. That's more like it." Like a caricature on a children's flashcard, her huge grin illustrated the emotion.

"I'm so pleased for you, Anna," said Andy, reaching over to give her a hug. He felt the hardness of her spine as he rubbed his hands over her back and thought how intimate that was, to feel someone's bone structure. Comforted by their friendship, he listened to her rambling on about soft furnishings but became preoccupied by the way the violet hue of the lights and the smoke in their 'snug' meant she looked like a presenter on *Top of the Pops*. Her over-animated, substanceless chatter compounded the image. He wanted to believe in her happiness but couldn't get a handle on Maddie's extreme change of heart.

"You know, Andy, she's turned a corner. It's like she's suddenly realised we're meant to be together. We've talked loads about it and she's really okay about moving on. She can still churn out a few big pictures in her spare time, but she agrees it's the only way forward."

"Really..."

As Anna continued counting down the top ten reasons why Maddie's conversion was genuine, Andy worried that Anna was deluding herself.

"... It hasn't taken her long to get back into taking photos. Her equipment is a little out of date apparently, but it's not a problem at the moment. A couple of her art college friends have given her some contacts and she's been meeting editors of magazines to sell them stuff. It's great. Trust Maddie to land on her feet." She swigged back the dregs of her wine and for a moment Andy was won over by her enthusiasm. "To be absolutely honest, Andy, if she hadn't done something extreme, I don't think we'd have stood much of a chance."

"Lord above! You mean you would have left her?" Andy felt his eyes widen and eyebrows lift to meet each other like French accents reaching over a couple of 'e's.

"That does sound tough, doesn't it? I love Maddie to bits, you know I do, and she knows it, but I couldn't see where we were going and it was making me feel anxious. Do you know what I mean?"

Andy nodded. He didn't have a clue what she meant and hoped he never would because it didn't sound like too much fun.

"Something had to give and I knew the crux of it was that she was scared of change. Scared of growing up."

"You didn't actually say to her, 'I'm going to leave you if you don't agree to buying a flat with me,' did you?"

"Good God, no! I'm not that callous!" said Anna in astonishment.

"Phew!"

"We just sat down and had a real heart to heart. It took a while to get to the root of the problem, but it's fine now. We've talked it through and we're both really happy. You should have seen her when we got the call from the bank. She was as wild about it as I was."

"That's great, Anna. I'm really pleased for you," said Andy, although he still wondered how much was bravado. He made a mental note to call Maddie, on the off-chance, just so they could get together sometime. A casual thing, to touch base. She'd obviously just ended an affair that had been going sour...

"I know we've been offered a bit more than we can afford, but it's great looking around for places..." Anna banged on.

"Whereabouts are you looking?"

"Kilburn, West Hampstead. That kind of area."

"Oh. Nice."

The more Anna talked, the more uneasy Andy got, and it annoyed him that he couldn't put his finger on the root of his negativity. Finally, he admitted to being a little nervous about the future. Friends buying houses were like friends who decided to have babies, or friends who split up and when it comes to taking sides you can't remember which one you were friends with first. Routines, rhythms, life patterns, whole social vistas change. Andy massaged the inside of his lip with his teeth as Anna painted a picture of what lay ahead. From where he was standing, however, the image she was creating was like the early stages of a Rolf Harris – lots of big, bold strokes that look really fucking mad and random, like they're never going to connect to make a proper image.

"Have you been to look at anything yet?" he asked.

"No..." Anna hesitated.

"Maddie not keen to do the actual deed then?" Andy was disappointed in himself, picking at a wound they had just examined and dressed.

"No. She's dead keen. But she thinks we're going to get somewhere in St John's Wood and I don't think that's in our price bracket."

"Really? St John's Wood? I'd have thought some sort of garret would have been more her thing."

"Andy, I think you've got the wrong idea about her. She might go on about being an artist, but she still wants to have the right postcode."

"I guess she does come from Cheshire," muttered Andy as he digested this new take on his friend.

"Fancy another bottle?" asked Anna, reaching for her wallet.

"I don't know..."

"Oh, go on. Julia will be here soon."

"All right then."

Anna went off to the bar and left Andy to think. Being a bit of a light-weight, he was already quite pissed, so his thoughts weren't necessarily coherent. He wanted to tell Anna she was making the most awful mistake. How could someone become something so different? Anna was beautiful. She was intelligent. She was tall. How could she be so blind? Had she really *thought* about buying somewhere with Maddie? Maddie was a bit of a fruitcake. A little unpredictable. What had really changed Maddie's mind? Was it an affair that had gone bad? Now he knew he was pissed. He would never use the phrase 'an affair gone bad'... even to himself.

"Sorry about that. I got chatting to a woman at the bar," said Anna when she eventually arrived back at their table.

"Oh yeah?"

"Not like that, stupid! She works on the top floor – asked me for a light and –"

"Show me."

Anna guided him towards her so he could see through the throng.

"Not 'you're never too old for Lycra' woman?" he gasped.

"No. Sophisticated 'I've got a posh suit and I'm not afraid to wear it' woman, two to the left of the Lycra."

Andy leaned more heavily on the table. "Blimey! Now she's a different story. Can't say I've noticed her around, though."

"Funny that," said Anna. Andy ignored the reference to his sexual blinkers and let her continue. "She's quite new. I think you were away when she came down to introduce herself. Seems really nice."

"Nice enough to make you take up smoking?"

"Hardly. But I might invest in a lighter!"

Anna poured out the wine and Andy took a long, reflective slurp. Like a dog with a bone, or a drunk person with something on their mind, Andy had to get it absolutely clear in his head. "So you're not worried about Maddie's personality transplant then?"

"I'd hardly go that far, Andy." Anna picked up her glass and leaned back defensively in her chair.

"I don't mean it nastily, Anna, but you have to wonder what's gone on, don't you?" He searched for the right words. "I just need to know that you've thought this thing through properly." As he lifted his head to look over at Anna, a big wet kiss landed on his cheek. He looked up in surprise and saw Julia.

"Hello you two," she said, as she wriggled out of her coat and commandeered a chair from the next table. "I can see you've had a bit of a head start." She leaned over and planted another smacker on Anna's alcohol-red cheek.

"Good meeting?" asked Anna.

"Yeah, actually. Another signature, another bonus. You know what it's like."

"I'll get you a glass," said Anna, and she disappeared off to the bar. Rushing off like that obviously meant she didn't want their earlier conversation to continue. Either that or she wanted a closer look at the posh suit at the bar.

"How's things then?" asked Julia.

"Busy. I'm sure Anna's told you about the changes at work."

"Oh yeah. Sounds really odd to me that they should announce this reshuffle thing is going to happen but not tell you when."

"Tell me about it. They've brought this management consultancy on board who are investigating ways of 'maximising the optimal potentiality of our staffing structure' in order to oil the wheels of our great organisation and grease the palms of those who own it. Which means penny-pinching and streamlining to most people."

Julia laughed and, after delving around in her bag, pulled out her lipstick and stood in front of Andy to get to the vast mirror on the wall behind his chair. She started to apply a fresh layer while he talked.

"It doesn't make for a very stable working environment..." While he yabbered on, Andy appreciated the look of Julia. She had a mobile, expressive mouth that was getting redder with every swish of the stick over her lips. She was slim but curvaceous, walked with the poise of someone who knows people will want to talk to them, and had the longest eyelashes he had ever seen. Her thick hair was cut short and her eyes were chameleon-like, changing colour with every outfit and every occasion. With Julia's cleavage just inches from his face, the wonders of a Wonderbra were finally demystified for Andy. Her chest was quite impressive – even he realised Julia had great tits. He wondered if Anna fancied her. Whether they'd ever done it together...

"... Everyone's so twitchy, it's like a never-ending game of wink murder over at our place at the moment," he continued. "Someone wearing a novelty tie will hang around a department for a few days and then suddenly, with no outward signs of communication, a desk will be cleared and all that will be left is the outline of the place their fluffy gonk was once stuck to their computer."

"You and Anna are okay though?" Julia screwed the column of colour back into its sheath, snapped the top of her lipstick back on and sat down.

"Yeah. Apparently we are the golden girls of the company at the moment. They didn't have a bad word to say about us."

"That's a relief."

"You're not wrong there. Especially for those of us who are planning on taking our first steps on the property ladder."

Anna was taking a long time getting a glass, and he thought he'd try and pick Julia's brains on the matter before she came back.

"Oh, yeah. It's fantastic, isn't it? I just can't believe they didn't do it sooner. I've never seen Anna looking happier. Or Maddie, come to that." Once Julia got going she could gush like a geyser, but her words couldn't quite dampen the anxiety Andy was harbouring in the pit of his stomach.

When Anna finally re-emerged from the mosh pit of the bar complete with extra glass, Andy noticed a business card sticking out of the pocket of her trousers, but said nothing.

By chucking-out time, both Andy and Julia were buzzing and ready for more.

"You've gotta come to this club with us, Jules, you'd love it," burbled Andy.

"Sounds good. Where is it?"

"Count me out, I've got to get back," said Anna, yawning to show she wasn't going to be won over.

"Looks like it's just you and me then, Andy."

"Do you need to call Ed to let him know?"

"No. It's my night off tonight, so who knows what might happen?" said Julia with no hint of guilt. Andy looked at Anna, raised an eyebrow and mouthed 'lucky cow'. They all did one last wallet, keys and phone check before heading for the door.

"Let's get together and do something at the weekend, then, instead?" said Julia as they dropped Anna off at the tube.

"We're going to our respective parents at the weekend, but I'll give you a call when we get back."

Picture perfect

Even though she felt comforted by the fact that Dysons were the best uprights on the market, Sheila missed her old cylindrical pullalong. It'd had to go, though. They'd stopped making bags for it years before she got rid of it and, in spite of her efforts to fashion something similar out of an M&S carrier bag and an old pair of tights, she'd finally had to admit it had stopped doing the job. Besides, the smell of smouldering plastic and nylon had been awfully cloying.

Sheila liked hoovering. She liked the noise and the total isolation it could bring. She didn't care if Malcolm was shouting down at her to ask if his shirt and tie went with his trousers, or if the milkman was hammering on the door for his money. She was hoovering and that gave her carte blanche to ignore everything around her. It was quite an art form really, Sheila thought, as she rolled the multi-coloured monster back and forth over the deep pile of the living-room carpet and watched the balls of fluff swirl round inside its transparent belly. She considered how typical this invention was of modern-day living. When she was a girl, everything was covered up, hidden away – feelings, worries, problems, dirt from the carpet – not even seen, let alone heard. But these days everything was on show, just like all the dust tumbling around in the vacuum. Why do you have to see it? Sheila asked herself. It's dirty, it's horrible. Surely the whole point is for it to be hidden behind some opaque outer casing? Turn on the TV and you get nothing but sex. Where once the camera would turn away, now you see everything in gynaecological detail. Sheila shuddered and shook her head as if to throw off the unpleasant thought. It might be there, but why do they have to ram it down our throats? Sheila had stopped watching *Brookside* years ago for fear of witnessing same-sex coupling at teatime. As she turned the appliance off to attach the hose, she wondered whether that Beth Jordache had anything to do with her daughter's sudden change of sexual orientation.

"Maddie'll be here in an hour or so." It was Malcolm's voice, as he came down the stairs. "Do you want me to do anything?"

"You could pop out to the shops if you like. I forgot there were going to be four of us, and I only bought three salmon steaks for lunch."

"What do you mean, four?"

"You, me, Maddie and Anna."

"Oh, I thought I'd told you, Anna's not coming. She's going to see her parents this weekend, so it'll just be the three of us."

"Oh, that's a shame," said Sheila as she struggled to change the nozzle. "I must be psychic!"

Malcolm laughed gently and kissed his wife on the cheek. Sheila watched him pick up the newspaper from the table in the hall and glide off in the direction of the garden.

"If you really want to make yourself useful, you could empty the dishwasher," she called out.

"Right you are, darling." Malcolm returned to the kitchen with less purpose than before.

Sheila heard the sound of dishes being packed away, crossed the task off her mental 'to do' list and headed upstairs to make a start on her husband's study.

Trying not to pay attention to the fact that she was dusting round the knick-knackery instead of underneath it, she wondered why Maddie was coming to visit alone. She picked up a photograph from the desk. It was of Maddie when she was sixteen. Sheila paused for a moment and studied her daughter's happy, smiling face. The picture was taken on a summer holiday to Italy and Maddie looked even blonder and bronzer than usual. A tear of pride pricked Sheila's eye as she remembered how the Italian men in the village had taken to Maddie. What was the name of that boy she'd become friendly with? Antonio, perhaps. Maddie even wrote to him for a while, Sheila remembered, her focusless gaze replaying snatches of the holiday. She sighed nostalgically as her thoughts slipped back into the present and she pondered over the reason for her daughter's welcome but unexpected visit. She hadn't gone and split up with Anna, had she? Naturally, if she had, Sheila would support her daughter, look after her, tell her everything would be all right. Maddie could come and stay with them for a little while. Have a change of scenery while she thought about where to live and what to do. It would be nice to have her knocking around the place. It would be hard at first, break-ups always were, but eventually she'd see it as a fresh start...

The chimes of the doorbell interrupted Sheila's fantasy. She put the photo back in its place, pulled off her pinny and went to greet her daughter. She had only made it to the top of the stairs when she heard Maddie talking to Malcolm.

"Dad, Dad! You'll never guess what!" she heard her say excitedly.

"Well, it must be something important to bring you all the way up here," replied Malcolm.

"Anna and I are buying a flat together!"

"That's wonderful, darling," said Malcolm as he hugged his jubilant daughter.

"Hello Mum! You look great." Maddie pulled away from her father and transferred her hug to her mother. "Did you hear what I just told Dad?"

"No, but it sounds exciting."

"Anna and I are buying a flat together. We've been to the bank to apply for a mortgage and everything!" cried Maddie, reverting to her seven-year-old self, as she did every time she stepped through her parents' portal.

Sheila smiled and gasped. "Oh, Maddie! That's a big decision to make. No wonder you've come to tell us in person."

Hamburger hill

"Why don't you leave that to me, Grae, and go and open another bottle of Liebfrau for Mum," suggested Barbara impatiently. But Graham wasn't going to relinquish his position at the barbecue without a fight. He maintained a firm grip on the tongs as she tried to prise them from his chipolata fingers.

"Anna can do that," he said through an exaggerated smile. He called towards the house: "Anna, get a drop of Kraut for Grandma, will you?"

But Doris was already heaving herself off the garden bench and Barbara wondered where she was heading. There was no way she could have missed the atmosphere.

"It's all right, pet," Doris told Anna, who had appeared in the doorway looking confused by Graham's effort to communicate. "He asked you to fetch me some more wine, but it's all right, I can get it."

"No, you stay there, Nana," replied Anna. "A drop more Blush for you, Betty?"

Betty, who was partial to a nice chilled rosé, nodded so enthusiastically that her fine, permed hair bounced on her head. Barbara watched Anna gloss over the situation.

"What about Vi?" asked Anna.

Vi was the final member of the triumvirate of elderly relatives. Not that they were all blood relations. Shortly after her husband died in the late 70s, Doris had moved in with her old school friend Vi, who owned a huge house in west London. Then they'd met Betty on a coach trip round the Benelux a few years later. On their return to England, Betty came up from Godalming to visit her new friends for a weekend – and never went home. That was in 1983. So it was that Vi and Betty had been subsumed into Doris's family and together they had collectively become known as 'the Nani'.

"Vi's in the living room trying to find the cricket on your mum's new telly. Bring her a glass out, though. Look's like grub's going to be up in a minute," said Betty.

Barbara turned round and saw Graham leave the patio and stomp off towards his shed at the end of the garden. With the coast clear and the wine distributed, Anna joined her at the barbecue.

"Smells great," said Anna, as she put her arm round her mother's shoulders affectionately.

"The burgers will be done in a couple of minutes but the drumsticks are still raw in the middle. I told the stupid bugger to put them on first, but he wouldn't listen."

"What's got into him today?" asked Anna. "Usually he makes an effort at least to be civil when the Nani are here."

Barbara prodded a burger that was not in need of prodding and wondered whether to tell Anna what had prompted her father's mood. She decided it wasn't worth trying to hide it from her. "I told him I'm going to give you the deposit for the flat and he went ballistic."

"Oh, Mum, you didn't. I thought that was going to be our little secret."

"I know. But I get sick of him treating you so badly. There's no reason for it. The miserable old sod! We shouldn't have to tiptoe around him, Annie. Giving in to him is just making him worse."

"I'm sorry, Mum. I really am."

Barbara busied herself by assembling burgers in buns with dollops of relish, salad and onions, as they talked. "It's not you who should be sorry, darling," said Barbara. "What's the good of having a bit of money to spare if I can't spend in on my only daughter?"

"I do love you, Mum." Anna watched her wedge chocolate-stuffed bananas onto the glowing embers. Vi appeared at the doorway and made her way over to join her friends at the table. The smell of the food must have smoked her out of her multi-channel heaven. She pulled up a chair and tucked into the savoury snacks – and immediately, three grey curly heads locked together. Some sort of pow-wow was taking place.

"What's got into them?" Anna asked her mother as she smiled and waved at the Nani.

"Old age," said Barbara.

"Do you think I should I tell Nana about me and Maddie, now that we're buying a place together?"

Barbara considered the facts. Doris was pushing eighty. Would she be able to cope with the idea of her granddaughter – the apple of her eye – being gay?

"I reckon you're best off saying nothing. Let them carry on thinking you're just friends."

"Whatever makes you happy."

Silent witness

"Trust Graham to put the mockers on everything," confided Doris to her friends. She wondered how her daughter put up with such behaviour. What would happen when the novelty of bi-monthly WI meetings and weekly visits to Nelly's Nails began to pall?

"Shame Anna's Maddie isn't allowed to come," said Vi.

"Keep your voice down, Vi," hissed Betty.

"I don't know why Babs doesn't tell the moody old sod to put a sock in it," remarked Vi.

"You would have thought he'd have got over it by now –" continued Doris.

"I mean, it must be at least four years ago that Anna told them," butted in Betty.

"Exactly. Enough's enough," finished Doris.

"You would have thought so," added Vi. They all shook their heads in disappointment.

"It's Babs I feel sorry for," said Betty. "Do you think we should tell her we know what's going on, Doris? She might welcome the support."

"I don't know. I think it would just make her embarrassed. If she felt comfortable discussing it with me, she would have done so before."

"Mum's the word then, eh?" Betty confirmed. There was a pause while they brooded.

"But Maddie is such a lovely girl," said Vi as she untwisted her cutlery from its floral paper napkin. They agreed, leaned back in their padded plastic chairs, looked over at Barbara and Anna and cooed and ahhed as Anna approached the table with plates of food in her hands.

Graham still hadn't emerged from the wilderness of the back of the garden, but they decided to eat anyway.

It was Anna who broke the awkward silence that Graham's sudden disappearance had caused. "I hear you've gone and booked yourselves on a Mediterranean cruise, you old devils!"

"Yes, we're off in July. But I can tell you about that later. I hear *you've* got some news for *us*," replied Doris for all of them.

"What, you mean the fact that I've decided to take the plunge and buy a flat at last?"

"Oh, how exciting!" said Betty, as she reconciled the conflicting actions of spitting her words out and keeping her teeth in.

"Can you afford it on your own, dear?" asked Vi, who had already attacked her bun and slopped tomato relish down her blouse.

"Well, actually, Maddie and I are going in on it together. We were both thinking that renting is a waste of money, so it seemed logical. Like a joint investment," explained Anna.

"What a wonderful idea!" Doris turned to her friends and smiled.

"I think that deserves a toast," suggested Betty.

"To Anna and Maddie and their joint investment!" declared Doris.

The lost world

Maddie knew Old Street better than the mosaic verruca on the ball of her left foot, but now she felt like a stranger. She became aware of different things, like the huge puddle that collected in the gutter outside the doorway to her… to *Kat's* studio. Rain or shine, it was always there, as if it had some special relationship with the water table, but it was only now that she became conscious of the fact. A car sped by and splashed her trousers. In the past she wouldn't have noticed because it wouldn't have mattered, but now, with her smart 'I've been to a meeting' clothes on, she did notice and it did matter. She looked down at her splattered legs and wondered how much it cost to get a garment dry cleaned.

Her finger hovered over the buzzer. Kat hadn't bothered to change the name on the bell. Maddie couldn't yet feel nostalgic about things like that. Instead she felt sick. Was she ready to face what she knew she'd see in her best friend's eyes? What she herself knew deep down. She'd sold out. She'd given up on her dream. Abandoned it. She slunk into one of the dark brick, nameless doorways opposite the studio and smoked a cigarette.

Cat on a hot tin roof

"What the fuck are you doing?" Without another person's ears to absorb the sound, Kat's voice bounced right back at her, as she forced herself to stop fussing around the studio, washing glasses, emptying ashtrays in readiness for Maddie's arrival. Her frustration knocked her into the decrepit chair in the corner. Her arse crunched against its spiky wooden frame. She winced.

She looked at her watch. Maddie would be there soon. "Act like you're in the middle of something. Make it look like her visit is a pleasant sideshow in your day," she told herself.

In an effort to find some serenity, she focused her mind on Miro. She wondered if she would learn to love her like she did Maddie. She allowed the thought even though she knew it wasn't conducive to her personal growth. Ever since Christmas, when Maddie told her she was giving up the studio and her life fell apart, she'd spent a lot of time in the self-help sections of London's bookshops. Lacking the funds to spend on a therapist, she devoured any form of DIY psychotherapy she could find. Well-thumbed books with swirling colours on their covers littered her journey across the capital in pursuit of mental health; and in her quest, the thoroughfares of book-dense WC2 had become roads much travelled. Although she suspected herself of being a woman who loved too much, she had opened her mind to the possibility of healing. She had to learn to accept her feelings for 'the one who was not to be' (i.e. Maddie) and achieve closure. She shouldn't try and replace her with someone different (i.e. Miro) but should see new relationships as an emotional playground – she would pick up bumps and knocks along the way, but ultimately, she would learn to embrace the obstacles as friends, and to reach out with love to those who wanted to help her find her balance on the see-saw of life.

As she scrabbled around, positioning some paints here, a sketch of a new design there, to make it look like she was in the middle of creating cutting-edge pottery, Kat tried to judge whether she and Miro were see-saw compatible. The ride hadn't been too bumpy so far, but maybe that was because Maddie hadn't been around. What would her self-help gurus think of Maddie's role in her life? She hadn't found any books that covered the idea of a time-share relationship – for that, Kat had come to realise, was how she had looked upon her relationship with Maddie. Anna was merely looking after Maddie until such time as Kat was ready to take over. In the past, there hadn't been any need to change things by telling Maddie how she felt. A confession would have presented more potential cons than pros. She had never considered the possibility that Maddie was actually happy with Anna so, in Kat's mind, Anna had always been a 'caretaker' girlfriend, someone with whom Maddie was comfortable but just biding her time until Kat was ready to sweep her off her feet. She'd thought Maddie would tire of Anna's funny, slightly prissy, corporate ways, but now it looked as if Kat's bluff had been called. She had timed her run all wrong, but when Maddie walked through the door, Kat would be nothing less than positive and supportive.

The sound of the buzzer made her nerve-endings tingle – she was out of the blocks.

"Hey you!" she cried excitedly, and she watched Maddie climb up the stairs. "Fucking hell, mate, what are you dressed as?"

"Old jokes are always the oldest," retorted Maddie as they laughed and hugged.

"I hear that congratulations are in order," exclaimed Kat as she pulled away.

"Congratulations?" Maddie seemed genuinely confused.

"Aren't you about to make some glorious commitment to your girl-friend and tie yourselves to each other for the next twenty-five years?"

"Oh, jeez, that! I'd forgotten she'd told you." Maddie hung her mac up behind the door and instinctively adjusted the webbing that formed the seat of the spiky chair before easing herself into it.

"Yeah. She said you'd just had the call from the bank or some-thing…" Kat handed Maddie a tumbler of Scotch and settled in the wicker bucket-chair that swung gently from a hook in the ceiling. Kat flexed her toes as she searched for something to fill the silence. "Do you remember when we first got this thing?" They both looked up as the fitting on the ceiling creaked under her weight.

"How could I forget?" replied Maddie. "Was it your idea or mine to do that film?"

"I can't remember, but we got some great shots of the studio."

"And you nearly broke my back in the process," added Maddie.

"Your back? It was the ceiling that needed plaster!" Having filled the gap with a little nostalgia, Kat waited for Maddie to pick up the flat-buying gauntlet. She didn't, so Kat took a different tack.

"So what's this I hear about people actually paying you to take photos?" she prompted.

"Yeah! It's crazy isn't it? I can't believe it's been so straightfor-ward. All it took was a couple of introductions to a few people, the offer of doing a couple of things for free so they could suss me out, and commissions have started to come in. I was photographing some kids who'd been chosen to review ice-creams for a teen mag last week... It was fun."

"So it's going well, then?"

"Yeah. I've found a really cheap place where I can hire a large format camera if I need to. But I haven't got anything to judge it by at the moment, so I hope it's not just a flash in the pan. You know, like beginner's luck."

"'Course it's not!" Kat said encouragingly, although half of her wanted Maddie to fall flat on her face so she would have to scurry back to the sanctuary of old, familiar surroundings.

"So how's it working out with Stewart being here?" asked Maddie.

"I think he's going to be fine. I don't see him that much. He pays the rent on time and hardly shows his face, which is okay with me."

"Isn't it a bit odd, though?"

It was monumentally odd as far as Kat was concerned. It was odd, horrible and had shattered her life. "Oh, you know. It's okay," she said.

"Don't you miss me, then?"

"Of course I bleedin' miss you, you stupid cow!" They laughed gently together. That was when Kat put her finger on why the atmosphere was so strained: a chasm of politeness had opened up between them. She set about filling it with common ground. "You know you can come here and work on your canvas any time you want..."

"Thanks. I want to get it finished, but, you know, it's just having the time." Maddie got up and headed for the Scotch bottle. She stopped to look at the sketchbook Kat had left out.

Kat watched her scrutinising her work, but didn't press for any comment. She could tell her friend was in a bit of a stew. She looked like a person who was experiencing a metamorphosis but not feeling very happy with her in-between, hybrid self. A little like Dr David Banner must have felt just before total Hulkification turned him into the flailing green monster.

"Do you think I'm doing the right thing?" asked Maddie as she topped up Kat's glass.

"Yeah," replied Kat.

There was another awkward pause. "Did I tell you that Anna's mum is going to stump up the deposit?"

"No way!" Kat saw from Maddie's eyes that she was looking for a more incisive remark. It seemed like things were already spiralling out of her friend's control. "That's… generous of her."

"It makes me feel uncomfortable, to tell the truth."

Kat shrugged and reached for her glass.

"Do you think I should say no, Kat?"

"The money's irrelevant. The only thing that would make this a bad decision would be if you were having doubts about your feelings for Anna. But you're not, right?" Kat held her breath as she waited for Maddie's answer. What would she do if Maddie said she didn't know how she felt, that she was having second thoughts? Would Kat encourage her to back-pedal?

"I know I've talked about wanting to sleep with other women before," replied Maddie. "But I can't ever imagine not being with Anna."

"Well, then. You're making the perfect next step."

"Is that what you really think?" pressed Maddie.

"Yes," said Kat. No way, she thought.

Maddie humphed as if she were storing Kat's comments away in her mind to consider later. She coughed, ran her fingers through her hair and changed the subject. "So, what happened with you and that Miro woman you were so into at New Year?"

"Nothing."

"Nothing?" Maddie laughed. "And there's me thinking she was going to be the one to sort you out."

"Sort me out?" Kat forced a laugh at the suggestion. She didn't want to get drawn into a conversation about Miro, so she did what came most naturally and lied. "She turned out to be a bit peculiar."

"Don't they all?"

"I'm happy the way I am, anyway."

"Don't you want to find someone to settle –"

Kat got up suddenly. She had to get her off the subject somehow so she made a show of searching for her phone. "Do you mind if I make a quick call? I forgot to tell –"

"No, that's okay. I guess I'd better be going."

Kat hadn't meant to drive her away, and protested as Maddie put her glass in the sink, found her coat and stood by the door with her hand on the latch.

"Honestly, you don't have to go."

"I've got to go and meet Anna." Maddie kissed Kat on the cheek.

"By the way, Mads, I'm really sorry about missing your birthday..."

A birthday card can be a Trojan horse for old feelings, so don't go there! Kat remembered reading that somewhere and taking it to heart. In retrospect, however, not wishing her best friend happy birthday did seem a bit harsh.

"Oh, that's okay. These things happen..."

"It's good to see you, Maddie."

They agreed to get together again soon. As she watched Maddie disappear down the stairs, she felt the familiar cloak of despair wind round her body, squeezing the joy out of her. Kat looked at her watch. It was only just gone four. She could just fit in a visit to Waterstone's in the City if she hurried.

Collision course

Miro strode down the road towards Kat's building. She didn't make a habit of calling in on the off-chance, but at four in the afternoon she was sure Kat would still be up in her eyrie. She looked up at the window but couldn't see any sign of activity. With her eyes fixed up there, she walked straight into a woman who had burst out of the building.

Their shoulders clashed, knocking Miro's bag to the ground. The woman muttered something that could have been an apology and continued on her way. Head down, Miro reclaimed the impressive range of sanitary paraphernalia that had spilled onto the pavement, before pressing the buzzer.

"I knew you'd come back!" The voice sounded excited and a little breathless.

"Kat?" Miro checked she'd pressed the right button.

"Maddie?"

"No. It's Miro. Can I come up?"

The parent trap

For once The Fridge was quite warm. Shards of sunlight fell across the breakfast table making the colours of the orange juice, marmalade and bright blue crockery look like a scene from a Sunny Delight advert. Anna licked her finger and crushed a toast crumb that had escaped from her plate onto the checked tablecloth. She knew they should get a move on if they were going to be on time, but after her Saturday lie-in she was enjoying the warmth of the sun too much to move. There was a thud as the post spewed through the letterbox onto the floor. Maddie came trudging slowly back into the room, a letter already torn open and its contents in her hand.

"What's that you're reading?"

"It's from Mum," replied Maddie as she skimmed over the letter and spread out the enclosed newspaper cuttings on the table.

"Don't forget we were going to pick up your dry cleaning on the way to Julia's." Anna leaned back on her chair and waited for Maddie to move. She didn't. "We'd better not be too long then."

"You're first in the bathroom."

"Why me? I'm first in the bathroom every single day during the week."

"I'm reading this."

Anna grudgingly stood up and peered over Maddie's shoulder. "What crackpot remedies is she sending you this time?"

"It's something about the flat –"

"Not more horror stories," said Anna.

"She's only trying to look out for us." Maddie continued to read the letter. "She's sent us something about finances. If we want the other to inherit the flat should either of us die, we should make a will, as gay relationships aren't recognised in the eyes –"

"Jesus wept! The next thing you know she'll be knitting a rainbow jumper and wanting to march with us at Pride, if you're not careful."

"She's just taking an interest."

"I've always admired her ability to look on the bright side," scoffed Anna, and she shuffled off to take her shower.

"Oh, and she wants me to come up for a party she's having for all the neighbours –"

"She what?"

"She doesn't go into details, but she says she'd really like me to be there."

"You're not going to, are you?"

"Of course not. I'll make up some excuse."

The 'burbs

"So, Anna and Maddie have asked you to go along with them to map read while they look out for 'For Sale' signs along the way?" confirmed Ed incredulously.

"Yeah! Why not?" asked Julia, keeping her eyes fixed on the street below. She would probably be able to hear Anna's old Peugeot before she saw it, but she couldn't resist the excuse to have a nose at the flats across the street as well as monitoring the amount of trade going on at the parade of shops on the opposite corner. She was convinced it wasn't just clothes and duvets that were laundered at the Wash-o-matic.

"The fact that you and those who compiled the A-Z have never really been on the same wavelength might be one reason," said Ed.

"If you are thinking of mentioning the words 'Gipsy Corner' and 'fiasco' in the same sentence, I would think again if I were you," warned Julia.

"Okay! Okay! Keep your hair on!" Ed knew just how to get under Julia's skin.

"What are you up to today, then?"

"I'm meeting Alison for a drink in Hampstead –"

"Alison?" This wasn't a name Julia had heard before.

"I met her through a bloke at work. Seems really nice. She said something about having tickets to a gig in Camden, so I think we'll probably make a night of it."

"Sounds like fun." Julia felt a twinge of jealousy as she thought of this Alison going out and having a good time with Ed. She wondered if she wanted to sleep with him. If he wanted to sleep with her.

"What have you got planned?"

"I'll probably –"

"Have you seen my wallet?"

"On the table by the bed. I'll probably do something with Anna and Madge."

Julia's thoughts about Alison were interrupted by the chugging sound of a stationary vehicle outside her window. The horn honked and Julia saw Anna's hand appear out of the window and wave.

"So we won't see each other tonight, then?"

"No, not tonight." Julia gathered her stuff and headed for the door. She kissed Ed goodbye. "Wanna do something tomorrow?"

"Sure thing, gorgeous! Have a good time."

"And you! Don't forget to double lock the door behind you..." Julia hurried out, hoping Ed had a lousy time.

In the twenty seconds it took her to descend into the lobby, she had ripped her relationship with Ed apart. She was aware she was playing a dangerous game by letting Ed have such a free rein, but what could she do when it was the very notion of 'exclusivity' that gave her palpitations? That was one pattern she was not about to repeat. By keeping Ed at arm's length, at least she could see things coming (punches were rare but, at a distance, easily ducked) and it suited her that way. But the pay-off for preserving her independence was that Ed was easy prey for other women who might want to lure him away. Every time a new name came up in conversation, Julia became anxious that he would be tempted away from the paradise she had created for him.

Unfortunately, she never had enough time between her front door and the bottom of the stairs to answer the question that always cropped up as a result of this thought process: why couldn't she just put the past behind her? Today wasn't going to be any different, however. She opened the front door, set foot into the warm, spring sun, saw Anna and Maddie's excited faces smiling at her from the car... and all attempts to reason why ceased.

Anna, Maddie and Julia had waved goodbye to the estate agent with a cheery "see you in a couple of minutes" a good half-hour ago.

"Oh God, I didn't realise it was a one-way street," said Julia anxiously, as she leant forward with her knees squished into the gap between the two front seats and the A-Z held inches from her nose. Anna did yet another three-point turn.

"So if I go back the way we've just come, can I then turn left, left and left again to get in from the other side?" asked Anna with pointed calm.

"There's no one around," butted in Maddie. "Why don't you just go straight across, park up and we'll walk the rest of the way."

"But we're miles away yet!" said Anna, who never liked to walk any further than she had to.

"It's only the other side of Crampney Gardens," said Julia, keen to put an end to this torment.

"A friend of mine from college used to live there," said Maddie. "Nice, as I remember."

"We're never going to fucking know at this rate," said Anna. "The bleedin' estate agent must think we've got sucked into a parallel universe somewhere between Kilburn and West Hampstead."

"No! I've got it. Turn left here," said Julia excitedly, as she found her bearings. "Here, Anna! Here!" There was a squealing of rubber as Anna finally responded to Julia's instructions. Julia tried to ignore the pain of bare flesh on plastic as she was flung across the back seat. "There you are, number twenty-five."

"Kevin!" exclaimed Anna to the suited youth who stood on the threshold.

"I was just about to give up on you lot. Come on then, now you're here." Kevin held open the door to the tall, thin house by extending his arm, so the women had to brush past him to get through the narrow aperture. "Now, I must tell you that even as we speak we've got three other couples sitting in the office waiting to view this property.

I can't tell you how quickly things are going at the moment. Two-bedroom flats in your West Hampsteads, South Hampsteads, Swiss Cottages, are like bleedin' gold dust at the moment and there's one reason for that. Everybody wants 'em, nobody's selling 'em."

"Really?" said Anna as they all filed up the rickety staircase to the top flat.

"How much is this one, again?" asked Julia. As far as she could see, even the common parts would soon be in need of at least £5,000 worth of attention.

"Well, there's the thing, ladies," explained Kevin as he put the key in the lock. "I got a call from the owner this morning and he reckons he can get £135,000 for it. So I'm afraid, if that's what he thinks he can get, that's what I have to sell it for."

"But it was only £128,000 when we spoke yesterday morning," said Maddie indignantly.

"But that was yesterday, darlin'. You see, in the current climate, prices are going up by the day. Mortgage rates are low, rents are high, everybody's buying. Simple equation. Sorry about that, doll. Still interested?" Maddie and Anna nodded as Kevin threw open the door to £135,000 worth of prime, north London real estate and they all trooped in.

Julia nearly crossed herself and fell to her knees when she saw the state of the place. She wanted to give thanks to the great Mortgage Lender in the sky that she had bought her flat eight years before this madness had gripped London and the south-east of England. The kitchen was about three feet square and needed major surgery before it would be useable, let alone pleasant. The second 'bedroom' was cunningly disguised as a broom cupboard, the master bedroom could only be described as pokey and to top it all there was a fat fucker of a tree growing about five inches from the living-room window. As soon as Julia heard the words 'subsidence' and 'underpinning' slipping nonchalantly out of Kevin's mouth and Maddie asking if the owner might be open to offers, she grabbed her friends by the hands and dragged them down the stairs.

"What on earth were you thinking of?" she screamed with disbelief as soon as they were out of the flat. She knew they were excited about finding somewhere to live but she hadn't thought they would lose their minds totally.

"I know it needs a lot of work –" said Maddie.

"A lot of work! It was falling down!" replied Julia.

"Don't you think we could have done something with that kitchen, though..." said Anna, tentatively.

"Come on, back in the car!" Julia frog-marched them to the Peugeot and guided them away from this, their first house of horrors. There was no way she was letting her friends turn into sawdust-covered, paint-daubed DIY hermits.

East of Eden

All three women had climbed a steep learning curve by the time they got to the top of Primrose Hill. From there they had London at their feet, but, as the last six hours of flat-hunting had made them realise, not in their pocket. They sat in a row with their cans of drink, surveying the area which had been Maddie and Anna's home for the last seven years but was shutting its doors to them.

"I can't believe everywhere is so expensive," said Anna, breaking the silence at last. The sun was sinking, giving the skyline a beautiful, Readybrek glow. Anna sighed as the prospect of moving out of the area began to dawn on her.

"There's still the two-bed basement in Kilburn that you've got to look at on Monday," said Julia.

"Two-bed basement," repeated Maddie. Her falling cadence meant she didn't have to explain how she felt about the prospect.

"I mean, I'm not badly off, so think what it must be like for other people who don't even have the money we do." Anna's exasperation was shared by them all, as they contemplated the way the demographic of the city was shifting. "Maybe we should broaden our search a little," said Anna as she reached out for Maddie's hand.

"I guess we haven't got much choice," said Maddie.

Anna couldn't believe that just as Maddie had agreed to them buying a flat, prices had rocketed. She turned and smiled at her partner reassuringly, but she couldn't help blaming her a little. If it hadn't been for Maddie's ridiculousness, they could have got something really nice, really local, and things would have rolled along much as they always had. Now they not only faced the upheaval of moving, but the trauma of moving to an unknown area, to boot.

"I could ask Mum if she could help us –" murmured Anna.

"And call it Casa Barbr'Anna? No way! It's hardly as if it's an equal partnership at the moment..."

"Of course. Very bad idea. Really stupid of me..."

"So where shall we spread our net?" asked Julia.

"I don't know," pondered Anna. "North?" Maddie pulled a face. "South?"

"Now you're just being stupid!" said Julia with a hoot of laughter.

"What about west?" suggested Maddie. "That wouldn't be too bad, would it?"

"It does look like it's either west or east," surmised Julia.

"Why don't we go down to Ladbroke Grove tomorrow and see what's on offer down there?" said Maddie.

"We could pop in and visit the Nani while we're there," said Anna. "We might even get a roast dinner thrown in."

Having settled on a plan, they hauled themselves off the grass, brushed themselves down and headed back down the hill towards the car, pausing for Maddie to do a couple of sit-ups on the outdoor assault course en route.

"Where are we off to tonight, then?" asked Julia. "Come on Madge! Put your back into it!"

"We could give Ed a call and go and get something to eat," suggested Anna, as Maddie grunted, forcing her stomach muscles into action.

"He's out."

"God! What are you two like?" exclaimed Anna, suddenly frustrated with it all. "He's not the same kind of bloke as –"

"Anna!"

"Twenty-five, twenty-six..."

"Sorry." Anna knew she'd strayed into hostile territory. "But don't you want a normal relationship?"

"What's normal, Anna?"

"Point taken."

"Twenty-nine, thirty!"

"It works really well for both of us this way." Julia's words were punctuated with a heavy full stop.

Pink and glowing after her exertions, Maddie bounced back into the conversation. "Why don't we go into Soho?"

"Or we could get a takeaway and a video," replied Julia.

"Sounds great." Anna's became the casting vote.

Home alone

As Julia, Maddie and Anna headed for home, Ed was wandering through the streets of Camden. He'd had a good time with Alison but he was tired and didn't feel like spending the night in a noisy, filthy pub listening to a band whose name included some ridiculous Dr Ed Ful pun. All he wanted to do was go home, hooch up on the sofa with Julia and watch a crap movie. He got his mobile phone out of his bag and reached the point where one press of the call button would make Julia's phone ring, but he couldn't quite do it.

His mates thought he was so lucky having a beautiful woman like Julia in his life who didn't try to pin him down and stop him seeing other women. It was every young bloke's dream ticket. But after a year or so of this kind of freedom, Ed wanted something else. He wanted to stop pretending he liked their arrangement...

He kicked a can and watched it rattle off into the gutter. Crossing Parkway, he headed for Regent's Park and hoped it wasn't too late to see the giraffes in London Zoo as he walked past.

... But what if he told Julia and she didn't feel the same? Although they seemed to be spending more and more time together, he knew one inopportune word could change the whole scenario. What if he told her he wanted it to be just the two of them, and that made her feel caged in and she ended it with him? That was the last thing he wanted, but he also didn't want things to go on as they had been. Even though he played along with his mates' leery sexual banter, he wasn't some tomcat kinda stud who wouldn't be satisfied with one woman – especially a woman as wonderful as Julia. He was a primary school teacher, for Christ's sake! He'd liked the whole deal with Julia at first because it made him feel *less* of a primary school teacher. It had been dangerous and decadent and exciting. But now it made him feel anxious and a little bit weary.

The Big Picture

Maddie reached for the pestle and mortar that had been relegated to the highest, least accessible corner since her departure from the studio. Kat wasn't as keen on crushing things and incorporating them in her work as Maddie.

The piece of brick that Maddie had chipped off the exterior of their flat was an outlandish, rubiginous red against the mottled grey/black marble bowl. She felt a little guilty about defacing the property she and Anna were about to leave, and persuaded herself that maybe 'chipped off' was too strong a term. The building was old and worn. The landlord hadn't thought it necessary to plough back any of the caseloads of rent they'd paid him over the years into the upkeep of the place. He'd obviously been saving up for a new car or a private jet instead. In reality, therefore, she'd probably just brushed up against the wall when squeezing down the side passage to put the rubbish out, and it had flaked off in her hand. 'Flaked off'. That was a much better way of putting it.

She realised her obsession with the brick she was now crushing was only one bent cog in her mechanism for procrastination. There had been many and varied reasons for staying away from the studio. She hadn't been able to work on her picture because it was too dark, because it was too cold, because she needed to buy a new brush, because she had brown shoes on, because she didn't have a 1999 10p in her pocket... Even now she was quibbling in her mind about how she'd procured the brick, instead of getting on with the job. The prospect of seeing Kat living her old life had been hard but, having jumped that hurdle, the prospect of working on this oeuvre was even harder. She'd thought it would be simple, a luxury in her new schedule. After all, things were looking up. She was amassing a good collection of published work and feeling good about the move, so it was logical to pick up the brushes again. If she looked at it as a house-warming present for Anna, maybe that would help focus her attention.

She leaned harder on the brick, which was resisting her pressure to destroy it. The grating of sand on marble sent shivers up her spine. Running fingernails down unvarnished terracotta would have been a more pleasurable experience. She distracted herself from the sensation by reliving key moments in the flat's history, like news previews in between the News At Ten bongs.

Bong. Kilburn house floods as pipes burst in freezing temperatures. Beige shag-pile is scarred for life. Bong. Women with no money buy Dualit toaster as first joint purchase. They say they have a thing about chrome. Bong.

NW6 landlord discovers Council Tax dodge. Tenants are forced to cut him in on the scam. Bong. And finally, Julia Reymar wins top prize in the 'stuff as many cheese footballs in your mouth as you can at one time' competition. Brushing aside accusations of having freakishly overactive saliva glands, Ms Reymar was said to be 'delighted' with her win.

Memories kept bonging away in her mind until she had to admit the brick had been well and truly pulverised.

She was absorbed in her attempt to recreate the brick's original shade of red, when the alarm clock (set as a reminder to collect her prints) clattered into life on the drainer next to the sink. Maddie jumped and the colour she was mixing took a turn for the purple. "Bastard thing!" she muttered as she blended the excess blue into the mix. As she worked the tones together, she watched the clock work itself up into such a frenzy that it jittered off the drainer and into the cloudy brown water in the sink. There it spluttered for a couple of seconds until, with a watery sigh, it gave up the ghost.

Lying there, drowned and lifeless, the rippling image of the clock floated up through the water. Maddie stared at the warped image of Time. She added a little more black to the red she was mixing. She thought about the growth that Time's passage demanded... A touch more black. That was what was needed... The destruction it brought to carefully established, comforting routines... A tiny squidge more... The havoc it brought to people's lives. Good, law-abiding people who hadn't done anything wrong...

Mission impossible

Even if a stark contrast was what he'd been aiming for, Andy's approach to flat-hunting couldn't have been more different to Julia's. Julia was very much in the laissez-faire, basking-shark school of predators, whereas Andy came armed with a strategy.

Anna, Maddie, Julia and Andy were gathered round Julia's kitchen table. They had agreed to leave work early and rendezvous at A-Z co-ordinates 59:4J at 18.30hrs. Anna had been a little late, which pissed Andy off slightly.

"Sorry, people. Meeting with Ms Gonzalez. Couldn't get away," was all the apology she offered.

Andy wondered how she could have scheduled a meeting at such a sensitive time, but didn't dwell on her inefficiency. He had allocated fifteen minutes to explain the route, five minutes to take questions, five minutes for them all to go for a wee and two and a half minutes to go downstairs and get in the car – this was obviously dependent on Anna securing a parking space in close proximity to Julia's front door... which she had, so that was all right. It was 18.59hrs. Julia hadn't needed the loo, so in spite of Anna's lateness they were practically back on schedule. Andy folded the map, which now had a trapezoid shape drawn on it to indicate the route they would follow, and they all marched down the stairs and got into the car. Andy was up front with Anna while Maddie and Julia cowered in the back seat.

"Right," said Andy, trying not to show how disappointed he was that he'd forgotten to bring his clipboard with personalised mark sheets. He'd spent ages grappling with the Excel package on his computer at work, devising a system which would enable them each to record the relative merits of the properties they were going to see. Each feature had been assigned a space in which to record a mark out of ten. Never mind – he'd fudge it somehow. "Two-bedroom basement in Kilburn is first up. So, Anna. If you'd like to turn the car round and get us back onto the main road..."

"Oh, Andy, I forgot to say," said Maddie tentatively as Anna battled with the steering. "The woman phoned up today and said it'd gone." Like a frightened tortoise, Maddie withdrew her head pretty sharpish from the space between the front seats. The muscles surrounding Andy's lower jaw twitched slightly but that was the only outward sign of his irritation. Inwardly, he was wondering how Anna could put up with living with someone whose thought patterns were so unstructured. After all, what did she have to do all day? Nothing except fart around taking a few snaps once in a while. The kind of temporary memory loss that had resulted in him forgetting his clipboard had been an aberration, and was totally different to the inherent dizziness he saw in Maddie. He shook the map out and rejigged his plan.

"Never mind. We'll just go straight to Westbourne Grove," he said, and smiled.

"So which way now?" asked Anna obediently.

"I think it'd be better if you turned the car round again and then I'll direct you from there." The back of Anna's neck started to glisten with sweat as she heaved at the powerless steering and Andy's hackles rose – he knew Julia and Maddie were pulling stupid faces in the back seat.

"You did remember to tell your mum you can't go to her party at the weekend?" asked Anna once they got to the first set of lights.

Andy smiled at the driver of the number 31 that had drawn up next to them. The driver smiled back and made Andy blush.

"I'll tell her tomorrow," replied Maddie.

The lights changed and the bus screamed off the line, swerving in front of the Peugeot.

"What the fuck does he think he's doing, the cock!" Anna blasted the horn and put her foot down.

The passengers in the single-deck hopper were swinging like chimpanzees from the fixtures on the ceiling as it carved up the traffic.

"Focus!" yelled Andy as his cheeks finally caught up with the rest of his face.

Even the mockers in the group had to admit that Andy's method did enable them to cover a lot of ground. At 19.31hrs they arrived at venue one – two-bed garden flat, all original fittings, patio, lots of character, £140,000.

"What do you think?" Anna asked Maddie as they contemplated their surroundings.

"Well, I think the low ceilings could be a bit of a problem."

"Hmmm. Jules?" asked Anna.

"Dingy and pokey."

"Andy?" Anna collected the final opinion.

"Damp. Wouldn't touch it with a Marigold."

20.16hrs. Venue two, W10 – one/two-bedroom flat in purpose-built executive block with all mod cons – £129,950.

Andy turned to Colin, the estate agent, and enquired: "So when you say one/two bedrooms, what do you actually mean by that?" He'd done a brief recce of the place and couldn't see anything resembling the '/two' bedroom.

"It might not be immediately obvious to your irregular visitor," explained Colin as he guided them into the living room. "But there used to be a wall where this strip of wallpaper is." Colin rapped the wall in question with his knuckles to demonstrate the absolute top-notch plasterboard that separated their living room from their neighbour's. "You see, what you had before was a slightly smaller living space and a second bedroom in the area between the wall and this area here," he said, demonstrating the 'room' with a sweep of the hand. "All a prospective new owner would have to do to restore it to its original design is rip off that plastering, construct a…"

Andy was keen to try and decipher what it was that the man was trying to explain, but was finding it difficult to understand his deeply coded language.

"Jules. Do you know what he means…?" Andy looked around, trying to find someone to help him solve the riddle with which this man was taunting him. "Jules…?"

"I think the ladies have gone downstairs," said Colin helpfully.

*

Venues three to six had all followed a similar pattern, so by the time they reconvened at 59:4J at 22.04hrs, morale was not high. Maddie and Anna had to be out of their rented flat by the end of June. None of them had thought that it would take so long to find somewhere, but now time was ticking away.

Andy had suggested setting another date to do more house-hunting as it would give him a chance to use the charts he'd prepared, but Maddie had to work Monday and Tuesday evening and Barbara was coming up for lunch on Wednesday so Anna would have to work late to make up the time. He was a bit disappointed, naturally, but he was confident there'd be other opportunities for trips out.

Eat the rich

"You'd have thought Oxo would have been more at home opening a pie and mash shop really, wouldn't you?" Barbara laughed and expected her daughter to do so, too. She didn't, so Barbara turned to the waiter for support instead. "At least I'm guaranteed a nice drop of gravy with my pork, though, eh!" She laughed again and was sure she'd seen a hint of amusement flicker across the waiter's face. Leaning across the table, she pushed the menu aside so she could see Anna's face. Barbara was disappointed that she wasn't even smiling.

"I'll have the chicken with some steamed vegetables please," said Anna. She handed the menu back to the waiter, who backed away from the table. "Mum, for heaven's sake –"

"Oh, Anna, come on! If you will bring me somewhere called 'The Oxo Tower' for lunch, what do you expect?" chortled Barbara. "I'm only trying to have some fun. He must have heard it a thousand times before."

"I don't think so."

"I may as well have stayed home with your father if you're going to be like that."

"Now that was below the belt! How is he, by the way?"

Barbara thought for a second. Graham was dreadful. He was making her life a misery with his moods and they only just managed to exchange pleasantries these days, but technically there wasn't anything wrong with him. Besides, she'd come up to London to escape him, not talk about him.

"He's fine." Barbara moved her glass so the handsome young waiter could put their bread on the table and waved her hand to dismiss the subject. "So, tell me about the flat-hunting."

"It's more difficult than I'd thought. We've seen quite a few places but they've all been too small or too grotty."

"How small is too small?"

"We definitely need two bedrooms as Maddie needs one for all her work, but some of them have been little more than cupboards."

Barbara played with the corners of her napkin while Anna continued describing some of the places they'd seen. Persuading her to look into the possibility of a three-bedroom place looked nigh on impossible, but she might as well have a go. A spare room was integral to her plan. "I really think you should take that extra money, Anna. You want to get something decent, don't you?"

"I can't. Maddie is absolutely against it. She's worried it's going to be more my place than hers as it is. And it doesn't help that her mum keeps sending her all these newspaper articles that make the whole thing sound more complicated than it really is."

"She probably just wants you to be aware of what you're doing, that's all."

"I suppose so."

"Menopausal anxiety – that'll be it. Has she gone down the HRT route?"

"I don't know!"

Barbara shrank back in her chair. Her daughter was getting snappish and that mood had to be snuffed out. She needed her to be calm and sympathetic and open to living suggestions that she might not have considered before.

"Maybe we could go and look at some more places this evening," prompted Barbara.

"I can't tonight."

"Why?"

"I've got a date."

"A date?"

"A do. I meant a do."

Barbara knew Anna well enough to let the subject rest while the waiter was serving their food. Instead she looked round the restaurant. There were lots of interesting-looking men dotted around the room. A middle-aged man in a striped suit – obviously a banker – caught her eye and winked. The interaction made Barbara feel tingly inside. She heard Anna thank the waiter, so she topped up their wine glasses and turned her attention back to the reason for her trip.

"If you were thinking about buying a three-bedroom flat or house, for example, on the budget you have, where would you look?" Barbara asked as she admired the plump piece of meat lounging on her plate.

Fear is the key

Sheila's hand tightened around the phone as she listened to her daughter let her down. The party would still be a success, of course, but it wouldn't be the same without Maddie there. It would have been a perfect opportunity for her to meet some new people, spread her wings a little.

"You could just come up for the day, Maddie, if you can't spare the whole weekend," urged Sheila.

"I'm sorry, Mum. But this potholing trip has been arranged for ages. It's not that I don't want to come, it's just that I can't. We've got to be at the centre on Saturday morning…"

"I see."

"I've promised Anna."

"Well, next time then, pet."

"Absolutely. Next time."

When Sheila put the phone down, she felt utterly disappointed. "That girl has got Maddie wrapped round her little finger," she said to Malcolm, who had come into the hall to water the plants.

"She can't come?" asked Malcolm.

"No. It was obvious she wanted to, but she couldn't because Anna had said so. It's not healthy, the way she tries to control Maddie's life. It worries me. She used to be so independent and happy and now she speaks like she's not got a mind of her own."

"Maybe they had something else planned. She can't just drop –"

"I'm telling you, Malcolm. That woman's trying to shape her in her own mould. Maddie said she would have loved to come to visit if Anna hadn't been taking her potholing."

"I though she wasn't too good in confined spaces." Malcolm looked confused.

"There you go! You've proved my point."

Malcolm left the room laughing. "She's got quite an imagination, that girl of ours!"

Why Malcolm found the whole thing so amusing was beyond her – forcing a claustrophobe down a pothole was barbaric. Sheila picked up the paper she'd been flicking through before Maddie's call and continued scanning it for articles. Her eyes had become accustomed to picking out key words like 'queer-bashing', 'homophobia' and 'gay rights', so when she picked out a wonderfully pessimistic piece about Clause 28, she smiled contentedly. She drew a ring around the word 'inequality'. That would wing its way over to Maddie first thing in the morning.

Extreme measures

Maddie had begun to panic about the idea of being homeless, so Anna was trying to play down her own anxieties about the timescale they were now working with. That's why she didn't tell Maddie she was going to do an emergency sweep of estate agents in the East End. As she didn't know the area, she decided to take a number 25 bus after work and see where it went after the City.

She got off outside the Whitechapel Gallery. Maddie had dragged her down there many times before, but Anna's knowledge of the area east of Aldgate was patchy. She felt intrepid as she strode past the familiar landmark and towards the tall thin bell-towers of the mosque. Estate agents weren't exactly two a penny but she did pick up an onion bhaji and a samosa to boost her sugar levels as she wandered through the market stalls lining the pavement. Traffic was backed up on the Whitechapel Road as it tried to weave its way out of the City towards Essex or Kent. Horns chastised those who didn't react quickly enough to a green traffic light, and fumes from frustrated drivers floated into the air. The atmosphere was totally different from what she was used to. It was dirtier and more frantic than the streets where she lived, but the people actually spoke to you and the colours of the posters, graffiti and saris that surrounded her were far more intense. It almost made Anna feel like a visitor from the suburbs.

When she walked into the small estate agent just off the main road and met Mina, the owner of the business, she hoped this was someone who wouldn't mess her around.

Anna sat down on the rather precarious swivel-chair opposite Mina and was passed a cup of tea. That was a first. Anna waited for Mina to finish filling in the first part of her pro forma before launching into the spiel she'd rattled off more times than she cared to remember. "I know it might sound ridiculous," was Anna's opening gambit, because estate agents had started to laugh at her space-to-price ideal, "but we're looking for a two-bedroom flat – preferably top floor, but we're flexible about that. We're not too fussed about whether it's new or a conversion, but it has to be in fairly good condition –"

"You're not a DIY enthusiast then?"

"Don't mind a bit of painting, but that's as far as it goes."

"A woman after my own heart," nodded Mina knowingly.

"I'm not that familiar with the area, so I'm open to your suggestions. But preferably nothing that's next to a school," concluded Anna. It wasn't that kids were a problem for her, but rather the ice-cream vans that preyed on them while playing Yankee Doodle Dandy on a continuous loop that drove her mad.

"That doesn't sound too difficult to find," responded Mina cheerfully. "How much have you got to spend?"

Anna wobbled on her seat before admitting that their price range couldn't really top £130,000. She waited for the spray of laughter that generally assaulted her when she uttered this figure. With Mina, though, there were no laughs or splutters of incredulity.

"Oh, we'll get you fixed up with a little palace for that money, my love," came the reply. Anna watched excitedly as Mina flicked through her property records. "Ah. Now. Here we are. Two-bedroom apartment, top floor. It's just round the back of Brick Lane, not far from here at all. I've seen this flat myself, Anna, and I think you'd agree both bedrooms are a very good size. The kitchen is very well equipped – clean and tidy." Mina emphasised this feature by patting Anna's hand. "It's very light and airy. Entry phone, services included. Leasehold..." Mina looked up questioningly at Anna, who nodded and smiled like a maniac. "Oh. But there's one thing."

"What?" said Anna, although nothing short of a water feature spurting raw sewage in the entrance hall would have put her off at that stage.

"You would be responsible for a share of the garden."

"But that would be great!" replied Anna. It all sounded too perfect to be true, so she made herself ask how much.

"£125,000."

Anna's windpipe had gone into spasm at the thought of having finally tracked down her ideal flat, so she grinned and managed to squeeze out "perfect" whilst pointing to the phone.

"You want to go and see it now?" enquired Mina.

1 JUNE 1999

Nowhere to run

In spite of the conductor's protestations, Maddie hung onto the pole at the back of the number 13 and leaned off the platform. She felt the warm air rush past her face and watched as the tarmac disappeared underneath the bus. When it slowed for the lights, she leapt off. She saw Anna waiting outside the cinema and waved, knowing she would be in trouble for being late as they were supposed to have a chat before the film about their interim accommodation. She hoped Anna wouldn't mind swinging by a twenty-four-hour lab later on; she'd spent the day photographing suntanning products for a trade title and was a little worried about one of the lighting set-ups.

Anna was already in the queue for the outside kiosk when Maddie plucked up the courage to do a death-run through the early evening traffic. After a cursory kiss hello, Maddie took her place at Anna's side. There were still eight people ahead of them; if the ticket seller didn't move any faster, they'd miss the beginning of the film. They both hated that. They stood in silence for a good few minutes, Anna sighing and tutting, Maddie panting and glistening.

"We're going to have to ask the Nani if we can stay with them," declared Anna. "Andy's place would be too much like living in Heaven; Julia's flat has less space than a Lakeland Plastics warehouse; so Vi's house is beginning to look like our only option." Anna pushed the money under the glass screen to the woman in the booth, who handed over their tickets.

"Screen one. Main feature starts at seven-thirty. Seats aren't allocated at this showing," intoned the woman.

"Thank you." Anna scooped up her change and headed inside to the snacks counter. "You are sure about the flat, aren't you, Mads?"

"Of course.

"Popcorn?"

"Small please. I think it's fantastic. It'll be a laugh, moving back out there."

"Your old manor."

"Exactly."

"You'll be nearer Kat. Drink?"

"Medium Diet Coke, please. And you'll be nearer work."

They settled into their seats, the lights dimmed and Maddie allowed the adverts to roll over her. It wasn't only the move or the rolls of film nestling in her pocket that were on her mind, but her mum was also worrying her. Suddenly, it appeared that Sheila had found gay politics. Financial, parental, social issues – all the bases were being covered. If it wasn't so profoundly odd coming from someone who, in the past, had only managed to refer to Maddie's relationship as 'her situation', it would have been great to know that her mum was embracing her lifestyle.

Maddie felt Anna's elbow dig her in the ribs followed by her breath on her ear. "Didn't you hear what I was saying about Vi's place?"

"Sorry, I was thinking about Mum."

"I've told you. It's just a phase. She'll grow out of it." Anna's response tripped off her tongue. "So, why don't I ask if we can visit Doris one evening this week and then you can ask Vi if we can move in for a month or so?" suggested Anna.

"Let's not talk about it now, Anna," hissed Maddie.

"I have to take my chances when I can these days."

"Don't you want me to get this business off the ground?" snapped Maddie. "Anyway, why do *I* have to ask? Doris is *your* grandma."

"They're more likely to say a polite 'yes' to you, though." Anna raised her voice to be heard over the thundering music of the opening credits.

"Jesus, Anna!" protested Maddie. The music built to a crescendo and stopped.

"Oh, come on, she adores you." Anna's booming voice triggered a wave of shushes from the darkness.

It started with Eve

Kat dropped everything, grabbed her purse and hurried over to the cafe. Her heart was pounding as she pulled open the door and searched for Maddie's face. What had made her friend so desperate to see her? Why had she sounded so agitated? Surely the builder's sand Kat had supplied for the suntan shoot couldn't have looked that bad. It had to be something much worse. She saw Maddie sitting in the corner and knocked tables and chairs aside in her effort to reach her.

"It's okay, Mads, I'm here. What's up?" Kat sat down opposite her and placed her hand on Maddie's forearm.

"What do you mean?"

"You sounded really upset on the phone." Kat sucked in the air and tried to normalise her breathing.

"Freaking hayfever, that's all.

"Oh, I thought –"

"I never used to get hayfever. Fucking thing..." Maddie blew her nose loudly. "You didn't leave anything important, did you?"

Kat thought about the newly painted vase she'd smashed in her panic to leave the studio. It was ruined. "'Course not. I needed a break anyway." Kat tried to settle the butterflies in her stomach. "So what are you doing down here?"

"I came over to meet with Eve – you remember, from college..."

"Yes."

"She wants to put some more work my way."

"Excellent." Kat watched Maddie's eyes sparkle as she related the story.

"No, but wait for it. She asked me if I could come up with a website for her fashion designs – she's got this concept for her show that would involve big screens, projectors and stuff. It would mean taking shots of her gear –"

"Well, you can do that."

"Yeah, but it's the other stuff. I don't know anything about designing websites."

Kat shook her head – was that it? Was that all she wanted her for? Maddie was such a worry-guts at times. "You really want to get involved in that kind of design? It's not really 'art', is it?"

"You've got to go where the money is."

"Suppose. There's nothing you can't learn from a book these days…"

"Do you reckon?"

Maddie blew her nose again and churned the contents of her bag over with her rummaging hands while they talked. Kat was mesmerised by the way Maddie stuck her Olbas oil inhaler up her nose and sucked heavily on the fumes. Her wrinkled, red-edged nostrils and glassy blue eyes looked beautiful under the cafe's strip lighting.

"Take a chance for once in your life," urged Kat, even though she felt uneasy about urging Maddie to do something she couldn't seem to do herself.

"I don't know. It's not like I couldn't do with the cash…" Maddie slid her bottle of Diet Coke over the Formica. Kat sucked on the straw. "What's up with you then, Kat? Haven't heard much about your love life recently…"

"No, come on! We haven't sorted *you* out yet! What have you got to lose by doing this thing?"

"Face, for a start." Maddie sunk her head into her hands before continuing. "Taking the pictures would be fine, but if I fuck up the website thing... I can't afford to start pissing people off."

"It's only Eve."

"I know, but she's been really kind, introducing me to her publishing mates... No. I'll do her shots for her but I'm not going to risk the other stuff. I'm not that desperate."

"You wuss!"

"No, I'm not!" Maddie finished trying to pour salt into the pepper pot, brushed the excess onto the floor and pushed the condiments decisively to one side. "So, Kat. Have you found yourself a 'Ms June'?"

She hesitated before pulling a story out of her library of conquests so Maddie could gorge on the details.

"Do you fancy coming back to the studio?" Kat asked next. "I could finish working on my design, you could do some work on your painting..." It was a perfect summer night to find a quiet nook in which to drink, smoke and chat away the evening. "We could make a night of it –"

"I can't," Maddie said. "We're going round to Vi's this evening. I've got to ask if we can move in for a while."

Family business

"It wouldn't be for too long, Vi," said Maddie, as they sat on the faded garden bench sharing a smoke. Vi had offered Maddie one of her cigarillos but Maddie had learned the hard way that they weren't quite the same as the soft-shite lights she smoked, so each stuck to their own. The garden was a network of creeping, climbing, blooming shrubbery and, as she spoke, Maddie brushed aside a stray frond that was trying to work its way into her ear.

"The people we're buying from have already bought somewhere

and are as keen as we are to get things moving, so I couldn't see it being more than a month, tops." Maddie left a pause which Vi was meant to fill with a reassuring answer that incorporated the word 'yes'. No such response came so she ploughed on. "I know it's a really big favour and I hope I haven't put you in an awkward position. I mean, take time to think it over. Discuss it with the others..."

This time Vi did chip in. "Maddie, please, it wouldn't be an imposition to have you and Anna here. It's a wonderful idea. I always think that it's a damn shame I don't make the most of this house."

"That's fantastic! Do you really mean it?"

"Of course, my dear," said Vi. "I could get Mr Thompson in to clear out the loft if you like, so you can store things up there. And there's always the little box room. You could stack your bits and pieces of furniture in there..."

"Don't worry about all that," replied Maddie. "We're going to put most of our stuff in storage."

"I suppose that seems to make sense." Vi paused for a moment or two. "The only thing is, we won't be here for long. We've got our cruise coming up soon, but it'll be a comfort to know there's someone here to keep an eye on the house."

"Sounds like it could work out perfectly for all of us, then!" Maddie gave Vi a hug. "You're so kind. Thank you so much."

"It'll be fun, won't it? We'll be able to do so much together. Let's go and tell the others." Vi stubbed out her smoke and galvanised her strength to pull herself out of her chair. "Now, you're a cricket fan, aren't you, Maddie?"

"Not really, but I'm willing to learn." Maddie found cricket mind-numbingly dull, but having to sit through hours of summer test matches seemed like a small price to pay for such hospitality. "I do like to watch the tennis when it's on, though."

"Oh, yes, so do I," enthused Vi as she negotiated the step from the garden into the house. "Doris! Doris!" She entered the kitchen. "I've got some wonderful news!"

A show of force

Barbara pulled her robe round her and shuffled into the kitchen. She was pleased for Anna and Maddie that they'd finally found somewhere to buy, even if it wasn't quite what she'd had in mind. A bolt-hole in London would have been perfect for her. She wouldn't have interfered. They wouldn't even have known she was there. Of course, a little company would have been nice if they'd wanted it, but she would never have forced herself on them...

She pulled at the handle of the fridge and looked inside. It took her seconds to remember what she was looking for. Milk. Where is the milk? She looked round the kitchen and saw the carton sitting on the worktop next to a mound of crumbs, a cereal bowl and an open jar of marmalade.

It wasn't as if she hated her life in Canvey. She flicked the kettle on and picked up the carton. It was light. She shook it from side to side. It was empty.

She heard Graham thudding down the stairs, followed by the clicking of his golf spikes on the parquet flooring. The front door slammed shut and the kettle came to the boil. Barbara drew back her arm and took a swipe at the cereal bowl. It soared across the kitchen, leaving a trail of milk and soggy bran in its wake before crunching against the wall.

Good morning... and goodbye

Driving the van made Andy feel butcher than he had in a long time. As he drew up outside Anna and Maddie's flat, he saw that his friends had already transferred some of their belongings to the pavement outside. A cheese plant, desk lamp and pouffe were in the road, reserving a space for the van. He was moving them when Anna emerged from the house.

"Sorry I'm late," said Andy. "I couldn't find you last night to ask when the storage centre opened, but we're not too behind schedule, are we?"

"We're fine," said Anna as she kissed him hello. "You're the first here."

"Where did you get to? I thought you were coming to the pub last night."

"I had some stuff I needed to do. The flat – you know."

Andy was satisfied with her answer but hurt that she hadn't bothered to tell him in advance. He'd wasted twenty minutes of his life talking to Jason from IT about the meltdown that was going to occur when the Millennium Bug struck, all because he thought he was meeting Anna. Breaking arrangements was a new habit, but one she was going to have to get out of.

Their conversation was interrupted as Maddie appeared at the door.

"So, how's it going?" asked Andy. "Tempers intact, so far?"

"Yep! It's all going quite smoothly," replied Maddie.

As Anna turned to follow Maddie back into the house, Andy touched her arm. "One thing I just have to ask before we start – what did that woman want to speak to you about at work yesterday?" Andy had been almost beside himself when Anna was called up to the top floor. Half of him wanted to hear that she'd got some bank-busting promotion, but another bit of him didn't want her to leave him behind.

"Which woman?" asked Anna as she stopped in her tracks.

"Come on. You know who I mean. That woman we saw in the bar a few weeks ago. Great suit... Ms Gonzalez."

"Oh, you mean Roz."

"I beg your pardon. *Roz*," said Andy, mocking his friend's familiarity with her superior.

Anna blushed. "It was nothing, really." Andy's excitement faded. He'd concocted all sorts of scenarios in the intervening time, sexual and professional. "She just wanted to talk about the possibility of extending my role, taking on more responsibilities when the restructure is finalised."

"More responsibilities! What kind of responsibilities?" Andy's appetite for gossip was insatiable. He chastised himself for not having seen this coming.

"Nothing's been set in stone yet. It was just a tentative enquiry about my professional ambitions."

"But you don't have any professional ambitions!" exclaimed Andy.

"That's what I told her, but –"

"Oy! You two – less gabbing, more humping!" shouted Maddie as she balanced a bin-liner full of winter jumpers on the window ledge. "Catch this, will you?" The bundle plunged earthwards. Andy screamed and took a step back. Anna stuck out a foot to break its fall.

The van

By the time Julia and Ed arrived, Andy had decided it was much more effective to have two people stay in the back of the van to organise the positioning of possessions and that he and Julia were ideal executors of the task. Subsequently, they were enjoying a brief hiatus while Maddie, Anna and Ed heaved the sofa down the narrow staircase.

"Did Anna tell you Babs was pushing for them to get somewhere bigger?" said Andy as he arranged his beanbag next to Julia's and sank into it. Grunts, orders and recriminations could be heard from where they sat.

"Yes. Sounds like she was a bit put out when they didn't take her advice."

"Or her money. Obviously she had her eye on a little granny annex..."

"Is that what Anna said?" Julia was shocked. Anna had told her that Barbara was looking for somewhere safe to invest her money.

"No. Just putting two and two together," replied Andy. "Mind you, I reckon Anna could have afforded something bigger, now this promotion is as good as in the bag."

"A promotion...?" repeated Julia. Who exactly was meant to be the best friend in this set-up?

"That's what she said."

"She hasn't mentioned anything to me," humphed Julia.

"She only met with Roz Gonzalez to talk about it yesterday."

"Yeah, but she must have known something was in the offing."

"Everything's in flux there at the moment, it's hard to know what's going on."

"Hmm." Julia's mind was distracted by the extreme warmth that was being generated by the beanbag, making her inner thighs sticky with sweat. "I reckon she might just go for it this time."

"What makes you say that?"

"Well, you know, she's buying a flat, settling down. I think firstly, she would find the idea of extra cash appealing and secondly, with Maddie's business taking her out so much, I think she'd like a new challenge to occupy her."

"No. I reckon she'll be too interested in fixing up the new place to want to take on more work. Let's face it, if she's got an Ikea catalogue in one hand and a brief in the other, which one is she going to flick through first?"

Julia laughed and agreed with Andy, although privately she thought Anna was ready to move onwards and upwards. In buying the flat, she was completing a phase. Julia wouldn't be surprised if Anna was very tempted by whatever this Roz woman was offering.

Shallow grave

Kat looked at her watch and wondered what she could do to make Miro leave. In the six months they'd been seeing each other, they'd developed a Saturday morning routine. Usually they would go back to Miro's on a Friday night, because her place was more comfortable and on a better night-bus route than Kat's. Saturday mornings involved sex, eggs on toast, and *Emmerdale* taped from the night before. Kat had never been particularly keen on soaps but, as a captive audience, she was gradually becoming a convert.

This set-up meant that Kat could decide when she left. But this particular weekend, their routine had gone awry – they'd ended up at Kat's flat and Miro still didn't look like budging.

"Got any plans for today?" asked Miro as she picked up the newspaper and stretched out on the sofa.

Kat looked at her watch again. It was approaching midday and she'd promised to be over at Maddie's by ten o'clock to help with the move. Now she either had to tell Miro where she was going or cook up a story that enabled her to leave. She couldn't take Miro along. She would introduce her to Maddie soon but now wasn't the right time. Things were just getting back on track with Maddie and she didn't want a new girlfriend to be seen as an obstacle to their renewed closeness.

"I'm going to have to go in a minute," said Kat. Even then, she hadn't decided whether to lie.

"Where?" Miro looked puzzled and disappointed.

There was no way she could tell the truth. "I promised myself I'd go and give blood today and you have to be there before a certain time." *An image of a shovel being slammed into dry, hard turf played in front of her mind's eye.*

"Give blood?"

"Yes." *A crunch as the shovel dug deep into the earth.* "It's something I do every six months or so. Some people give money to charity. I can't afford that at the moment, so I give blood to the blood bank." *Fibrous roots popped as they were torn from the ground.*

"Maybe I should come with you." Miro put her paper down and started looking for her shoes.

"No. You can't," replied Kat sharply. *Another clod of earth was flung onto the side.*

"Why not? I've never done it before and it seems like a really worthy thing to do."

"Yes. It is, but they don't do first-timers on a Saturday." *Thud.*

"Oh. Okay."

Kat's explanation seemed to have succeeded in putting Miro off, but she couldn't see how or why. She rarely gave up her seat on the bus, let alone her lifeblood. But at least it had prevented the 'why won't you introduce me to your friends? Are you ashamed of me?' conversation.

"When will you be back?" asked Miro.

"Late," said Kat. *Rip.*

"Why so long?" Miro looked confused again.

"I have to go to Ponder's End to do it. It's the travelling." *Grate.*

"Oh."

"I'll call you later." Kat went over to Miro and kissed her.

"Why don't I call *you.*"

Splat. Kat walked out the door and fell face down into the coffin-shaped hole she'd dug for herself.

Why worry?

Vi had spent all morning rearranging the house so it would be ready for Anna and Maddie's arrival later that evening. She'd put fresh linen on the bed in the back bedroom, cleared out the wardrobe and chest of drawers, scrubbed the mug stains off the bedside table and made space in the attic room for other oogee-bits they might have brought with them. Doris and Betty had gone out shopping for some telephone extension cable. They would probably be back soon, so Vi was having a well-earned forty-winks. She was drifting in and out of consciousness when she heard her friend's key in the front door.

"Cooee," called Betty, as she struggled in the doorway with her purchases.

Vi forced herself to shake off her sleep and go to the door. "What have you got there?"

"This and that," replied Betty.

"We've got a couple of treats for the girls," said Doris as she bundled past Vi into the living room. "So what have you been up to? All the jobs done?"

"Oh yes. It's looking marvellous up there," replied Vi, pleased with her handiwork.

"Which room have you put Anna in?" asked Doris, pulling some Murray Mints out of her nylon shopping bag.

"I decided to put them in the back room," said Vi. It was so much lighter there and she was sure they'd feel happier.

"You can't put them in together," said Doris.

"Don't be such a prude," replied Vi.

"It's not that." She let go of her shopping bag – which wilted on the table – and tottered off up the stairs.

"I think what Doris means is that they don't know that *we* know, so –" Betty's explanation was cut short by Vi's impatience.

"For heaven's sake, isn't it time we all came clean about this?" she said tartly. "I'm too old to start playing games. Why can't we all just call a spade a spade, eh, and be done with all this pussyfooting around?"

"It's got to come from Anna," said Doris, clutching the bannister halfway up the stairs. "It's got to come from her."

Betty, who was hot on Doris's heels, looked down at Vi and nodded her agreement.

"Oh buggery hell!" Vi shouted. Although she was a pretty strident character, she did try not to steamroll. "What are we going to do?"

"They'll be here in a couple of hours," added Betty.

"I know," said Doris. "We'll have to get the camp bed out of the garage and put it up in the attic room. That could be for Maddie."

"Oh, yes," chipped in Betty. "We could say we thought it would be a good hideaway for her so she wouldn't be disturbed during the day when she was trying to work."

Vi felt very old and weary. Transporting the camp bed all that way was like asking her to carry a baby grand the length of the Great Wall of China – it was unwarranted and preposterous. Plus, it meant she would miss the Superbikes on TV.

A man for all seasons

With everything neatly packed in the van, they went upstairs for a final cup of tea before closing the door to The Fridge for ever. Anna stood on guard at the window, looking out for potential thieves. Ed took a slurp of his tea and rubbed his back. He was sure he'd heard something click as they were humping that sodding sofa down the stairs.

"I think living with the Nani will be fine," said Anna. "The worst thing will be not sleeping together. That's going to be really odd."

Ed caught Julia looking at him and smiled. They'd been sleeping together a lot recently. Staying over and everything. Instead of agreeing with Anna, he heard himself disguise his feelings of contentment with laddishness: "Sex is a fuck of a lot better if you don't sleep together all the time. Keeps you fresh, don't you think? Keeps you interested – if you know what I mean. Eh, Andy?" As soon as the words left his mouth, Ed cringed inside.

"Jesus! Penises of the world unite!" interjected Julia with a grimace.

"I guess," replied Andy, who was going round the skirting boards with a damp cloth.

How could I forget that Andy doesn't do that 'male conspirators' thing? thought Ed. He's gay, he's gay, I must remember he's gay. I don't know why I keep forgetting, he's as camp as tits. I wonder if he fancies me? What would I do if he made a pass at me...? Ed felt the conversation drift over him.

"So how long do you think you'll be with your grandma?" asked Julia.

"Well," replied Anna, "we're waiting for the result of the survey and some information from the freeholder, but once that's all in, we should be able to exchange and complete pretty quickly. I reckon we should be doing this all over again in about a month."

"Has Maddie sorted out where she's going to work?" Andy piped up.

"Not really. I can't say the idea of her having to work out of Vi's house hasn't caused some tension."

"But she's been doing so well. There's no reason why that shouldn't continue, is there?" asked Andy. He spoke encouragingly and looked to Julia to do the same.

"A month isn't going to do any harm." Julia picked up her cue smoothly. "She's given everyone her mobile number, hasn't she?"

"Come on!" Ed's order was intended to shift the homoerotic thoughts that had suddenly made themselves at home in his mind and he cut through the small talk with ease. "I thought we were meant to be picking Kat up at the tube any minute."

"I'll just pack up the cups," said Anna.

"Right, who wants to come in the van with me?" asked Andy as he chucked the keys authoritatively from hand to hand.

"Don't worry, mate. I'll drive the van," barked Ed, plucking the keys out of the air mid-toss. "Jules, you come with me. Anna, you can drive Maddie and Andy and pick Kat up on the way."

"Maddie's already gone, you dick!" said Julia, laughing.

"Has she? When?"

"About half an hour ago. She had to go on her bike, so we gave her a head start."

The prisoner

Maddie had been hot and sweaty when she arrived at the storage depot. Now, sitting in the ten-foot-square cell that was going to be home to their belongings for the next month or so, she just felt clammy. The only light came from an unshaded bulb that hung from the ceiling. The only noise was the distant grunting and groaning of others undergoing the tortuous process of dragging large objects from one place to another.

The door worked free of its wedge and slowly swung shut. Her mind was telling her she should be afraid. What if the door wouldn't open? How would she breathe? What if the lights went out? What if she'd been transported back in time and was actually a POW in solitary confinement, being watched by barbaric and merciless Nazi guards? She didn't have an oven mitt, let alone a baseball mitt, with which to keep herself sane.

Although all those things were going through her head, she wasn't afraid. She was enjoying the silence. Being alone. Sometimes there wasn't enough time to think – not recently. The move, the purchase of the flat, sorting out the money, moving in with the Nani, it had all been exhausting. At least Eve's shoot had gone well. The floaty, feminine designs had come up a treat against the brutal East End architecture that Maddie had chosen as a backdrop. She'd handed over the results to the bloke who was designing the website, but she was beginning to wish she'd taken up the challenge to do it herself. Commissions had hardly been flooding in, and she was dreading getting back on the touting-for-work treadmill. Realistically, though, there was no way she could take on big projects like that while she was working from Vi's house. She didn't have the equipment or the space. Instead of being able to channel her energy, she felt like one of those wind-up cars that just keeps going and going and going, regardless of the obstacles it happens to meet, until the mechanism runs out of juice.

She had been so overcome by her own momentum that she didn't have a clue what Anna had been up to, these last few weeks. There had been talk of her being in line for promotion, which was a real turn-up for the books, but even that conversation had slipped off their agenda. Maddie had hardly spoken to Kat, and her mother had left at least three messages which she hadn't had time to return.

Oh, well. Only a month or so to go. Surely it wouldn't be so bad living with the Nani for a while. At least they had a garden. And soon she would own a beautiful place with the woman she loved and was committed to. They could spend time thinking about how they wanted to decorate it. They could go to Homebase to buy paint and nails and sealant on a Sunday afternoon. They could spend hours ripping off dados and pulling down pelmets. It would be calm and blissfully unpressured. She was so pleased that she'd faced her demons and taken the plunge. Anna was kind and intelligent, funny and supportive. She knew now, she'd never want anyone else.

Wait until dark

Anna sat on the edge of her bed and waited. She thought she'd heard Vi turn off the radio, so it wouldn't be long before she came upstairs and went to bed. She listened. Vi was still pottering around downstairs. Kitchen noises. That sometimes meant she was making a drink to take to bed. Or it could mean she needed more whisky and dry to see her through to the end of the programme.

She looked at her watch. It was half past midnight. It had been fun – romantic almost – at first, sneaking upstairs in the middle of the night to sleep with Maddie in the attic, squeezing into a single bed, leaving around dawn to avoid bumping into Betty, who liked to be up and dressed by six o'clock. But her hostesses' sleeping habits had been eating into Anna's sleep pattern for a week and now she was exhausted. She had three back-to-back meetings at work the next day, and plans for the evening – she couldn't afford to be either late or tired, so, grudgingly, she got into bed. She picked up her phone and sent Maddie a text message explaining she would see her in the morning. Moments after it was sent, she heard the muffled beep on Maddie's phone receiving it.

Why did old people need so little sleep?

Modern times

Doris was determined not to let age wither her, and if that meant popping into Smith's at Notting Hill Gate to buy a book about computers and the internet, then so be it. With a cup of tea at her side and Vi and Betty safely tucked away in the garden, she turned to the first page. 'Software' wasn't mentioned until chapter eleven – she'd looked it up in the contents. It was tempting to dip in halfway through, but she knew it would be more instructive if she started from the beginning. She marked the page with her thumb, though, in case she needed to flick forward. A section about sound ports and subwoofers was keeping her quiet when Betty came in from the garden. It must be elevenses.

"It's lovely out there, Doris, why didn't you come out and join us?" she said, setting three cups and saucers on a tray.

"I've been trying to get to grips with this." Doris held up the book so Betty could read the title.

She squinted at the letters and Doris headed off the rigmarole of a hunt for her glasses by telling her it was about computers.

"Computers?"

Betty returned to the tea-making ritual as Doris explained. "I had a chat with Maddie this morning – the poor girl was distraught because she'd missed out on some work –"

"Oh no."

"It was some sort of problem involving the computer she's working on while she's with us. Apparently, it's a lot smaller than the one she's used to and can't do so many fancy things to her photographs."

"It is tiny, you know. I've seen her using it," confirmed Betty. "Smashing snaps she's taken though, Dee. Really smashing –"

"But I didn't understand a thing she was saying – that's the point," continued Doris, who was accustomed to talking over Betty in order to progress a conversation. "I nodded and agreed in all the right places, but she was chattering away as if it was the most normal thing in the world, and I didn't have a clue. It made me feel like a proper old fogey, which is why I got this."

"Anyone fancy a hand of trumps?" called out Vi, as she made her way through to the living room.

Now Doris had to make a choice. Cards in the middle of the day was quite stimulating. A little half-hour break wouldn't hurt. She left the book face down on the table as she helped Betty carry the tea through.

"Did you give Anna's note to Maddie, by the way?" asked Betty above the noise of the rattling tray.

"Blast – I clean forgot. Was it important?" Doris adjusted the antimacassar on the back of her chair and wished, if Vi was going to sit in *her* seat, she would leave things as she found them.

"Anna's got to work late again, so she won't be able to go out for dinner as they had planned." Betty passed Vi a cup of tea.

"Poor love. Maddie's not having a good time of it at the moment, is she, what with this work business and Anna being out all hours?" Doris had hardly seen her granddaughter since they'd arrived – and they'd be gone again before she knew it. She must try and get Anna to spend some time with them. Join in a bit, like Maddie did.

"At least we'll be able to continue with Maddie's bridge lessons," said Betty.

"Hearts are trumps," declared Vi.

Doris fanned out her cards and a satisfied smiled settled on her face as she saw the ace of hearts beating gently in her hand.

Tennis chumps

Vi was all of a dither. The taxi driver was going to arrive any minute, to take them on a holiday for which she hadn't finished packing, but she wanted to watch the Wimbledon final with Maddie and Anna. Having gone out on a limb to watch the match, she couldn't even relax because Anna hadn't arrived home, and now Maddie was missing the best bits.

"Hurry up, Maddie, she's got set point!" called Vi. She liked Steffi Graf. Such poise, such athleticism, that Yank was bound to trip up sooner or later. Damn. "Davenport's taken the first 6-4! Bloody nonsense!" The door was kicked open and Maddie came in with a fresh jug of Barley Water. "There's a girl. Thank you." Vi licked her lips. Watching tennis was thirsty work. "Can't believe this Davenport character has got her on the run."

"Graf's probably just making a match of it. She'll come back, don't you worry."

"Who was that on the phone, dear?" asked Vi.

"Someone for Anna. One of her colleagues, I think."

"On a Sunday?" Vi was worried about Anna. It was all very well working till all hours and getting dropped back at the house in the middle of the night by women in fancy cars, but she shouldn't be letting her career rule her life.

"Anna'll be home soon," said Maddie. "She said she'd be here to wave you off and I know she wanted to see the final."

The door opened again; this time it was Betty. "I hope you've packed, Vi – the car will be here to take us to the airport any minute and we can't be doing with any panics."

Vi grinned at Maddie and rolled her eyes. "Don't worry, Betty. I only need to fling a spare pair of nylons in a bag and that's me done." There was a roar from the screen. Vi turned back to the match. "Bugger me! Look at that forehand."

Swearing and sport – two things that were guaranteed to make Betty leave a room. She tutted and shut the door behind her.

"Do you reckon the rain will hold off? They've got to get Sampras and Agassi on after this." Vi settled back down in her chair.

"They were saying it shouldn't be too bad today."

Another upper-class exclamation from the television remarked on what an exceptional volley Davenport had executed to win a crucial point.

"So she can run forward, that whatshername. Picked that one off at the net pretty darn well."

"She's not a bad doubles player either."

More polite chit-chat on the television as another Graf assault was dealt with by Davenport. The doorbell dinged and Vi got up to look out of the window. An unshaven, chewing youth stood on the doorstep and a car chugged in the road.

"Minicab's here!" shouted Vi. She waited for the stampede to start. Maddie helped them downstairs with their cases and the youth loaded them into the car.

Betty started fretting about some lost hair nets, tennis commentators were lamenting the end of an era as Graf's loss looked inevitable, Doris was shouting at Vi to turn the television down and the minicab driver was bellowing a warning about traffic on the M25, when Anna appeared at the door. The three women filed past her and proffered their powdered cheeks for her to kiss, glad she had made it home in time to see them off on their holiday.

Betty and Doris protested when Vi said she just had to duck back into the house, but she took no notice. It was her holiday as much as theirs and she wouldn't survive a day without the BBC. She slipped back in and was rummaging around in the tallboy in the back room for her transistor radio when she heard Anna and Maddie talking in the kitchen. She peeked through the hatch. They were standing close, Maddie's head on Anna's chest – Vi smiled. They looked so happy together.

"At least I'll be able to move down into your room now," said Maddie, looking up at her partner. Vi shook her head as she realised how hard they'd had to work at keeping their relationship a secret.

"I don't know," replied Anna. She pushed Maddie away slightly. "I feel a bit awkward about it – what with it being Nana's home and everything."

"What do you mean?"

"Maybe we should leave things as they are. It's only going to be for a couple more weeks."

Vi frowned. She'd always thought Anna was too sensitive for her own good. It wasn't like that in my day, she thought. Any spare moment and we were at it like pistons. How things have changed.

The taxi was honking its horn, so she stuffed her radio in her pocket and crept quietly down the hall.

Don't bother to knock

Maddie was trying to concentrate on what Anna was saying, but she was having trouble finding a salad bowl. Since the Nani left, she had been in charge of organising meals, but the way the equipment in Vi's kitchen was arranged left a lot to be desired.

"She said they were looking for a team player who could 'interface with other departments'," explained Anna.

"What does that mean?" Maddie found a bowl on the top shelf of the larder and put the chopped cucumber in it. She was trying to focus on Anna's job offer, but it was difficult in the light of all her own missed opportunities.

"Someone who's flexible and not too bossy, I guess."

"Oh." If only she hadn't told Vi she'd be around to let the plumber in, at least she wouldn't have missed out on that session as an assistant.

"Because the job is all about being able to offer a range of legal support services on issues affecting every aspect of the company, internationally as well as domestic."

"Jeez, Anna, it sounds really –" She tried to sound excited for Anna. It wasn't her fault that Maddie hadn't bothered to learn how to manipulate images electronically when she'd been given the chance.

"No, but that's not the best thing." Anna stopped dicing the carrot and started to read from the email that was lying on the kitchen worktop. "The role will include joint ventures, trading agreements, assisting the corporate team with major projects... blah, blah, blah. You will be expected to work using your own initiative, take the lead and create your own opportunities!"

For a second Maddie was flummoxed. Her knife kept slamming down on the chopping board as she collected her thoughts.

"Well – what do you think?"

"It sounds amazing, Anna. I had no idea you were so…" High-powered, ambitious, successful – she could have ended her sentence with any of these words.

"Clever? I know! Amazing, isn't it?"

"All that overtime was worth it, then?"

"Oh yeah." Anna moved closer to Maddie and brushed her cheek with her hand.

Maddie considered how surreal her life had become. Even her partner's touch was so unfamiliar that it made her shiver. Maybe when they started sleeping together again, they'd feel closer.

"But now that I'm allowed to 'create my own opportunities', that is going to stop, Mads."

Maddie lifted her eyes to meet Anna's and challenged them to tell the truth.

"I promise –" The doorbell interrupted Anna. "Fucking hell. Who's that?"

"The Nani should be poking round Moroccan bazaars by now, shouldn't they?" Maddie shuffled down the hallway, still reeling from Anna's news.

Maybe it was Mr Thompson come to check on the dripping tap in the bathroom. Maddie opened the door with her 'don't think you're coming in for a cup of tea' face on.

"Barbara! What on earth are you doing here?"

Barbara planted two huge kisses on Maddie's cheeks.

Maddie picked up Barbara's case and called out: "Anna! Your mum's here."

"A joke's a joke, Mads, but that just isn't –" Anna rounded the corner and saw her mother beaming at her. "Mum!"

"Anna, darling."

Maddie watched as Anna clocked the suitcase.

"I'm guessing you've come to stay."

"That's right, Annie," said Barbara. "Just a couple of nights, though, while I find myself a hotel."

"A hotel?" chorused Anna and Maddie.

"It's going to be so much fun, girls. I should have done this years ago. I already feel twenty years younger," chuntered Barbara. "Oh Anna, you can take me to some shows, museums, restaurants. We can spend some quality time together."

Maddie peeped out of the doorway into the twilight. A man was heaving another bag up the path. He plonked it down with the seven already on the steps, said, "That's the lot, mate," and got back in his cab. Maddie turned back to face Anna, whose glowing face had been drained of its vitality by Barbara's burbling.

"Mum. Just stop a minute," she ordered. "Explain slowly and sensibly exactly what is going on."

Barbara just stood there, smiling girlishly.

"I think she's gone and left him," surmised Maddie.

13 AUGUST 1999

Let's make love

Anna reached up and undid the buttons of her lover's blouse. Their faces were so close together that it was hard to see her expression but, after all the time they had spent avoiding this moment, the move felt right.

She had anticipated this scene over and over as she lay in bed alone at night, but now it was real. Finally she was alone with the woman she desired more than anyone. She should never have let her own prudery keep them apart. Now, though, the setting was perfect. It was as if the centrifugal energy which had forced them away from each other, kept them circling each other for weeks, had brought them to that pinpoint of calm where everything becomes clear.

A smile greeted her through the candlelight. Anna could feel the rise and fall of her lover's chest as she peeled off her clothing. Slowly. Sensuously. Trying not to do anything that would pierce the vacuum they had created for themselves. She pushed the black fabric of her lover's blouse over her shoulders and ran her hands over the torso it exposed. She leaned in, brushed aside the strands of hair moulded around her nape, and kissed her naked neck. The alcoholic taste of her perfume made Anna's mouth pucker slightly, but that was okay. She felt her partner ease herself forward on the sofa, and reached round to undo her bra. Her lover's mouth was a tongue's tip from her own...

Sex had been a blur of emotions, tastes and smells, intensified by weeks of abstinence. Now, in the aftermath, Anna lay as still as she could. Finally she felt her lover stir and pull away from her embrace.

"Are you okay?" Anna asked. Her voice tried to sound upbeat and resolute but it was garnished with guilt.

"I'm fine."

"You are wonderful, Roz. Truly wonderful."

Long day's journey into night

The minicab ferrying Anna from Roz's house in Clapham to her own new home in Whitechapel seemed to be running on odd-shaped wheels. The jerking, jolting ride through the clear, early morning streets of London was enough to draw Anna back into the real world. Gone was her Princess Charming with her scented candles, silken tongue and box set of Carpenters CDs. Anna caught a glimpse of herself in the driver's rear-view mirror and shrank away from the hard evidence of her evening of debauchery. Her outfit had definitely become more 'rags' than 'glad', the convertible Saab in which Roz had whisked her to Clapham was transformed into a Datsun Cherry and now it was Anna who felt like the pumpkin. At least she had both shoes, she thought to herself as she located her purse and gave the driver more money than he'd asked for.

The unlocking routine for the new flat hadn't yet become second nature and she stared at her bunch of keys like an English person examining foreign currency. She looked at her watch after she'd cracked the sequence. It was four-thirty-seven a.m. She crept into the kitchen and got herself a glass of water. She would just have a quick lie-down on the beanbag in the living room before taking up the challenge of a shower. Dropping her bag on the floor, she thought how comfortable and warm the polystyrene balls were as they sculpted themselves into her shape. Maybe she should phone Roz. Just to say she got home safely, just to say... The phone nestled in her hand as she dropped into a deep sleep.

Intimate games

Maddie was used to feeling unsettled when she woke up in the morning; after all, they'd only lived there for a matter of weeks and it was bound to take time to get used to yet another set of surroundings. This morning, however, it was more than 'unsettled'. When she rolled over and realised Anna wasn't lying next to her, she also guessed why. Anna had had a work celebration the night before and she was probably with Andy somewhere, trying to beat off a hangover with a greasy spoon.

Tempted as she was to ignore this logical explanation, she decided to try calling Anna's mobile before going into panic mode. As Maddie smothered herself in her partner's robe, her mouth watered involuntarily. Why did I have to start thinking about fry-ups? she moaned.

She looked for the phone on its charger in the spare room, but it was missing as usual. To track it down, she pressed the button that made the handset ring.

A nanosecond after the electronic 'here I am' beep sounded, there came a piercing scream. Maddie grabbed the letter-opener from the pot on the desk, joined in the screaming and charged out towards the doorway. The symphony of beeping, screaming, stomping and shouting mounted as Maddie, terrified, half asleep and uncoordinated, searched for her door keys. She could hear someone stumbling around in the living room.

"Just take what you want!" she yelled at the intruder. "You can have it all! Don't hurt me! I've got a knife! Please don't hurt me!"

She was emptying the contents of her bag on the floor, searching for the keys, when she felt a hand on her shoulder. She screamed like she'd shut her finger in a car door and tried to get away, but her socks couldn't get any purchase on the smooth floorboards. Instead she went crashing to the floor, bringing her assailant with her. Instantly, the noise stopped.

"Anna?" The mascara-smudged, red-eyed, puffy-faced woman lying next to her was vaguely reminiscent of her girlfriend, but Maddie wouldn't have bet more than a tenner on it. The face, imprinted by a beanbag seam, smiled apologetically.

"What the fuck are you playing at?" asked Maddie.

"I think I must have fallen asleep in the other room."

Maddie couldn't understand why Anna kept shrinking away from her touch when she tried to comfort her. She was doing everything she could to make her feel better, but it was only after her bath that Anna became anything like her normal self.

Maddie handed her the remote control for the video and sat beside her on the sofa. She looked less green than before, but not much happier. Obviously she needed food.

"So what is it you want? Fried chicken or a burger?" Having made the decision to go hunting and gathering, Maddie was keen to have a description of the particular beast that needed rounding up. Instead of replying, Anna burst into tears. Again. Maddie took her girlfriend's hand and tried to be patient. The tears began to seep onto lashes that were still wet and clumpy from the last bout of spouting.

"Come on, it'll be okay," soothed Maddie, rubbing her partner's hand. "Things always look shit when you've got a stinking hangover. All your vitamin B has been blasted – that's why you're feeling depressed. I'll get you some painkillers when I'm out and you'll feel fine." Maddie's voice sounded caring and concerned, but the core of her was getting pissed off with Anna's ridiculousness.

"That would be great. Thanks Mads," said Anna, fixing Maddie with her mournful eyes. "You're so good to me, you know. I love you so much, Maddie."

"Oh jeez, you are bad, aren't you pet!" laughed Maddie.

"No, I mean it –"

"For Christ's sake, Anna, you've had too much to drink. Everyone does it from time to time. It's a laugh at the time but you feel like crap afterwards. It's a given. You've had the fun, now you've got the pain. End of. So, chicken, vitamin B, ibuprofen…anything else?"

Anna shrank down under the duvet and shook her head.

"Heavens to Betsy," muttered Maddie as she grabbed her wallet and headed for the Whitechapel Road.

It was busy in the fried-chicken shop, but Maddie was happy to queue. She was still trying to decide whether she fancied barbecue beans or coleslaw with her chicken when she felt someone tap her on the shoulder. She looked round in surprise.

"Eve! What are you doing here?"

"Same as you by the look of things." Maddie felt Eve's eyes scan her from head to toe. From her jogging bottoms to her coffee-stained T-shirt and the two litres of Diet Coke she was holding, she looked so 'morning after'. "You know, Maddie, I never really thanked you for doing such a great job for me on that shoot. The designs looked fantastic."

"It's the least I could do." Maddie's eyes drifted back towards the overhead menu. She was getting nearer the serving hatch but needed more time to resolve the beans vs coleslaw dilemma.

"It's such a shame though, because Miles, who was doing the website, has pulled out, so the whole idea might have to be scrapped."

"But I thought you'd already invited a load of people to the launch." Maddie felt miffed. She'd put a lot of effort into taking those shots of Eve's creations. She'd been banking on it bringing in more work, and now it didn't look like being the loss-leader it was billed as.

"I know. I don't want to cancel until I've gone down every avenue."

"Six pieces of chicken, two large chips, one strawberry shake, a corn on the cob and a tub of coleslaw. No! Beans. Barbecue beans." Maddie's mouth was already beginning to water as the assistant assembled her order. She caught Eve staring at her and smiled sheepishly.

"I don't suppose you would reconsider, would you?" drawled Eve.

"I told you I'm not that proficient at all the computer stuff," replied Maddie.

"We could make it as simple as you like. I have some ideas and I'm sure we could work something out. It wouldn't take that long because Miles had already made a start. I would pay you, Maddie, and think of all those new contacts you could make. It will be fun, I promise you, and, after all the favours I've done for you, it would really help me out of a hole."

Maddie looked at Eve's wide desperate eyes and visualised her own empty bank account before she replied. "As long as you understand that this would be like an experiment for me."

"But that's just the look I'm after! I'm thinking avant garde, off the wall, experimental! Perfect!"

Maddie picked up her bag of food. Given that her once booming business was now little more than a whisper, she really could do with the money.

"Okay," she said, omitting the 'what the hell' she was thinking. "Let's meet in the next couple of days so you can tell me what you want."

The bucket of gnawed chicken bones in the middle of the living room looked like a sacrificial altar to the ancient god, Alcohol. Maddie was watching the black and white images on the TV with Anna, but she wasn't taking anything in. She knew she should really enrol on some kind of computer course, but it was too late for that now. Instead she visited an internet bookshop and ordered *How to Build a Website*, to quash her anxiety about the project.

Anna was still watching the film when Maddie wandered back into the living room. They had been planning to go and buy stuff for the flat, but now they were wasting a day. Maddie didn't blame her for wanting to postpone the trip but she couldn't help feeling disgruntled.

"There's a letter from your mum on the side," wheezed Anna from the sofa.

Maddie collected the letter from the table and tore at the thick, textured paper with less dignity than it deserved. Inside was the obligatory cutting, but she couldn't concentrate on it so she put it on the pile with the rest. She'd get round to reading them sometime, but she wasn't going to let Anna distract her with such mundanities.

"How come it all got so out of control last night?" asked Maddie. Anna hadn't said much about her evening, but Maddie thought, in the absence of any other entertainment, she'd get her own back by picking at her girlfriend's wounds.

"I really don't know." Anna sighed.

"Where did you go?"

"We were at the restaurant for ages. It was a fantastic meal actually..."

"I bet!"

"The wine was flowing and everyone was celebrating – you know what it's like, you just lose track."

"Whose idea was it to go on somewhere?"

"Errr. Well, I guess, it was... You know, I can't remember."

"I was beginning to think your mum had dragged you off to Stringfellow's again."

"Heaven forbid! It was Andy's fault. He was way out of it." Maddie watched Anna try to piece together the night's events. "It ended up being just him and me," she continued eventually. "We went to this club in Covent Garden, started dancing, and the next thing I knew, it was four o'clock in the morning."

"He's such a bad influence, that boy," said Maddie, wondering what it was about Andy that tended to draw out the worst in Anna, rather like magnesium sulphate on a pustule.

"You know, I think everything caught up with me. The pressure at work. Roz said my promotion should come into effect in the next couple of weeks. What with Mum acting like a teenager, work, moving house – twice! I think I just lost it for a moment."

Maddie wondered if she'd been a bit hard on her. Anna's job had never imposed itself on their lives before. She had been happy at the company, not ankle-snappingly ambitious, and things had jogged along smoothly. But now that Anna was being encouraged to broaden her professional horizons, that smoothness had become rumpled.

"I understand, sweetheart," said Maddie. "I know I haven't been great to live with lately, but you do know I'm there for you if you need to talk about stuff, don't you? I'm really proud of you, Anna." Maddie saw tears squeezing themselves up through the ducts at the corner of Anna's eyes and decided to change the subject. "Maybe I should give Andy a ring and say we're not going to be able to see him and Phil tonight," she offered. "Judging by the state *you're* in, I doubt if he's feeling up to much, anyway."

"*No!* No. It's all right. *I'll* give him a call. I want to make sure he got home okay, anyway."

Loose cannons

"Hi Phil, is Andy there?" Anna waited nervously for him to be brought to the phone.

"So what happened to you last night?" asked Andy excitedly. "I've been dying to know, but Phil said I should wait and ask you tonight."

"That's what I'm calling about." Anna was trying to sound calm, but she wasn't making a good fist of it.

"Are you okay?" Andy's tone changed when he heard Anna's voice. "Has something happened?"

"No. Well yes," she replied, getting a grip on the situation at last. "Two things, Andy. Firstly, we're not going to be able to go out with you tonight –"

"A little the worse for wear, are we?"

"Not at all. I hardly drank a thing, which makes it even worse."

"Which makes what worse?" Andy sounded confused – and she knew confusion was something he wasn't good at tolerating.

"I'll tell you later, but the second thing is that if you speak to Maddie, I was with you last night and we were at a club in Covent Garden until about four o'clock. Okay?"

There was a slight pause. Anna waited for Andy to confirm the instructions. "You want me to lie?" he asked finally.

"Put it bluntly, why don't you," hissed Anna. "So, will you do it?"

"Yeah, I s'pose..."

"You're a real mate, Andy. I owe you one."

"What you owe me is an explanation, my girl."

"Monday. I promise."

"So do I. You are okay, though?"

"Yep. Absolutely fine."

Analyze this

Anna took Monday off. Those of her colleagues who had seen them leaving the restaurant early had been told that she wasn't feeling well and that Roz was driving her home. In retrospect, it had all fitted in quite neatly. She hadn't made a fool of herself in front of anyone who mattered; but now she didn't want to bump into Roz at work before she knew what she was going to say.

The weekend had been exhausting. She'd spent all her energy

putting on a show for Maddie and needed some time on her own so she could take stock of the situation. She felt awful about duping Maddie into thinking she was ill when, in fact, it was her guilt that had driven her to bed. She'd stuffed herself with painkillers, but they were no good at treating the conscience-ache she was suffering from. She imagined the packet of a new kind of pill that showed a red, pulsating blob radiating out from around the heart, declaring its ability to 'fight guilt fast'. Until that little gem was perfected, however, she'd have to live with the sensation.

She turned on the TV and let it twitter as she dissected her feelings. There were two prongs to her guilt. Regret for doing the dirty on the Madonna was bad enough, but when it was mixed in with continued lust for the Whore, the result was a pernicious tableau full of snakes, fruit and voluptuous women. She remembered the first time she met Roz. She couldn't deny it, she'd fancied her from the moment she came down to introduce herself to the team...

The woman walked in the door flanked by two men from the top floor and everyone immediately stopped surfing the internet, downed tools and waited to be spoken to. One of the men made an introductory speech, but Anna didn't listen. With the shamelessness of someone observing a third party through a one-way mirror, Anna stared at the woman. She was tall and wore a suit that clung to her body like melted chocolate. There was a hint of cleavage but it was confident and slightly bold, titillating but not sluttish. She looked foreign – Spanish or South American or something – and her natural skin colour was enhanced by a healthy, wealthy person's tan. She obviously had a penchant for gold, but it manifested itself sparingly in a chunky watch and a plain, thickish chain around her neck. By the time the woman stepped forward and started to speak, Anna was totally mesmerised by her brown velveteen eyes.

"My name is Roz Gonzalez," she said in a throaty foreign accent of no clear origin, as her eyes swept the room, "and I will be working with you on the company's restructure..."

Those were the first words Anna had heard the vision say – The Voice had just been the pickle in the Pork 'n' Pickle Fancy. But it was a big step between admiring someone from a distance and ending up in bed with her.

After she'd revelled in the replay of her first impression, the guilt came rushing in once more. It had all been a bit of a game – harmless fun – hadn't it? Something to keep the mind occupied at work, a reason to go to the kitchen next to the boardroom, just in case she happened to be in her office. Anna remembered the night she'd seen her in the bar. Andy had been mithering on about how unreliable Maddie was, when Julia arrived...

"I'll get you a glass, Jules," said Anna. She walked slowly through the crowd to the far end of the bar where Roz was still sitting, alone. Anna picked up a box of matches from one of the tables and muscled her way in next to her. She saw Roz reach for her cigarettes – this was her chance. "Need a light?" she asked.

Roz turned and smiled. She should have looked surprised, but all she said was 'thank you'.

Anna struck the match. There was no need for Roz to touch her hand as she offered the flame and, when she did, Anna felt a frisson of excitement ripple through her body.

"Let me buy this for you." Roz hailed the bartender as she spoke.

"I'm just getting a glass for my friend..." Tongue-tied and gauche, Anna racked her brain for something to say.

"Another time, maybe," replied Roz. "I was thinking, we should get together for lunch."

"Oh. Yes."

"For work. There are things I'd like to discuss with you."

"Okay."

"Here's my card. My mobile number's on it..."

That was the first time she'd spoken to her out of the office. It was the kind of encounter Anna would usually have gone squealing to Andy about so he could blow it up out of all proportion and tease her about it for weeks, but this time she didn't want Andy to know. She stopped talking about Roz, and the baiting over Roz's sexuality gave way to some other fantasy scenario that she and Andy created.

Anna had kept telling herself they were just becoming friends, that it would be ridiculous to get sidetracked by a stupid obsession when she was making such a huge commitment to Maddie. She'd forced the idea out of her mind.

Now she focused on the television in an effort to get some perspective on the real world. The words 'My father's a cheating lowlife and now I'm afraid to commit!' flashed up on the screen. Three women were lined up on the chatshow, waiting to entertain the public with their various states of psychological decay.

Amid the fights and accusations on TV, it occurred to Anna that Barbara's sudden appearance in London hadn't helped. Maybe Anna was testing her own relationship, frightened they would end up like her parents in a loveless, barren liaison that had become little more than habit. "Don't talk rot," she scolded herself, and she searched for another excuse.

Perhaps her thing about Roz stemmed from the fact that she had been so encouraging, so flattering about Anna's abilities…

"You know Anna, you really should set your sights a little higher," said Roz, as she paid for their dinner. "You have a lot to offer and you shouldn't hold yourself back…"

When had Maddie ever said anything like that? Roz was so nurturing. Maybe that was the attraction. She paused for a moment to consider the fact that she had used the word 'nurturing'. The TV psycho-babble must have penetrated her thoughts, because she was starting to sound like a babbling psycho. She reached for the remote control, pressed a button, and the self-help guru combusted into blankness.

But none of this was about Maddie. Roz was slightly older, more successful and sophisticated. It was *Roz* who'd invited her out for lunch, then dinner, then suggested the sights she wanted Anna to guide her round. It was Roz who chose where to go. It was Roz who'd bought her small gifts and impressed her with stories about her lavish childhood in Puerto Rico. For once, Anna was able to be led rather than be the leader.

So, she surmised, the fling had stemmed from her desire to take a holiday from responsibility. There again, maybe it just stemmed from her desire, full stop. Roz was a fine-looking woman, that was for sure.

Girls talk confidential

"I didn't even know she was a dyke," confided Anna.

"Well, I guess you've got an inkling now," said Andy facetiously.

"Yeah, but I would never have flirted with her if I'd known." Anna gasped and cradled her face in her hands – attempting, Andy assumed, to hide her embarrassment. They wandered down the aisle of cold cabinets, trying to pick out something for lunch, getting buffeted by more decisive lunchers whose arms turned into spears at the sight of a poached salmon sandwich daubed with dill mayonnaise. Andy fingered a bap before rejecting it in favour of a box of sushi – he didn't like it much, but it was *so* the thing to be seen eating.

"You won't say anything, will you Andy?" continued Anna as she shuffled to keep up with him.

"Of course not. I won't even tell Phil, if it makes you happy," he said to a complete stranger who had suddenly appeared in the space once occupied by Anna. He searched for her face in the crowd. When she popped up in front of him, he realised what an unsatisfactory experience this was.

"Yeah. I think the fewer people who know about this, the better."

Andy was wishing Anna had started this conversation *after* they had gone through the lunch-buying routine. Telling one of your best friends about having crazy-go-nuts sex with the boss (who also happens to be said friend's boss) should not share mind-space with such a banal activity as buying lunch. So when Anna started dishing up more details, Andy put his foot down.

"We need food, we need drink, we need a bench to sit on, and *then* we can talk."

And talk Anna did. For almost an hour, in the mind-thickeningly hot air. By the end, even Andy couldn't think of Roz's name without experiencing a fit of the quivers. She was so poised, not at all the sort of person you'd expect to give in to their baser instincts. Especially with someone from the workplace – that arena where image rules and reputation can be destroyed in the time it takes the lift to travel from basement to boardroom.

"So, I take it you haven't seen her since your rendezvous the other evening?"

"No…" Anna bit her lip and looked at Andy expectantly.

"But you've decided you don't want to pursue it?"

"Of course I don't!" said Anna.

Her response was indignant, but Andy couldn't understand why. So what if she'd just bought a flat with her girlfriend of nine million years? The choice didn't seem hard. If at one end of the bed he had a really hot, rich, exotic, intelligent, rich, classy woman and at the other end there was moaning Maddie, he knew which end he'd put his pillow. Dump the deadwood and enjoy life in the fast lane.

"You've just got to talk to her," said Andy, pushing his personal opinion to one side. "For all you know, a one-night stand might have been all she wanted. She might have a husband and family of Von Trappian proportions tucked away in whichever country it is that she comes from."

"Puerto Rico."

"There you go! Catholics, the lot of 'em."

"Maybe you're right."

"The only way you're going to find out is by asking her."

Anna still looked anxious. He felt like he was directing his friend to the room where the axe murderer had last been seen.

"Come on, Anna, it'll be okay. She doesn't bite. Does she?" Still there was no reply. "Why don't you arrange to see her on some work pretext and then slip in the sex thing as a coda?"

"Well, I think I've buggered up any chance of the promotion going through, now." Again the hands went up to the face.

"It's a dead cert, Anna. Don't worry about that." Andy picked up the remains of his lunch. He was feeling uncomfortably sweaty and wanted to get back to the air conditioning of the office.

"It's weird, though, Andy," said Anna, just as they arrived at the entrance to their building. "I'm not sure if I really like her that much."

Never say never again

Sheila enjoyed the feeling of her scissors' sharp blades cutting through the flimsy paper. The shining metal against the drab newsprint was very satisfying. The sound they made as they did their job was as sharp as their blades. Her hand slipped slightly and cut into the picture. "Damn," she exclaimed. She rectified her mistake, neatened the edges of the shape and smoothed it out in front of her. She read the article one more time, just to make sure she'd got it right. It definitely said that the woman had left her long-standing girlfriend and was unsure about her sexuality. Apparently, they were both famous, but she hadn't heard the names. Anyway, names didn't matter, it was the sentiment that was important.

She folded the article and, on a plain piece of paper, wrote: "My dear Maddie, I thought you might be interested in this. Give me a ring if you need to talk. Your loving Mum."

The gum on the envelope tasted foul. Given the amount of money this stationery had cost, they could have paid more attention to little things like that.

She slipped on her shoes and called up to her husband: "I'm just popping down to the post office, Malcolm. I shouldn't be long."

Future tense

Ed threw the last of the debris he'd gathered at the ducks on the canal. "You haven't got any regrets, have you Jules?"

Julia watched the ripples the movement created. The ever-decreasing circles reminded her of the boa constrictor's eyes in *The Jungle Book* and she wondered if she had been hypnotised somehow. That would certainly account for her behaviour over the last couple of months. Perhaps an association had been planted in her mind that meant whenever she heard anyone mention anything about The Dawning of the New Millennium, she agreed to whatever Ed wanted...

"My neighbour's been stockpiling food in the garage for the last six months 'cos he thinks the world's going to go into meltdown on 1 January 2000..."

"Would you go to the bar and get the drinks in, Jules?"

"Okay."

"This bloke in the pub was saying that on New Year's Eve, some geezers are planning to fill the Millennium Dome with helium and cut the guy ropes on the stroke of midnight..."

"I'd like us to stop seeing other people."

"Right you are, then."

"Did you know that only one in eight of Russia's nuclear power stations are Y2K compatible?"

"I was thinking it would be a good idea if I moved in, what do you reckon, Jules?"

"Yeah. Absolutely."

With a fair amount of time to go before the old millennium became the new one, she hoped against hope it wouldn't occur to Ed to ask her to go on a camping holiday.

"Oy, I was talking to you!" persisted Ed.

"Regrets? Of course I haven't. I think it's working out really well, don't you?"

"Oh God, yes. Best thing I've ever done." Ed started hunting for more missiles to intimidate the aquatic birds. With his head between his knees as he searched for ammunition, he said: "I love you, Julia."

Julia giggled nervously, rubbed his back and kissed the exposed bit of flesh at the back of his neck. "Oh *you!*" She tried to sound loving, but all she could think was "Fucking shit, he said the 'L' word! And what always comes after 'L'? 'M', that's what..." She wanted to get him home and perhaps then to the cinema or theatre or anywhere where talking wasn't the object of the exercise.

"Come on, Ed. Let's make a move. My arse is going numb."

He chucked the last of his sticks in the water and they slouched back to their flat.

"I was thinking," croaked Ed. "Maybe it's time for us to tell Anna and Maddie that I've moved in and we're like a proper couple now."

"Yeah. You're right. Why don't I give Anna a ring when I get in?"

No sooner had the words left Julia's mouth than her eyes widened, her eyebrows lifted and her mouth gaped. She listened. There was complete silence. No car radios, no passers-by, there was no one and nothing anywhere within earshot that could have made a passing reference to the historic event in question. It appeared Maida Vale was even being given a moment's respite from the ubiquitous Robbie Williams song. She had to face the possibility that there was no external force controlling her, that this was what she actually wanted. It was time to stop avoiding her friends and make herself come clean. She wondered what Maddie and Anna were doing. And it was ages since she'd last seen Kat.

Friends, lovers and lunatics

Kat, meanwhile, was having a crisis of her own. Making up outlandish stories about the people in the paintings in the Portrait Gallery used to be something she did with Maddie, but now she sat in the quietness of the gallery on her own. The general rule was, the older the work, the better the story, but as hard as Kat looked at the pinched-faced woman in the painting in front of her, she couldn't come up with anything. The woman's fin-like nose, eye-wateringly tight corset and lady-boy companion should have made something stir inside her. She would have resorted to that old faithful, bestiality, but there wasn't even a dog in the piece to fuel the imagination.

Kat knew what was wrong. There were too many other thoughts bunging up her brain and now she was suffering from constipation of the mind. That was why she came here. If the British Museum was her Novocaine for the soul, then the National Portrait Gallery was definitely Ex-lax for the mind.

She shut her eyes for a second and tried to visualise the different strands of thoughts bobbing around like anchorless balloons in her head. Okay, let's split them up into groups. Main heading, 'Maddie', sub-heading one: 'Love for'. This wasn't a difficult one to pin down. She was in love with Maddie but Maddie was in love with Anna, so she shouldn't waste her time fretting over it. That balloon should have been popped, but it had grown tough with age and was reluctant to be destroyed. Oh, well. Moving on.

Sub-heading two: 'Friendship with'. "This is a lot harder to nail," thought Kat as she stared unseeingly into the space in front of her. "If I were to tell Maddie how I feel, at least it would be over. Either Maddie would be freaked out and I'd lose her friendship, or she would say 'fucking hell, I've been in love with you for the last six years, too' and my world would be full of sirens, silhouettes and sunsets... Can I risk losing her?" That was the bottom line. After rooting around in the recesses of her mind, banging against the wall of her subconscious in search of some pre-Oedipal truth, she realised the answer was 'no'. So if she was going to find any sort of happiness with anyone else, this particular thought-balloon had to be deflated, reeled in and shut away in the box with the rest. This took some concentration. Her eyes drifted shut as she visualised herself gathering in the thought that had been clogging her mind and shutting it in the box.

Miro was the next subject. Having just put Maddie away, it was much easier to deal with Miro. Kat could imagine herself doing 'normal' things with Miro – shopping, washing, cooking, go-karting – and could see them having a proper relationship. What she couldn't understand was why Miro was so into *her*. Kat hadn't been the most attentive girlfriend ever. She'd hidden Miro's existence from her best friends, she'd always put her work first, and yet Miro kept tipping up for more. It was as if Kat had been trying to drive her away.

"Oooh. Now you're onto something," she said to herself, frightening a couple of public school boys who had wandered into the room in the process.

That was *exactly* what she'd been doing. Thank fuck her plot to bring herself down hadn't worked. From now on she was going to devote herself to her real relationship, not some tentative possibility. As

Kat stopped clenching on to her thoughts, her whole body relaxed. Her back rounded, her brow dropped, her breathing got deeper and she looked at the painting with keener, fresher eyes.

She felt someone sit down next to her and automatically moved away to give them some space.

The person moved in closer and whispered in Kat's ear: "The man is trying not to faint because –"

"– He's wearing his wife's knickers and knows that if she catches him in her drawers again, she'll tell his father who the large made-to-order women's shoes were really for." It wasn't her best, but it rushed through her like a dose of salts. Kat heard Maddie laugh and swung her legs over the bench so they were facing the same way.

"What the bejesus are you doing here?" exclaimed Kat in delight.

"Looking for you, stupid. Stewart said you'd gone out to try and clear your mind, so where else would I look?"

"Am I that predictable?" As Kat basked in the unexpected sight of her friend, she could feel the thoughts she'd boxed off, straining at the lid of their mental container. "I thought you were too busy to do stuff like this these days." Kat could never resist taunting Maddie about her change of career. It was like a non-physical form of play-fighting that allowed them to bond.

"Yeah. I know. I shouldn't be here, really..."

"But...?"

"Oh, you know, waiting to hear back from a couple of people about some work, just finished a project, waiting to get in to meet a potential client... I think it's always like that, though, with this kind of work. Peaks and troughs."

"And you're peeking into a trough?"

"No! Everything'll work out. No worries at all," said Maddie. She put her arm round her friend as they left the dark austerity of the Tudors and headed for the fluff of the 20th Century.

"None?"

"Apart from Mum, who's acting very strangely. She sent me a

picture of Ellen Degeneres this week, clipped out of the paper."

"I hope you've stuck it on the wall with the rest of the clippings," laughed Kat.

"No, but seriously, Kat. Anna reckons Mum's trying to reach out to me by showing she knows the kind of stuff I'm into."

"Scary."

"Exactly. Great pic though." Maddie laughed and shook off the subject. "So, what's got you in such a stew that you have to come here?"

Kat took a deep breath, looked Germaine Greer straight in the eye and said: "I've got myself a girlfriend." Slowly she turned her gaze away from the painting and looked at Maddie.

"You're kidding me!" she guffawed. "You mean someone you've been seeing for longer than a week?"

"Yes."

"Ten days?"

"More."

"Not a fortnight!"

"Maddie, I'm serious. I've met someone. She's called Miro –"

"The same one you met last Christmas?"

"Yes." Kat blushed and wished Maddie would lose this obsession with time.

"This is fantastic!"

"Keep your voice down." People jostling to look at Paul McCartney were beginning to stare, so Kat guided Maddie towards the exit.

"What's she like?"

"Tallish, dark, artistic." It was drizzling as they walked onto Charing Cross Road, but the fresh air was a welcome relief. Kat pushed her damp hair out of her eyes.

"What does she do?" The pedestrians seemed less concerned than Kat about the half-walk, half-dance Maddie had struck up as they wove through the kagooled tourists.

"Teacher."

"What subject?"

"Art. She does supply in secondary schools and teaches –" Kat squirmed. Could she make her sound less interesting?

"Lives in London?"

"Clapham."

"And you like her?"

"She's great. I really like her."

Kat didn't leave enough time for Maddie to fit another question in before changing the subject. "How's Anna?"

"She's good. I think she's as relieved to be in our own place as I am – the Nani were lovely, but it turned out to be a bit of a strain, especially when Babs turned up. She's always on at Anna to take her out –"

"And I suppose she can't say no."

"Exactly. So if she's not out with Babs, she's working late to impress this new boss."

"What's got into her, for Christ's sake?"

"There's a woman at work who thinks Anna's shit's ice-cream. It appears she's being groomed for greater things."

"Sounds a bit fancy."

"I think it is. Loads more money, apparently. Trips abroad, that kind of stuff."

"That's excellent," said Kat, after a pause. "Doesn't sound much like Anna, though."

They walked in silence, each in her own world. Kat felt the ground shifting. Now she'd told Maddie about Miro, their relationship would change. It was bound to. She felt that suffocating feeling again as they marched down the road. But her panic subsided as she realised she was in the heart of London's bookshop-land. She'd drop Maddie off at the bus stop and nip down to Waterstone's to see what their self-help section had to offer. She'd definitely read something about 'people who didn't allow themselves to be happy', it was just a question of remembering which book. Tottenham Court Road was in sight now, so she wouldn't have to wait long before she could make a dash for it. Suddenly she became aware of her friend's laughter.

"Kat's got a girlfriend," chanted Maddie, like a schoolgirl. Maybe it wasn't going to be so easy to get away.

Whom the gods destroy

Maddie pressed her forehead against the window of the homebound 25 bus, trying to get to grips with Kat's news. Her hair made a squeaking noise as it rubbed the condensation off the pane.

She was using her thumbnail to clean the display on her phone when it rang. Eve's name appeared on the screen and her chest tightened. She heard people round her groan impatiently as the ringing continued. "Hi Eve, I'm on the bus. Can I call you ba–"

"No! I need to talk to you now."

Maddie turned pink and tried to override her embarrassment.

"What the fuck have you done with my website?"

She fidgeted as Eve's anger burst out of her phone and into the ears of her fellow passengers.

"I've just tried to log on and the whole thing looks scrambled and when you clink on the little images – and I'm only guessing that's what they are because they're so mashed up – the whole thing freezes. The links don't work and the colours are nothing like we discussed. It's a fucking state and my show's tomorrow –"

"I only said I would have a go, Eve," whispered Maddie. "I told you I wasn't –"

"You told me you would be able to do it. There's no way I can use this now. The entire concept for my show is totally fucked –"

"Eve, please –"

"After everything I've done for you, I can't believe you've let me down so badly. Why didn't you let me know? You wait until this gets out, Maddie, you're never going to work –"

"You're breaking up, Eve. I'll call you back." Slowly and calmly Maddie turned off her phone and slipped it into her bag.

Numb with shock, she stared through the transparent patch of window she had created. The dome of St Paul's dominated her port-hole. It was impressive, imposing and inspiring, and eased her dis-comfort. Christopher Wren hadn't just woken up one day and built St Paul's Cathedral. He'd probably started with a little chapel in some provincial suburb; then he might have experimented with a couple of little churchy type things in the backstreets south of the river, then built the odd monument here and there to ring the changes. Even someone as prolific and extraordinary as that had no doubt had his highs and lows.

As the bus inched past the structure, Maddie knew there was no way she could let herself feel this humiliated again. She would find a course and learn about the whole process from scratch. Start building the foundations, and the cathedrals would follow later.

Basic instinct

Roz was sitting on the corner of her desk, interviewee side, her foot al-most brushing Anna's calf.

Anna cleared her throat and started to speak. "I feel I need to say something about the other night."

Roz nodded slowly, but still she didn't say anything.

"The thing is, I don't really know what came over me, Roz. This isn't something I usually do. I mean, I've never been unfaithful to Maddie before and, actually, we're very happy. My behaviour was an aberration, I can assure you." Anna sniffed nervously and shifted in her seat. She could smell Roz's perfume but was determined not to let that distract her. "You see, I wasn't looking for an affair. That's not to say it wasn't fantastic, because it was, and, you know, if things were different I'd love to…" Anna's voice tailed off, but Roz didn't help her out of her hole.

"What I'm trying to say is, I hope you don't think badly of me," she continued. "It's like we've gone and crossed the Maginot Line of office politics and I feel a little stranded now I'm on the other side."

Roz raised an eyebrow. "I've always liked a woman with a firm grasp of world history." She smiled while Anna melted at her feet.

"I'm scared I've messed things up so we can't be friends or work together any more. I think that's what I've been trying to say."

"Anna, there were two of us involved that night. You mustn't blame yourself for what happened," soothed Roz. "And I can assure you that you have not 'messed things up'. Whatever happens between us on a personal level will always be 'without prejudice'." Anna tittered at this amusing use of legal jargon before her colleague continued.

"To be honest, I completed my work with your department some weeks ago, so I will be turning my attention to other parts of the company. I think you can guess why I might have stayed with you longer than necessary. I admit to having taken more interest than I would normally in a team member's career path, but I can step back from that if you'd like. Having said that, Anna, you have to understand that I did not encourage you and help you prepare for this move with the sole intention of seducing you.

"I think you are talented, intelligent and a great asset to the firm. I like you and I would like therefore to see you succeed. I think the crux of the matter for me, however, is that whereas I thoroughly enjoyed having you as a friend, I much prefer you as a lover. But it's up to you. I respect your feelings."

"I don't know what to say," stuttered Anna.

"Call me if you change your mind." Roz brushed her hand over Anna's shoulders as she retreated to familiar territory on the other side of the desk.

A very curious girl

Miro was in the middle of counting her paintbrushes when Brian (second in charge, science) poked his head round her classroom door.

"Sorry to bother you, Joanie, but there's a rather delightful woman at reception asking for a 'Miro Petrowski'," he declared. "As you are the only Petrowski we have, I presumed she meant you."

Miro was annoyed at herself for being shocked by her unexpected visitor – and none too pleased that Brian was there to witness her loss of composure. He insisted on walking with her back to reception and did a ridiculous semi-bow when he was introduced to Kat. Miro bundled her out of the door before he could kiss her hand or suggest they took tiffin together.

"This is a nice surprise," said Miro.

"I just happened to be in the area and thought we could check out your bike sheds."

"You'd be lucky if our kids knew what a bike was, let alone owned one."

"Maybe we could just go home, then."

Miro grinned all the way to the tube. She hoped she hadn't misread the gesture, but the idea that Kat had come just to be with her – not to go out anywhere or for any special occasion – seemed to add a sense of permanence to their relationship.

They rattled around in the half-empty tube train like dried peas in a maraca. It hurtled round bends, whipping the back carriages from side to side, so they lurched in time with its beat. The train screeched to a halt. A man and a woman got on and stumbled into the seats opposite Miro as they sambaed into the tunnel once again. Miro studied them and tried to work out if they were a couple. They didn't speak, they weren't touching, their faces showed no emotion. The tube did that to people. Even the most extreme personalities were sucked out of travellers the moment they stepped through its sliding doors. Miro imagined the amount of love, hate, anger and humour that the seats had soaked up over the years. She saw the man's hand twitch and thought he was going to let her in on their secret. But that was it. Just a twitch.

"Do you think people look at us and know immediately we're a couple?" she asked, once their fellow travellers had left the train.

"I've never thought about it really," mumbled Kat.

"I suppose it's less obvious with two women. It's not the first thing that would come into people's minds."

"Suppose not."

"I wouldn't mind, you know, if you wanted to hold my hand when we're out, for example."

Kat smiled and slipped her hand into Miro's.

"It's nice, isn't it, to show someone how you feel from time to time," persisted Miro. Still no response. She started to question her girlfriend's sensitivity and reconsidered her plans to tell her she was falling in love with her. The beat of the wheels over the track throbbed on. Two stations later, Miro felt Kat's arm sneak round her shoulders.

"I was wondering if you'd like to come to a party with me?" asked Kat. "Some friends have just moved into a new flat, and they're having people over. I'd really like you to meet them."

The doors opened and the couple headed for the escalator. "That would be great. When is it?"

The uninvited guest

"When is she going back to Canvey?" asked Julia, as she checked the people in the stalls for crimes against fashion, using her 40p opera glasses. "She's not going to be around for your party, is she?"

"That's just the point! I don't know," bleated Anna. They both stood up to let a couple get back to their seats, designed for nineteenth century theatre-going midgets. "And what's more, she's having the time of her life. She reckons she's not missing Dad at all, she doesn't want to talk to him and has no intention of trying to build bridges."

"Jesus wept!"

"Precisely."

"Have you seen that jacket – row G, halfway along?" Julia scrutinised the outfit. "I haven't seen an epaulette like that since the late eighties."

Anna agreed half-heartedly while Julia retrained her glasses on the ice-cream vendor who was propped against the balcony. There were about five minutes left of the interval and Barbara was third in the queue. Julia had about three minutes to bring up the subject of her and Ed living together before Anna's mum got back to her seat. It was easier thought than said, however. It wasn't the kind of thing she could just blurt out.

"How's Madge then? Feeling more settled now you've moved in?"

Anna went pale. "She's fine. Actually, she's more than fine. She's brilliant. She's the most wonderful woman I've ever met and I don't know what I've done to deserve her."

"That's nice," nodded Julia. "Are you okay, Anna?"

"Here we go, girls," blustered Barbara as she climbed over bags and legs to get back to her seat. "Two strawberry and a chocolate for me. I'd forgotten how much I love the theatre. Do you know what –"

"You're having the time of your life?" asked Anna. Her mother's howls of laughter confirmed her suspicion.

Reality bites

The bubbling soundtrack of the store washed over Anna as she yawned, scooped up a trolley and trailed after Maddie. She hadn't got home that late from the theatre, but slipping friends into a schedule that was dominated by her mother's voracious social appetite was extremely tiring. Between them, Barbara and Roz were like thorns puncturing her natural buoyancy. Usually, she would head the charge around the Aladdin's cave that was a DIY store. Not a shelf, nor an aisle, nor a bargain bucket would go unexamined. This time, however, it was she who lolled over the trolley and allowed it to steer its own course while Maddie forged ahead, list in hand.

When Anna caught up, they were in an area full of boxes of different types of screws, nails and other contraptions that were meant to help you affix things to walls. Maddie had two different packets in her hand and was reading the instructions intently. Anna knew she should throw herself into this activity too, or else she would start thinking about Roz again. She looked at Maddie's face. She had grown her hair longer and it made her look younger, more fresh-faced, more innocent. As Anna thought these thoughts, her guilt, lurking in the wings of her psyche, leapt centre stage and shimmied its way through her body. In the past, she'd shared everything with Maddie – chocolate, clothes, concerns – maybe she should just come clean and tell her what had happened. Then they could start with a clean slate.

"What do you reckon, Anna – should we use one of these things to hang the mirror, or stick with the mounts it's got?"

"What do you think would be best?"

Maddie tossed the packet around in her hand. "Stick to what we know?"

"Fine with me."

"Right. More emulsion. That's the next thing…"

Anna couldn't manage a fully fledged fight but she did rouse herself sufficiently to have a slight skirmish over what colour to paint the spare room. That was a good sign, she told herself, as they argued the toss over the difference between 'off white' and 'bandage'.

"Is this your shout then, Mads?" Anna asked as they joined the queue for the checkouts. It wasn't that she didn't want to pay, but she couldn't be bothered to fumble around in her bag looking for her wallet.

"Okay."

Anna fitted in a couple more minutes of lolling while she watched Maddie stacking their booty on the conveyor belt.

"Jesus, Anna! Can't you give me a hand? Why is it always me who has to do everything?"

Anna's body snapped into an upright position. Maddie had just had a pop at her. That was a bit uncalled for, wasn't it? Or maybe it wasn't. She should do something to show Maddie how much she appreciated the work she'd done in their new place. She should suggest they go for a romantic meal. That would do them both good.

"Anna, you really have no idea, have you? Here I am, trying my hardest to keep my weight down, and you suggest going out for a meal! Jesus!" They packed up their shopping and walked out into the car park in silence.

"Look, Anna, I don't mind going to the pub for a bit when I get back from the studio, but I'm not up for a big evening."

"Okay." Anna felt her bottom lip protrude and reeled it back in. She didn't want Maddie to have a go at her for sulking, but she felt she was justified. Usually Maddie went on at her for being a party pooper. How was she meant to know that Maddie had suddenly become a stay-at-home-Sally?

"You haven't forgotten we're having everyone round tomorrow, have you?"

Ahh, thought Anna, she's trying to back-track. There's the real reason she doesn't want to go out tonight. "If it's the money, I don't mind paying," she offered.

"It's not the sodding money. I just don't want to go out to eat, that's all."

They drove home in silence.

The Big Picture

It was more through desperation than desire that Maddie found herself gazing at the embryonic ideas on the canvas. A whole generation of elephants could have been conceived and reared in the time it was taking her to produce one measly picture. Popping into the studio had been a bad idea. It was going to take more than Anna's picture to take her mind off what had happened with Eve. The phone calls that hadn't been returned; the contacts that had become uncontactable. Where was it going to end? She groaned.

It wasn't as if Anna even deserved the bleedin' painting. She wished she hadn't bothered starting it. She wished she wasn't there.

She swung slowly in the wicker chair. Her momentum made it creak. It sounded sinister in the silence and put her in mind of a story her grandma used to tell her about how people – criminals, she guessed – used to be hung over the banks of the Thames. "If their necks didn't break, the tide would get 'em" was how the tale went.

Interesting, she thought. Brutal, lurid and probably made up by the old card, but interesting. And kind of appropriate.

Where did Kat keep her stash these days? A quick smoke would see her right, help make death less fascinating and torture less appropriate.

She sprinkled the flakes of dope into the tobacco on the paper. Why do Americans say 'oreguno' and why does it sound more exotic that way? she wondered as she licked the sticky edge of the Rizla. Centre left. 'Oreegahhno'. Centre right. 'Oreguno'. She rolled the joint between her thumbs and forefingers. Tight and as pert as a gay boy's buns.

"You say tomayto, I say tomarto," she sung softly. She lit the screw of paper and pulled on the joint. "You say potayto, I say potarto." She inhaled the fumes. Maybe the picture would be better as a birthday present. After this work palaver had blown over, it would be easier to concentrate. "Tomayto, tomarto." Next July would be in a whole new millennium. "Potayto, potarto." Loads of time. Coherent thoughts were smoked out of her mind. "Let's call the whole thing off."

True lies

As soon as Julia pushed at the open door and set foot in Maddie and Anna's place, she could feel something wasn't right. Everyone looked and sounded cheerful enough, but there was definitely an undercurrent. But what could be wrong? Was it that Barbara had turned down the offer of a night cruise down the Thames and insisted on coming to the party after all? Or maybe something was up with Maddie. Or perhaps she'd misread the vibe. Ed had just closed the front door behind him when Maddie finally appeared in the hallway to greet them. She was glistening like a boxer who'd gone ten hard rounds – she was obviously the nominated cook for the evening.

"Hello stranger!" cried Julia, giving Maddie a hug. Maddie took their coats and flung them on the bed in the spare room as Kat appeared in the hallway waving a bottle of red around and offering drinks. Julia smiled to see that her friend had set upon the wine supply with her usual determination.

"Is it okay to talk about the living-together thing tonight, or is that still *verboten*?' hissed Ed in her ear as she walked further into the flat.

"Let's see how it goes, eh?" said Julia before turning her attention back to Kat. "Kathryn! You look stunning!"

"You're not looking so bad yourself, gorgeous," said Kat as she gave her a kiss that lingered just a fraction longer than friendship usually allowed. Julia revelled in the flirtation that often went on between them and she didn't make a move to pull away, even though she was keen to find out what had given her the heebie-jeebies when she first walked in.

"So where's this mystery woman of yours, then? I do hope you've brought her tonight or there'll be trouble."

"Jules, babe, I couldn't possibly bring her here when I know how jealous you get. It would have been cruel and insensitive of me to spoil Maddie and Anna's do." Kat goosed Julia before meandering back to the kitchen.

"I know you're just making her up to taunt me!" Julia shouted after her.

"You mean this Miro woman doesn't even exist?" asked Ed.

"Don't believe her!" shouted Maddie from the kitchen. "She's organising her students' art exhibition and couldn't make it, that's all."

Julia let Ed trail after Kat, demanding more explanations. She could hear Andy chatting to Anna in the living room, and she cooed a comment about the decor in the hall as she made a beeline for them.

Anna was in a huddle with Andy when Julia came in. Immediately he pulled away and went to join Phil, who was flicking through the CD collection. That was all it took for Julia's suspicions to be confirmed. Something was up. It was obvious that Andy was in on it; Phil was never in on anything so he didn't count; but Julia didn't know who else they were in cahoots with. The best way was not to confront them too early but to let their secret come out naturally.

"Anna, it's so good to see you at last! The place is looking great. Really smart," enthused Julia.

"Yeah. Maddie has been a diamond. She's been working like the clappers. Don't you think the walls look fantastic?"

Julia looked at the freshly painted slug-coloured walls. It didn't look as though anything too taxing had gone into their transformation from white to slug, but she agreed they were indeed fantastic.

"It was a shame we didn't get to talk properly on Friday," said Julia, plonking herself down in the space next to Anna. "I didn't even get the chance to ask you about your new job."

"It's all been a bit of a nightmare," replied Anna. "There's been so much going on and some tough decisions to make. You know how it is."

Out of the corner of her eye, Julia saw Andy glance over at Anna. The movement was almost imperceptible, but Julia definitely saw him shake his head. She looked back at Anna and caught the tail end of her glare. That was it.

"What on earth is going on here?" she asked softly, turning her back on Andy and Phil as she did so.

"I can't tell you now, Jules, honestly. Let's wait until we're on our own."

Julia groaned in disbelief. She was trying to hatch a plan to get rid of the others when, as if by magic, Ed appeared in the doorway with his coat on. "I'm just going to the offy, Jules. We forgot to bring the champagne and Kat says we're nearly out of red wine. Do you want anything?"

"No. That sounds fine. I'd go to the place on the main road if I were you, it's got a much better selection." That should give her enough time. She was about to suggest that Ed took Kat with him, when the woman herself squeezed into the doorway in Julia's jacket, pulled the collar up round her face and waved. The door slammed and two sets of footsteps went down the stairwell.

"Right. Come on. They've gone, Maddie's in the kitchen. Spill the beans."

Julia could practically feel her bodice ripping as she listened to the story of lies, deception and adultery that came out of Anna's mouth.

"It was all quite innocent at first. She was being really friendly and we just seemed to click," explained Anna. "I mean, I know I fancied –"

"What do you fancy, my love?" Maddie was in the doorway.

Anna's face was taut with concentration as she tried to provide an answer. "I was just telling Julia how I wanted to try doing curried lamb's kidneys tonight but you weren't keen."

"Offal isn't really everyone's cup of tea," replied Maddie. "I'm looking for an extra pair of hands to hold the strainer for me." Andy volunteered Phil, who followed Maddie into the kitchen to execute the task.

"Fucking shit, Jules, that was close," sighed Anna. "I told you we should leave it."

"You can't stop now," chorused Julia with Andy, who had joined them.

"There's not much more to say. We started going out as friends and I fancied the pants off her. I didn't have a clue she was a dyke, so it never crossed my mind that... 'it' would happen."

"And now 'it' has...?" Julia's reaction was split down the middle. She felt awful for Maddie that Anna had done this, but it sounded so exciting that she couldn't help but get swept along with the intrigue.

"That's just the thing. She said she'd like more from me, but she's totally fine if I don't want it to continue."

They all looked up as Maddie walked over to the dining table and reached for the only drop of wine left that Kat hadn't consumed. "What are you three whispering about?" she asked suspiciously.

"What do you mean?" asked Anna defensively.

"Anna's got a surprise for you, Madge," Julia piped up, to save her friend. "All will be revealed later on."

"It'd better be something good!" Maddie filled her glass and went back into the kitchen.

"That's it! I'm not going on with this," said Anna determinedly.

"Just one more question. How long has it been going on?"

"Depends what you mean –"

"She's talking about sex, Anna, not the wishy-washy stuff!" chipped in Andy, who had been suspiciously quiet.

"Not long. But that's it. It's over. I feel absolutely dreadful for Maddie. Do you reckon I should just tell her –"

"No!" exclaimed Julia.

"I can't believe I've got myself in such a state," said Anna. "If only we were more like you."

"What do you mean?" asked Julia.

"This kind of thing isn't a big deal for you and Ed. Maddie was always saying you had the perfect relationship and now I'm beginning to think she was right."

"Absolutely," added Andy.

The front door opened and curtailed any further discussion.

Julia wondered if she should take Ed's keys away from him there and then or have the locks to her flat changed first thing in the morning. The latter would cost a fortune on a Sunday.

"So they made him strip down to his boxer shorts and act like he had a sink plunger stuck to his forehead!"

"I swear you make these stories up, Jules," accused Maddie.

"It's the truth!"

"She'll start on the one about the hand model and the dog food if you're not careful," said Ed, as Maddie started to clear the table.

"That was fantastic. Cheers, Maddie." Kat stretched back in her chair. "What are we going to have now?"

"Scotch anyone?" asked Anna.

"Not for us, thanks." Andy and Phil got up. "We're going to make a move. Phil's got to work on a friend's carburettor in the morning before he goes to the gym. You know how it is…" Phil's eyes dropped to the floor and he nodded.

"I'm pretty shagged too." Ed looked over at Julia. She took the hint and let Andy and Phil say their goodbyes and leave before going to get her jacket. Kat followed her into the spare room and leant up against the door frame.

"So when's Anna going to tell her?" asked Kat. She swirled the ice around in her glass and waited for an answer.

Julia was stunned by Kat's nonchalance. "Jesus, I hope she doesn't tell her at all! Can you imagine?"

"What do you mean?"

"Finding out her partner's been having it away with some fancy piece at work isn't going to do their relationship a lot of good, is it?" Julia became aware of a confused silence. She looked over at Kat and laughed anxiously. "You didn't know, did you?"

"No. I was talking about this frigging surprise Maddie's been going on about all evening."

Kat's face looked as if *she* was the one who'd been cheated on. Julia could feel the *carbonnade de boeuf à la flamande* turning to lead in her stomach.

"I don't suppose this is something you could possibly keep to yourself, is it, Kat?"

Paper mask

Kat hid in the spare room, trying to decide what to do with the news she had been fed. She heard Julia and Ed call out 'goodbye' as they went down to their cab. Then she flung her coat back on the bed and went in search of Anna. There was no way she could go to sleep with this little doodlebug exploding inside her.

"I fancy one for the road. How about you, Anna?"

Anna nodded sheepishly; it looked as if she'd been primed by Julia to expect the worst. As Anna slipped off to the kitchen, Kat slumped down on the sofa next to Maddie, who looked dead beat. Kat put her arm round her and Maddie snuggled into her shoulder. Her heart was beating in slow motion as she pulled Maddie into her body. It felt so right. She was so perfect. How could Anna be so completely ungrateful?

When Anna came back into the room, Kat eased away from Maddie. Two coffees and three Scotches were placed on the table.

Maddie opened one eye. "I'm going to have to go to bed," she said as she stretched and yawned.

"You look shattered. I'll give you a call in the morning, yeah?" Kat leaned over and kissed her on the cheek. Over her shoulder, she saw Anna turn pale. "The meal was really nice, Mads. Thanks so much."

"Thank you for coming. Shame about Miro – next time for sure, though, yes?"

Kat nodded.

"Night Anna." Maddie blew her a kiss and slithered off into bed.

"I won't be long," Anna shouted after her.

They both waited until they heard the bedroom door shut before turning to one another.

"Kat, let me explain. You don't –"

"What the fuck do you think you're doing?"

Their hushed voices clashed and although each wanted to raise the volume in order to get the first punch in, neither wanted to run the risk of Maddie being drawn back into the room. Kat figured that Anna had the most to lose, so she ploughed on regardless.

"I can't believe you would do a thing like that, Anna. For God's sake, you pressure her into getting this flat with you, she turns her back on what she loves doing most, just to make you happy, and as soon as you've got it all nailed to the floor, you decide you've had enough of her! It's the fucking pits. Maddie is the most beautiful person I've ever met and you go and treat her like that. She deserves better –"

"Look, Kat. I don't know what Julia told you –"

"Not much."

"But it's not what you think. It was kind of an accident –"

"An accident?" scoffed Kat, disturbed by how much she was enjoying seeing Anna squirm.

"If you'll let me speak, I can explain!"

"Go on then."

"I was out with some colleagues at work, got really drunk, this woman came on to me, I was flattered, one thing led to another and we ended up having a grope back at hers – and that was that. End of story. She regretted it. I regretted it. It's not going to happen again."

They both sat in silence. Anna's tone had knocked Kat for six. She felt stupid, as if she'd over-reacted. She had come close to doing the one thing she'd always promised herself she wouldn't do – showing Anna how she felt about her girlfriend.

"Is that so bad?" continued Anna.

"No. I guess not." Kat was pulling her cards back into her chest, where they belonged. "She's my best friend, though, Anna."

"I know."

"It's only natural that I wouldn't want to see her get hurt."

"I'm not going to hurt her, Kat. It was a mistake. A moment's indiscretion, a fleeting lapse in judgement, is, I think, how the line goes."

"Are you going to tell her?" asked Kat.

"What do you think?"

Conspiracy theory

Libraries were useless places to have conversations – and the librarian didn't mince her words when she pointed out this fact to Kat and Maddie. But Kat had been trying to source a picture of Lulu, so it had seemed like a logical place to meet. Having been forced out into the autumn drizzle by the sharp tongue of the walking rulebook, they resorted to number two on their 'warm places to sit and not have to spend much money' list.

They hadn't been to The Smelly Cafe for ages, but it was still as potent as Kat remembered. The precise aroma that permeated the tiny, corridor-like eatery was difficult to pin down. The elements that combined to create this memorable olfactory experience had a tendency to change subtly according to the time of year. Early September meant a melange of piss, BO and a sprinkling more piss wafted out to greet them. Compared to mid-December – which offered old, sodden dish-cloths, a hint of rotting wood and overtones of cabbage – this was veritably fragrant.

In spite of the stink, or because of it, Maddie and Kat had been known to while away a good few hours in there. It was the challenge of providing the ultimate definition of the smell that had made them return to this place; then, when the fun wore off, they came out of habit.

"I don't know what to do," confessed Maddie. "Ever since that disaster with Eve, things have gone from bad to worse. I got a call this morning from a bloke who was going to commission me to take shots of his products for a catalogue. When we met, he sounded really keen. He loved my portfolio and I came up with some great ideas – or at least

I thought so – but now he's cancelled. You don't think Eve got at him, do you?"

"Now you're being paranoid!"

"I'm trying not to dwell on it, Kat, but everything was going fine until we moved into that damn place. I feel like I've been struggling ever since."

"Have you told Anna?"

"I can't bring myself to. I think this would force us further apart."

"Apart?" probed Kat, as she sprinkled more sugar into her frothy coffee. Maybe she *should* keep her mouth shut about Anna's affair – it would make Kat look like a complete bastard if she spoke up, and now it seemed Anna was alienating her partner quite successfully without her help.

"It seems like she's got everything she wanted – the flat, the mortgage, the shopping trips. While the whole thing has highlighted my inadequacies, it's made her stronger, more gregarious, more ambitious, more successful. That's great for her, but it makes me feel like a mardy old cow a lot of the time because I'm exhausted just by the effort it takes to keep going, let alone catch up with her." Maddie faltered. Kat watched as she tried to make her spoon stand up in tea the colour of American Tan tights. She was happy to help Maddie offload.

"So what are we talking about here, your job or your relationship with Anna?" she asked after a moment's thought.

"The two have become inextricably intertwined."

"I can't help feeling, Mads, that it's only when you get yourself sorted out on the job front that you'll see your relationship is wrong. Or right."

Temptress moon

It was nearly seven o'clock. Anna leaned back in her new chair, in front of her new desk in her new office, and yawned. Her bones creaked as she stretched her arms over her head. She wondered if Andy was still around. She was hungry and there was nothing in the fridge at home. Besides, she didn't fancy going home and listening to Maddie moan about how little Anna was helping around the flat. She left a message on Andy's voicemail just in case he happened to be working late. She was thinking of calling to see if her mother's yoga class had finished, when there was a knock at the door.

Roz was the last person Anna had expected to see. She didn't come all the way into the room, but leaned in and hung on the door handle.

"I noticed you were working late and wondered if you'd like to go and get something to eat." The body language was saying: this is just a casual question, I'm not going to be too bothered if you say no...

Anna weighed up her options. She didn't even know if Maddie would be in. An empty house was worse than a grumbling girlfriend and she hadn't had the chance to speak to Roz on a personal level since the aftermath of That Night. Both of them knew where they stood, though, so what would be the harm in saying yes? It was probably time to start rebuilding their friendship.

"Okay. Why not."

Roz smiled but made no move to come further into the room. "Wonderful. Are you in the mood for anything in particular?"

"Not really. Why don't you surprise me."

"I'll see you in the lobby in five?"

*

Seven minutes later, the lift doors opened and Roz emerged. "I called the restaurant I wanted to take you to, and it appears they are fully booked."

"On a Tuesday night?" asked Anna as they headed onto the street.

"I didn't realise it was so popular."

Anna tried to think of an alternative. There was a chill in the air and she was hungry. "How about that new place in Farringdon –"

"I've got an idea," Roz interrupted, her eyes bright with excitement. "What's the point in searching for somewhere when I've got a perfectly good kitchen at home?"

She seemed to finish her sentence and bundle Anna into a passing cab in one all-encompassing movement.

"I hope you're not too disappointed. I seem to remember you rather enjoyed eating out..."

Anna wasn't disappointed at all.

Mad cows

Andy popped into Anna's office the following morning to thank her for the dinner invitation she'd left on his voicemail. He was surprised to see her pacing round the room, waiting for someone to uncork her anger.

"It's not like I got home that late –" she ranted.

"Where did you get to, in the end?"

"Only out with Mum. I was back by midnight, but Maddie hit the roof. Totally over-reacted."

"Maybe she's got some kind of hormone imbalance." Andy swung on his chair and wiped the dust off the pot plant on Anna's desk. There was something different about her and he couldn't tell if it was just her new environment or this unexpected burst of frustration.

"Don't talk rot!"

"No, Anna, it could be. We all thought my Aunt Tina was one rocker short of a chair before she was carted off to the doctor. Mood swings, bitchy sniping, the anonymous hate mail – it all stopped once she'd had her bits whipped out and started taking the tablets regularly."

"I don't think Maddie's quite that bad."

"No, but she's been moody enough for you to bring it up. Maybe you should just face the fact that she's never been the happiest person in the happy club."

"So you're saying she'll never change?"

Andy tried to guess what Anna wanted to hear. "No... It's probably just attention-seeking."

"What do you mean?"

"Look at you." With a sweep of his arm, he drew her attention to her new office. "Look at this."

Anna slumped down in her seat, forcing the shoulders of her suit up round her ears.

"So you think I've been neglecting her?"

"Are you asking what *I* think, or what I think *she* thinks?" Andy smiled at Anna and tested the casters on his chair. Very impressive. One push got him right the way over to the filing cabinet.

The glass alibi

Anna stood in front of the mirror and pushed her hands through her hair. She hoped Maddie wouldn't make a fuss about her going out again, but two nights in a week couldn't be seen as excessive and she wasn't about to give in to these tantrums. She looked tired. 'Zingy' tired, though, not grey tired. She squirted some perfume on her neck and ran her hands over her top. Was her outfit too much for an evening out with her mother? She turned round for a back view. It would pass. She poked her head round the door and saw Maddie sitting on the sofa. The TV was up full blast, so she pulled the door shut.

Taking her mobile from the dressing table, she selected her mother's number and waited. What if she didn't pick up? Anna couldn't abort her plans now. Just as she was going to give up, she heard her mother's voice.

"Hello Mum, it's me. I just thought I'd give you a ring to let you know that we're having problems with the land line at the flat – no, the telephone line – so from now on, if you want to speak to me, call either on my mobile or at work. The numbers are in your phone already, okay? You mustn't call the flat because the engineer said any more incoming calls will fuse the whole network. So just call my mobile or work." When she was satisfied her mother had grasped the importance of these instructions, she finished the call. "See you soon, then, Mum. Bye."

She pushed the bedroom door open slowly and went into the living room.

"I'm off now, Mads."

Maddie reached for the remote control and lowered the volume. "I still don't see why I can't come."

"Mum wants to talk to me on my own. About Dad, you know."

Maddie muttered something about always being left out.

"Oh, come on, Mads. I've said I'll go bowling with you at the weekend, what more do you want? And it might be that Mum's decided she wants to go home. You never know."

Anna bent down and kissed her on the cheek. "Don't wait up, it could be a long one!"

The TV was up full volume before Anna got to the front door. She glanced at her watch. She crossed the road and walked briskly onto Brick Lane, only marginally later than arranged. As soon as she turned the corner, she saw the headlights of Roz's Saab flashing.

Checking behind her, she rushed across the road and climbed in through the open door.

"I thought you weren't going to make it," said Roz.

The engine turned over and they drove off.

Strike it lucky

Everything about bowling appealed to Maddie – the organisation, the smooth, slimy boards of the alleys, the key pad to punch in food orders and team names, putting her fingers in the holes in the balls, the shoe spray, everything. She knew, however, that Anna wasn't quite so taken with the experience, which is why she couldn't believe her luck when Anna agreed to go. In fact, she knew it was one of Anna's least favourite things in the world. Even with dry-slope skiing on the agenda for the following weekend, Maddie was surprised that Anna had okayed the deal. (As for her own preferences, Maddie's over-riding memory of her last trip to east London's answer to Val d'Isère was of friction burns and shin splints. But, having both agreed they should spend more time together, Maddie felt it wouldn't be in the spirit of the new regime to say no to Anna's chosen activity.)

She stepped up for her turn – a strike would mean certain victory. Two steps, arm back, pivot through your navel, weight forward, right leg back, shoulders square, release the ball – smooth, straight follow-through. The pink marbled ball went thundering down the alley. Catching the pack just off centre, the skittles went crashing to the ground. The huge neon X confirming the strike flashed up on the board as Maddie walked triumphantly back to the booth with her arms aloft.

"Beat that, sucker!" she said to Anna, who went to collect her lucky ball from the dispenser.

"Just watch and learn, Mads. Watch and learn."

Maddie dipped into the portion of nachos that had been delivered to their alley, sucked up some watery Diet Coke through her chewed straw, watched Anna's ball roll limply into the gully and learned that, once again, she was the bowling queen.

"Do you want to call it a day, then?" she asked.

"We have put in a good few hours…" replied a dejected Anna.

"Okay."

"Fancy a film? We could do a double-header down at Mile End."

Maddie felt a surge of happiness. At least there was still one thing they could agree on.

16 NOVEMBER 1999

Waterloo Bridge

Maddie's phone beeped and she read Kat's message: "Grow beard and get job in a circus. Am practising lion taming. Will come too when out of hospital."

This was Kat's way of cheering her up. And even if running away to join the circus didn't provide an answer to Maddie's financial worries, it did put a smile on her face.

Maddie carried on walking. She had been occupying herself lately by turning pictures of London sights into greetings cards. Tower Bridge was in the can now, but with an order of twelve to fill by the end of the week, witty replies would have to wait until she found a photographic shop where she didn't have an outstanding bill. She was berating the facilities around Waterloo when she came across Snap Happy. It boasted a speedy, professional service with a choice of print sizes. As Maddie looked at the display in the window, she found they also had the ability to transmogrify your favourite image onto the side of a mug, a coaster or even a T-shirt. Jigsaws were a further possibility and – although this process was slightly more expensive – they were, apparently, a perfect gift for a loved one's birthday.

In spite of the persistent rain, she had become locked into a staring contest with the framed portrait of a pit bull terrier that had pride of place in the window and she had to force herself to look away. In doing so, however, her eyes fell upon something much more frightening. It was a hand-written note that said: 'Photographic assistant required. Experience not necessary, but enthusiasm is a must. Please enquire within.'

Maddie bit her lip as she read the sign again. There was no doubt in her mind. It was definitely a job advert. The rain was beginning to trickle down inside her collar and she couldn't just stand there getting wet. Either she walked away and pretended she'd never seen the sign and the thought had never crossed her mind that she might be able to work there... or she enquired within.

Then again, there was the option of just going in to get her photos developed. She could have a look at the uniform. If they weren't wearing one, she would ask about the job. If they were, she'd leave her photos and come back in an hour and nobody would be any the wiser.

Maddie pushed the door open and stepped inside. A man was bent over his paperwork at the counter. He was in his early twenties and had longish wavy hair, slightly greasy, but his hands looked clean. He was wearing a blue, thick-ribbed jumper. It could be the sort with a logo embroidered on its upper left chest area, but Maddie couldn't see because of his pose.

"I'll be with you in a sec," he muttered as he continued writing on his piece of paper.

Maddie peered over the counter. He was wearing grey flannel trousers. If he'd been wearing jeans, she would have been sure it was not a uniform. But grey flannels. They could easily be regulation. She looked around for any other signs of life. All she needed was one other blue-jumper-wearing, grey-flannels-sporting staff member and she could leave with an easy conscience. But there was no one. Finally, greasy-hair boy lifted his nose from his paper. Maddie was greeted by a cheeky grin and a logo-less jumper.

"Sorry about that, mate. I've been trying all day to put all Genesis's singles in chronological order and I think I've finally cracked it."

"Is that including their solo chart successes or not?" Maddie watched the boy consider this added complication.

"Maybe I'll save that and do it as another list tomorrow." His head bobbed up and down, happy with this decision. "Anyway, what can I do for you?"

"I'd like this developed, please." She handed over her film. "One set, hour service, gloss prints, please."

The boy glanced up at the clock and scribbled the time of collection on the rip-off slip.

"Oh, and I'd like to enquire about the job you have advertised in the window."

Saved by the phone

"Hey Madge. Looking forward to Christmas?" asked Julia.

"God, yes. I could do with a change of scenery." Ten miles of telephone wire separated them but Maddie's voice sounded more distant than that.

"Where are you going?"

"It's all up in the air at the moment..."

"Bit different from last year."

"Tell me about it!"

"We must sort out what we're going to do for New Year. This thing on the Embankment sounds good, doesn't it?"

"Yeah – sounds great."

"Do you reckon you'll be up for it, then?"

"Don't see why not."

"Excellent. Anyway – is Anna there?"

"Is she buggery."

"You what?"

"She's never bloody in these days. I think she's got some meeting tonight about the millennium bug or something. Sounds like a right wind-up to me."

"What?"

"This bug thing. And then she's straight off to a meeting in Bournemouth for a couple of days in the morning."

"Oh." Julia paused. She was shocked to hear that Maddie was sobbing.

"What's up, Madge?"

"Jules, I don't know what to do."

"Why? What's happened?" Julia's heart was racing.

"Everything's gone wrong. I've got no money, no work, no future. I don't know how I'm going to pay the mortgage, let alone the bills... Everything's crumbling."

"Have you talked to Anna about it? Surely she can help."

"No. You've got to promise not to tell her. I'm serious. I don't want her to know. I don't want her to find out I can't cope!"

"Are you sure that's wise?"

"Absolutely sure. I've got a little bit of space on my credit card and Mum's sending me a cheque which should turn up in the next couple of days..."

"Are you sure that'll be enough?" Julia heard more sniffing down the phone. "If there's anything I can do, just call, okay."

"That's really kind. I'm sorry. I didn't mean to dump it all on you."

"That's fine."

"And you promise not to say a word to Anna."

"Absolutely. Take care."

Julia put the phone down. She tried Anna on her mobile. It was turned off.

Sleeping with the enemy

The hotel was the kind with a sweeping gravel drive and men in uniforms waiting outside to carry your luggage. Roz was obviously used to this set-up, for she pressed the button that opened the boot and walked straight into the lobby, certain in the knowledge that her bags would follow.

"You have a reservation in the name of Ms Gonzalez."

Anna let Roz do the talking while she admired the marbled surroundings and wondered if it had a snooker room.

"Twin beds. En suite bathroom. Top floor." The receptionist reeled off the accommodation's assets.

"No, I think there must be some mistake," said Roz impatiently.

Anna turned to see what was going on.

"I specifically asked for a room with a king-size bed." Roz's voice didn't twitch.

"I'm so sorry, madam. I'll see what I can do. So that'll be one single and one king –"

"No. One room with one king-size bed will be sufficient."

The receptionist glanced at Anna – who shuffled uncomfortably – and then back at Roz, before returning to his computer.

"If you'd like to take the lift to the top floor, the porter will bring your luggage up." He handed Roz the key. "I do hope you enjoy your stay."

Anna felt his eyes burning into her back as they walked across the lobby. She kept her eye on him until the lift doors swept shut.

"If you look powerful enough and rich enough then people rarely snigger in your face – and who cares about what happens behind your back?" whispered Roz as they watched the numbers light up on the panel.

The receptionist wasn't a homophobe, apparently, because the room was stunning. Three-inch thick carpet and towels, enough tiny bathroom accessories to play Chinese chequers with, and an enormous bed.

"Where did you tell your girlfriend you were going?" asked Roz. She sat on the bed and kicked off her shoes.

"I just said I had to go to Bournemouth on business." Thoughts of Maddie weren't appropriate in this scenario, so they were pushed back into their rightful place in Anna's newly compartmentalised mind.

Roz kissed Anna softly on the cheek. "I could get used to this."

Anna felt Roz's hands pulling at her blouse and she helped her to ease it up as she replied, "Me too."

While the cat's away

Maddie would never have guessed she'd be back at Snap Happy so soon. Whereas the day before she'd been 'front of house', this time she was sitting in what Pete referred to as their 'common room'. She guessed he called it that because the occupants had to have a lot in common as there wasn't much room. She was sitting on an L-shaped sofa-chair – the kind that can transform into an I-shaped sofa-bed, should a long, thin person want to lie down. She didn't imagine the bed facility would be used too often, as her knees were nearly touching her interviewer's as it was.

There was a sink with a separate water heater that growled and steamed menacingly from time to time. The kettle looked well used but not overly choked with limescale. The melted granules on the surface next to it suggested Pete and his brother Glen were instant-coffee drinkers.

Maddie wondered why Pete was taking so long to read her CV. She knew there were a couple of missing years on it, but the period travelling round Asia and the time she'd spent living as a modern-day Baha'ist (listed in the 'additional information' section) dealt with any anomalies.

Pete coughed a big rattling catarrh cough, looked at Maddie from beneath his furrowed brow and back down at her CV. "So Madeleine," he said with the voice of a man who was more happy shouting. "You reckon you could operate the machine all right?"

"Yes." Maddie nodded as intensely as the question had been asked.

Pete made a mark with a stubby pencil on a piece of paper, then stuck the pencil behind his ear. Unlike his brother, he had short, practically transparent hair. He ran his hand over his bristly head and leant forward so they were almost nose to nose, giving Maddie first-hand experience of his last cigarette.

"Who is your favourite photographer? Or what period has produced the photography you admire the most?" Pete growled, in his thick south London accent. Maddie swallowed hard and shrank away from his eye contact.

"Helmut Newton." Tall women in high heels with their tits out, Pete should go for that, surely. To be on the safe side, Maddie up-talked the name to make it sound like a question. Pete didn't say a word but just slowly shut his eyes: maybe he too was struggling to reconcile the thorny feminist issues surrounding the acceptability of the photographer's work. Maddie proffered another name.

"Man Ray." What was not to like about him? She waited for a reaction.

Pete did a Robert de Niro 'downward mouth curl with slow nod' and encouraged her to continue, with a flick of his curled forefinger. The gesture made Maddie nervous and her mind froze. Pete opened his eyes and resumed his stare. Think of an old iconic photographer, any old iconic photographer.

"Brassai…" she offered tentatively.

"Excellent choice, Madeleine!" He rubbed his stubbly chin contentedly and smiled. "Brassai – 1899 to 1984. Fucking master, in my book. Most people think he's French because of all the Paris by night stuff, but he was Hungarian. Did you know that?"

Once their taste in photographers had been determined, the other thing Pete was keen to find out was what kind of music she liked. By then Maddie was much more relaxed and, remembering Glen's reference to Genesis when she'd first popped in, was easily able to cover all the bases by saying she had a catholic taste in music and naming one band from every genre she could think of.

"… Abba and Iron Maiden," she concluded, adding that techno was the only real no-no.

"That's brilliant," declared Pete. "Glennie-boy and me play in this band, you see. Anyway, I'll let him tell you about that. I can see he's going to love you!"

"Does that mean I've got the job?"

"'Course it does, darling!" he shouted. He jumped up off the sofa, forcing Maddie to do the same. "Welcome to the family business!"

"Thanks Pete," she bellowed, getting entangled in his excitement. "When shall I start?"

"How would 4 January suit you?" he suggested as they walked back into the shop.

Maddie could still feel the impact of Pete's handshake in the knuckles of her right hand as she left the shop in Waterloo. Other than a couple of Saturday jobs as a kid and a stint working in a bar while she was at college, she'd never had a proper job. Nobody had ever welcomed her into their business before. Things were definitely looking up. Getting a job had been the first thing she needed to do to get her life back on track. Now she was on a roll, she could go straight to the night school in Camden and get a place on the Creative Computing course she'd read about. Her mum's cheque would cover the deposit and she might get some money for Christmas to cover the rest. She pulled out the brochure and read the blurb again. By the end of the course her photographic ability and her understanding of computers would be one synergic, authoritative mass. She'd just give Anna a call to let her know the news and then she'd go and enrol.

Predictably, Anna's phone was switched off, but this was too big an event to leave a message. She tried to remember the name of the hotel where Anna was staying, and realised she hadn't been told. No note had been left, no nothing. Maddie wondered if Anna was working too hard – she was getting incredibly vague and absent-minded these days.

She decided to drop by Anna's office. It wasn't far away and someone there might know where she was staying. She could go to the adult education centre afterwards.

The walk over the bridge and into the City was cold and windy, but it didn't manage to expel that other-worldly feeling that had taken over while she was at her interview. The sun had been obliterated by the heavy, mist-laden atmosphere. It was monochrome and moist. Maddie stopped and leaned over the bridge to take in the view. The string of lights looping from lamp post to lamp post glowed persistently in the gloom. She watched the people walking quickly along the Victoria Embankment. With their collars up and hats pulled down, the cold and distance had covered up the usual signifiers of époque. It reminded her of something. When the cars stopped and the crowd thinned, the scene looked just like one of those old-fashioned moonlit shots Brassai took when poking around the Pont Neuf. Maddie took it as a sign.

The closer she got to her destination, the more vivid the picture of her future became. She would start work, full-time, on 4 January 2000. She would get up around seven-thirty to be at the shop for nine, have lunch around one o'clock (to be agreed with Glen) and leave at five. She would help Glen order stock – film, stationery, biscuits, etc – and be chief in charge of the machine (aka The Beast). They had some equipment in the basement for doing hand prints, but that wasn't offered on a commercial basis yet. As Glen was a list-obsessive, she would help him work on the current topic of his (or occasionally her) choice.

If she had to do something, this didn't seem so bad. Glen and Pete looked like good, kind, strange people, which suited her down to the ground. She'd still be able to do her work and might even get to use the mysterious darkroom to which Pete had alluded.

Anna's building loomed up in front of her. In a lobby sparkling with chrome and Christmas decorations, the receptionist's plinth was so high that Maddie had to stand on tiptoe to see the woman's glossy, painted-on smile. It reminded her why she hated the place and rarely went there.

"Would you tell Anna Foster's assistant I'm here, please?" she asked. There was a pause while the immaculately turned-out woman punched in a number and looked at her screen.

"I'm sorry, Dinah's on holiday. Is there anyone else who can help?" said the painted lips.

"How about Andy Tyler?" This time there was success. Maddie was directed to go up – and the first thing she saw as the lift doors opened was Andy's grinning face.

"What are you doing here, hon?" He gave her a hug and a kiss.

"I was trying to get in touch with Anna, but her mobile must have run down because I can't get through, so I thought someone around here must know where she's staying."

"I'm not privy to that sort of information now she's Gone Upstairs, but I'm sure we'll be able to find out."

Maddie followed him into his office. Maddie felt as alien in this environment as Mork must have felt when he first arrived on earth. She was relying on Andy to be her Mindy and guide her through the experience.

"Her assistant's left for her Christmas holiday already but there must be someone up there who'll know. There's nothing wrong, is there, Mads?"

"No. Everything's fine. There's just something I want to speak to her about, that's all."

"Right you are then. Hold on here for a sec and I'll go and see what I can do." He pointed to a chair which Maddie realised she was meant to sit on. Everything around her looked so ordered and purposeful that she didn't like to move in case she caused some irreparable damage. She grinned at some office workers who smiled that smug 'you look really uncomfortable here and I'm going to try and make you feel even more out of place' smile back at her. Maddie was relieved when Andy returned brandishing a piece of paper with a number written on it.

"Do you want to call from here? You can use the phone in the meeting room if you want some privacy."

"That's kind. Thanks Andy."

The deer hunter

Anna heard the phone ringing in the bedroom, but she was enjoying being pummelled by the jets of warm water from the power shower too much to do anything about it.

"Roz! Will you get it?" she shouted from within the tropical climate she'd created.

She heard Roz say hello into the phone, then a pause, then Roz's voice again: "Hello?"

Anna stood still for a moment. The sound of the water was making it difficult to hear what was going on in the other room. She wondered who would be calling either of them. Maybe Roz had given the number to someone at the office. Either that or it was the hotel reception.

"No, Anna's not available at the moment..."

Who the fuck could it be? Her assistant was away and there wasn't anything pressing at the office that needed her attention. As she stood under the cascading water, she felt like an antelope that had just realised there was a lion lurking in the bushes. For a second she was paralysed with fear. Then she leapt out of the shower.

"Who's calling?" Roz asked.

Anna reached the doorway.

"Sorry Maddie, she's in the –"

She made it into Roz's field of vision just in time. Dripping and naked, Anna gesticulated wildly. Roz looked at her enquiringly and reworked the end of the sentence.

"– She's in the car park. Collecting some papers from the car," she said slowly.

Anna asked Roz to pass her the phone.

"Oh, no. Hold on a minute. She's just walked in the door. I'll pass you over," said Roz. "Anna, there's a young woman named Maddie on the phone for you."

"Hello sweetheart," said Anna. "How are you?" Anna's mind was racing, trying to think of ways to cover her tracks. Her heart pounded as she tried to keep one step ahead.

"Who was that?"

Maddie was already breathing down her neck.

"That was Roz Gonzalez." Anna tried to hide their intimacy behind Roz's surname.

"I thought you were going on your own."

"It takes more than one person to give a presentation like this, Mads." Anna couldn't help the hint of annoyance in her voice. She just wanted to get to the point and get off the phone. Her muscles tensed and her breath shortened as she dodged Maddie's words. "So what's up with you?"

"What was she doing in your room?"

"We're preparing for our final meeting with the client." An agile change of direction kept Anna out of harm's way, but for how long? Roz draped a robe around her bare, shivering shoulders. Anna smiled her thanks but she had to keep concentrating, keep thinking. "I'm sorry, Mads, but did you call for anything specific, because we're actually in the middle of something here?"

"I just wanted..."

"Wanted what?"

"Nothing. It's okay. It'll keep."

"Okay then," said Anna. Her heart rate decreased, she was out of the woods, safety was in sight. "Let's speak when I get home. It won't be late, I promise."

"Yep. See you tomorrow then."

"Yes." Finally the end of this ordeal was in sight. Maddie would put the phone down and she would have survived.

"I love you, Anna."

The words pounced on Anna from a great height. They ripped open her chest, dug their claws into her heart and wrenched it from her body. "I love you too."

The Big Picture

Maddie sniffed back the tears that were making her stinging eyes bulge. The moon would reappear from behind the clouds in five seconds, she thought. One Mississippi. Two Mississippi. Three Mississip–. The light poured into the studio through the skylight. "Fuck it," said Maddie. "Must have been breezier than I thought."

She kneaded the paint on her palate with the square-ended brush. The dark green goo oozed up the hair and coated the metal casing. The light faded again but Maddie was poised, her brush full, ready to attack the canvas the moment the shroud was lifted. She felt like a terrified actor, waiting on stage for the lights to go up and the play to begin, knowing what was meant to happen but not having a clue what the first line was.

The moon reappeared and a line of colour was daubed onto the canvas. She worked quickly, aggressively, confidently. The paint was so thick that the bristles were leaving tiny, narrow grooves in their wake. More sweeps of paint, more texture, rough, uncomfortable texture.

Tears streamed from her eyes. It was emotional vomit that marked the canvas. Spontaneous, uncontrolled, uncontrollable vomit. She worked until all she was producing was bile.

Exhausted, she took a step back to look at what she'd created. She couldn't explain why the hands of the clock she'd been working on had taken such a macabre turn. Her insides started to twitch once more as she realised the image was looking more like a morbid reworking of the opening sequence to Dad's Army *than a homage to Dali. The distorted timepiece turned into exploding droplets of water as it clashed onto the brick-encrusted paint at the bottom of the picture and huge, dancing, dagger-like arrows butted up against it. She rubbed her sleeve over her stinging eyes.*

"Fucking load of shite!" she screamed. Turning round, she kicked the wicker chair. It careered back and forth like a punchbag, taunting her and fuelling her anger. Snatching a brush out of the pot, she loaded it with paint the colour of oxygenated blood, pulled it back like a catapult and launched the missile at the painting. The globules splattered onto the surface. It looked as if a medium-impact bludgeoning had taken place.

Return to the edge of the world

"Mum! You can't tell me something like that while we're putting the blinds up," exclaimed Anna. She was perching on a chair in her living room, screwing the bracket into the wall, while Barbara was on terra firma scrutinising the instructions.

Barbara took a step back. "The left one is definitely lower than the right, love. We're going to have to unscrew it and have another go."

Anna jumped down off the chair and tossed the screwdriver onto the sofa.

"For heaven's sake, Mum, forget the bleedin' blinds!"

Barbara started to back out of the room. She hadn't realised Anna would take the news so badly.

"And don't think you can go and hide in the kitchen."

Barbara continued her retreat. She wasn't trying to hide, she really did fancy a cup of tea.

"Mother, come back," yapped Anna.

That voice was like a lead yanking round her neck. She stopped in her tracks and came to heel.

Barbara took her daughter's hand and guided her over to the sofa, carefully avoiding the upturned screwdriver. "It's not a decision I've taken lightly," she began. "When I first came to London, it was a spur of the moment decision. I'd had it up to here with your dad. His moods, his opinions. His workshop! And I thought it might shake him up a little. Make him think about the kind of whingeing old bastard he's turned into. Now, it might have taken a little longer than I'd thought to get the reaction I'd hoped for –"

"Just the four months then…"

"But we've finally started to talk. He realises now that he didn't make me feel valued."

"Dad used the word 'valued'?"

"Stop being so bloody picky!" It was as if the clock had been wound back thirty years and she was trying to explain why Anna wasn't going to get a chemistry set for her birthday. "We've talked about a lot of the things that had gone wrong between us and he's said he's willing to be more adventurous as far as food and holidays are concerned and he's not going to spend every Saturday out with his friends. He told me his life just wasn't right without me."

Barbara waited for a reaction but Anna's eyes were firmly fixed on the floor. She had been moved to tears when Graham admitted he wanted her back. All dressed up in a suit and tie, he'd taken her to a lovely restaurant with candles and low lighting. He hadn't even said it with his mouth full.

"We also talked about you, Anna. I said there was no way I was going back to Canvey if he was going to continue with his ridiculous prejudices. 'Anna's our only daughter. She's a beautiful person and we both should be proud of her,' I told him – and he apologised, Anna. Honest to God, he did. He even wants you and Maddie to come down to us for Christmas. How about that?"

"You've made your mind up to go, then."

"Yes. I've given it a lot of thought and he knows that if things don't change I'm going be out of that place before you can say knife."

Anna took hold of Barbara's hand and looked her in the eye. The sulky child had gone and she smiled tentatively. Then she hugged her mother, who was surprised to feel Anna's body jerking with sobs. Barbara rubbed her hand over Anna's back in small circles and half expected her to burp. She shook her head as she comforted her daughter. Why was she taking it so hard? Did she really dislike her dad that much? Anna pulled away and sniffed gently as she tried to compose herself. Her eyes had already puffed up.

"I'm going to miss you though, Mum. It's been brilliant having you around."

"It's been fun, hasn't it, Annie? But it's a shame that you've been too busy to spend much time together over the last couple of months... Maybe in future you should come and visit more often –"

Barbara was interrupted by the front door slamming. They both looked up. Anna looked so horrified that Barbara thought they had burglars. But it was only Maddie.

"Hi Anna! I ran out of red paint so I thought I'd pack up and come home early –" Maddie came in the room and paused. "Hello Barbara! I didn't know you were coming."

"It was meant to be a surprise," muttered Anna as she pointed to the half-erected blinds.

"Oh. Is everything okay?"

"I may as well tell you too, Maddie," confessed Barbara. "I'm going back to Canvey."

"No wonder Anna's upset. With all the time you've spent together this last couple of months, she's really going to miss you."

Barbara turned to meet her daughter's pleading eyes. She felt her hand being crushed in Anna's grip.

"I know," said Barbara with collected calm. "I'm sure she'll get over it. Why don't Anna and I go out and buy some cakes to go with our tea? The kettle's just boiled, Maddie. We won't be long."

Barbara didn't care that it was undignified to argue in public, so, once they were out of the house, she had no qualms about confronting her daughter.

"What on earth has been going on? I suppose you've been having some sordid affair and using me to cover your tracks?"

"You've got it all wrong, Mum."

"Really?" Barbara swerved to avoid a letterbox and and tried to catch up with her daughter, who had galloped off into the gloom. "Anna! Slow down." She trotted after her disappearing daughter, grabbed her by the sleeve and pulled her into a doorway to isolate her from the throb of people on the street. The reflection of the flashing pink neon sign in the shop window made Anna's face look eerie. Barbara shuddered. She hardly recognised her daughter. "You might not want to talk about it but you owe me an explanation."

They moved to one side as a man carrying a huge sack of rice on his back pushed past them and into the shop. Anna led her mother further up the street and talked as she walked. "I know I shouldn't have done it, but it's not as serious as you think –"

"So you're jeopardising your relationship – cheating on Maddie – just because you've taken a fancy to some floozy."

Anna shuffled uncomfortably and looked at her feet. "No!"

"Yes, no? Which one is it? I didn't realise you were capable of such a thing. And Maddie doesn't have a clue?"

"No. I don't think so."

"The poor thing! I don't know how you can live with yourself."

"Mum, you're really not in a position to understand. Everything's going to be fine. It's no big deal –"

"Well, you'd better make up your mind one way or the other, my girl, or else you're going to lose everything. Including my respect."

"I'll sort it out, Mum, I promise."

Terms of endearment

Leaving was always the hardest thing about being with Roz. There was always one more thing she wanted to confirm about their next meeting, one more course to eat, one more kiss. It was excruciating but Anna had never questioned whether it was worth it. She manufactured a yawn and glanced at the watch on her outstretched arm. It was ten o'clock. She should have left an hour ago. Slowly she eased herself out of Roz's embrace.

"You're not going yet, are you?" sighed Roz.

"I told you it was going to be more difficult now Mum's gone home."

Anna hadn't replied to any of Barbara's messages since their last meeting. She knew an interrogation was bound to follow and she would rather have her fingernails pulled out than be grilled by her mother, whose words had already broken into the hermetically sealed world she'd created for herself and Roz. However briefly, Barbara had made her consider the consequences of her actions.

When she was away from Roz, it was easy to see the negatives. But now she became aware of Roz's arm snaking over her stomach, and pleasure and anticipation flooded her body. She'd never met anyone who'd had such a sustained effect on her. Roz made her feel jealous and excited in a way that Maddie never had, but now she was being forced to decide if it was more than physical indulgence.

Still, a period of separation over Christmas was all it would take to get things into perspective. She would go to Canvey, her father would act like a normal person, the Nani would come down for Boxing Day. After Christmas it would be easy to distance herself from their affair.

"Maybe we should bring our next trip forward," suggested Roz. "LA would be lovely at this time of year."

"That would be a tough one to get away with..."

"If you don't want to..." Roz pulled her robe around her and reached for her glass of wine on the bedside table.

"It's not that. You know it's not that."

"You're not feeling guilty about her again?"

"Of course I'm feeling guilty." Anna hated it when Roz spoke about Maddie.

Roz kissed Anna's neck softly, her hands moving over her body. The sensation from her touch was just as strong as the first time.

"Why don't we do something a little different next time?" whispered Roz. "Arrange a Christmas treat for me." She flung back the duvet, got up and tossed Anna's clothes on the bed.

"Roz!" protested Anna.

Little shop of horrors

Sheila looked at the display of Christmas puddings. In the old days she would have cooked her own, but why de-stalk sultanas when you can afford to have someone do it for you? That was her philosophy.

She hadn't realised there were so many different types. Some had nuts, some didn't, some had rum, others had sherry, some were huge, deluxe pudding-mountains and others were small, bog-standard things. She stood, she looked, she deliberated. Although she wasn't a nut-lover herself, Sheila wasn't going to have people thinking she'd skimped on her Christmas shopping. Her hand hovered over the pyramid-shaped arrangement of the deluxe variety. Therein lay another dilemma, however. Maddie still hadn't let her know if she was going to be with them on Christmas Day. All Sheila wanted was a message to say they would be coming to Cheshire, and then she could rest easy.

She looked at the pile of puddings again. Should she get one or should she get two? She couldn't bear the waiting, the not knowing. Something had to be done.

Delving into her powder-blue vinyl handbag, she groped around for her phone. She turned it on and found Maddie's number with the deftness of someone who didn't use the apparatus very often. It started to ring. When Maddie picked up, Sheila got straight to the point.

"Madeleine, darling, it's your mum," she said. "I'm not going to keep you long, I just want to know if you're coming for Christmas?"

"Hello Mum – I've been meaning to call. Hold on, I'll just ask Anna what she's decided." Sheila strained to hear through the scratching sound Maddie's hand was creating as it brushed against the mouthpiece. She could just make out Anna's voice saying she had to go to Canvey because she couldn't let her mother down. Slowly she returned the pudding she had been cradling, with its individually wrapped, choke-proof coins, and downgraded it to one the size of a small child's head.

"Looks like it'll just be me, Mum."

"Oh really," said Sheila, but she wasn't so surprised to hear they would be going their separate ways.

"Thanks for the cuttings, by the way," said Maddie. "They're very interesting but I think we need to –" Her voice was blotted out by a bing-bong announcement that Wallace & Gromit soap dishes had just been reduced in aisle nine.

"Where are you?" Maddie asked through the background noise and the bad line. "You keep breaking up."

"I'm in the supermarket," answered her mother.

"What?"

"*I'm in the supermarket.*" Sheila raised her voice to combat the conditions but couldn't understand why the two youths who were standing next to 'tea and herbal beverages' were finding her so amusing.

Eat drink man woman

It wasn't that Kat didn't like going round to Maddie's house, it just seemed more appropriate for Maddie to come to the studio. Seeing as everyone around them had been inundated with invitations to office parties, it was there that they had decided to hold an office party of their own. Stewart had gone off bird-watching in Bolivia but, even though his absence had made a serious dent in the numbers, it didn't stop Maddie and Kat setting about the task with vigour.

The menu had all the right elements – luke-warm turkey roll that Maddie had brought from her flat, stuffing Kat had knocked up using an old palette and a soldering iron, and chips and mushy peas from the takeaway over the road. The gravy granules didn't overpower the taste of turps that had burrowed into every porous material in the studio, but that didn't totally mar the meal.

"So Christmas at Sheila and Malcolm's starts tomorrow?" said Kat to fill a post-prandial lull in conversation.

"Yeah. Anna has even said I can have the car, so I'm going to set off early tomorrow."

"Shame you're not going to be around in the evening." Kat adjusted her paper hat which had fallen down over her eyes.

"Huh?" Maddie made the hanging chair twirl, then brushed a bit of the resulting ceiling-plaster off her trousers.

"I was going to suggest we all went out tomorrow night; you and Anna, me and Miro, for Christmas Eve." Kat was proud of the way these words – me and Miro – slipped easily out of her mouth. "Why don't you just stay one more day?"

"I'd love to, Kat, but I said I'd be there to help out so I can't back out now." Maddie took another chocolate out of the packet on the table, looked at it and put it back. "You and Miro – it must be your longest relationship ever?" she remarked.

"Go on, scare me, why don't you?"

"She must be pretty special…" Maddie gazed wistfully off into the distance.

"She is."

Kat looked at Maddie, who had retreated into some dark corner of her mind. She left her there for a moment or two and enjoyed the unadulterated looking. She knew she would never stop loving Maddie, but Miro had definitely started picking at the knots that bound her to these old, established feelings. It felt liberating, if a little precarious.

"It's a shame she's been so busy preparing for this new course," said Maddie. "What is it she'll be teaching, again?"

"She mentioned something about gouache. She doesn't talk about it much."

"It'd be really nice to meet her sometime soon."

"We're going to come with you on New Year's Eve. Is that soon enough?"

Maddie dragged her feet on the floor to stop the hanging chair twizzling. "You're really coming?" she said excitedly.

"Yeah. I was keen to go away to some cottage in the country, just the two of us, but Miro reckons London is the place to be."

"That's brilliant! Jules is going to organise with Anna who's bringing what, in terms of drink and food and stuff, so I'll let them know you're both in."

Kat pulled herself out of the spiky chair. She flicked a switch on the heater and a third closely bound coil began to glow. More instant coffee was shuffled into the dirty mugs and the kettle was put on to boil.

"All this hype about it being a new millennium really rams it home to you how much people value numbers, you know, milestones, how measuring time is so important. I mean, it's just another new year. Not that I'm turning my nose up at fireworks and wheels and new bridges and all that exciting shit, but really, nothing's going to change. Life will still go on just like the day before."

"For some people, maybe," said Maddie, tantalisingly.

"What's up? What's going to change?" Although she asked the question she could hardly bear to hear the answer. Had she found out about Anna's affair? Was she going to leave her?

"I've gone and got myself a job!" Maddie slumped back in her chair so her whole body matched the curve of the wicker frame. She took a sip from her mug of coffee. The steam rose up in front of her face and Kat couldn't see her expression, but instinct told her that this was meant to be a good thing. "I start on 4 January."

"Mads, that's wild!" She went over to her friend and gave her a hug to hide the fact she was totally disorientated. She slipped down and sat in the space between Maddie's legs, reaching her hands out to feel the heat of the fire, and let her friend fill her in on the details.

The scenario didn't sound so bad. These blokes in the shop sounded like quite a laugh. It would give Maddie the opportunity to earn a bit of cash and use the lab for her own stuff.

"This way, I can take things at my own pace – not take work I'm not confident about – practise some more portraits and build it up slowly," she concluded.

"Sounds like a perfect compromise. You always knew you'd had a flying start, didn't you? So it's not as if it's come as a shock to have to slow down a bit."

"I suppose not."

After the flood of words and information that had saturated the atmosphere, the sudden silence was eerie.

Look me in the eye

There was always a thrill in the air on Christmas Eve in London, but this time the excitement was more tangible as Julia, Anna and Andy strode down Villiers Street towards the Embankment. It was as if the city was slowly morphing into some giant party animal. The London Eye was like its huge Cyclopean orbit, the Millennium Bridge was its backbone straddling the Thames, the Tate Modern was its powerhouse heart and the Dome was the boil on its bum. They were trying to decide where to watch the fireworks on New Year's Eve and Andy had suggested they do a little advance research.

They'd done the Tower Bridge end of town but had decided there wasn't enough open space and they would run the risk of missing the river of fire.

"But the flames are going to be two hundred feet high," protested Anna, who had argued quite a convincing case in favour of Tower Bridge as it was extraordinarily close to where she lived. "You're not telling me a couple of buildings are going to obscure a fuck-off thing like that?"

Julia thought it was all a little extreme. Why didn't they just turn up and see what happened? As they walked, Andy babbled on about the merits of various locations.

"The benefit of being on one of the bridges is that we'd get a good view of whatever was happening up and down the river as well as on either side," he rambled. "Whereas, if we aimed to be near Big Ben, at least we wouldn't have to worry about synchronising our watches – and it would be nice to know that we were celebrating bang on time. There again, we could venture south of the river. I've heard there's going to be a fairground near Tooley Street and it would almost be like going abroad. The other option, of course – although I would have to say it's my least favourite – is staying in and watching it on TV. In spite of the obvious cons, we would be guaranteed not to miss a thing."

When they finally decided that Embankment tube was the place to head for, Julia thought he was going to produce a piece of chalk from his briefcase and draw an 'X' to mark the spot. She sighed with relief when he skipped down into the tube.

Julia and Anna continued east towards Temple. They walked in rhythmic silence for twenty-five paces before Julia finally spoke.

"Anna, you did resolve things with that woman, didn't you?" The regular smack of their shoes on the tarmac continued.

"What do you mean?" replied Anna sharply.

"You've been so distant recently – and I don't just mean today – and I'm worried you've been trying to cope with things on your own too much. Whatever you say, it's strictly between you and me. I want you to know that." Coaxing Anna into discussing affairs of the heart was sometimes like persuading a shy, furry animal out of its den.

"It's okay, Jules. Really. Everything's under control."

"So I can take that as a no, then?"

Anna nodded her head and her pace slowed. Julia steered her friend towards a bench. They looked out over the river and watched the barges bobbing up and down as the passenger ferries surged past towards Greenwich. Julia pulled her coat round her to keep out the stingingly cold air.

"Is it serious between you two?" She scrunched and unscrunched her fingers inside her mittens in anticipation of Anna's answer.

"I haven't stopped loving Maddie, if that's what you mean."

Julia shrugged.

"Roz is more like an extra, rather than an instead of."

Anna stopped for a second and Julia wondered how long it had taken her to come up with that neat little explanation. It made Roz sound like a side-serving of liquor with a pie and mash supper.

"What if you lose her, though?"

"Who?"

"Maddie, of course."

"It's not going to come to that. I've had this out with Mum and it's all under control." Anna's voice oozed the confidence of the deluded. Julia had heard natural history zealots talk about the existence of the Loch Ness monster using the same unwavering tone.

She thought how ironic the whole situation was. She laughed and shook her head.

"What are you laughing at?"

"Ed moved in with me a while ago," admitted Julia.

It was as if Anna had been poked with a cattle prod as she suddenly came to life.

"Why didn't you tell me before?" she exclaimed.

"I don't know..."

"My God! I can't believe you've kept this from me!"

Julia had been expecting the accusations but at least Anna had handed her some ammunition. "That's rich coming from you, my all-sharing friend," she fired back. The put-down hit its target, countering Anna's flash of indignation.

"When did he move in?"

"A couple of months back. I didn't want to say anything before. I'd made such a show about being a divorce-ravaged commitmentphobe that I felt a bit foolish."

"Are you happy?"

"Very." Julia wanted Anna and Maddie to stay together, so she said what she thought was best.

"That's great, Jules," said Anna. "But it's not like it didn't work out the other way; it's just that you realised you wanted something more from each other. That's really great."

The fabric of Julia's body groaned with despair. Anna's thoughts were as cloudy as an English summer. It was going to take a lot more than Julia's example to make her see sense, but as she clearly wasn't in the mood to talk further, Julia suggested they carry on to the tube.

"I guess the roads should be quite clear if you're driving back to Canvey tonight." Travel plans were small enough to fit the size of talk needed.

"I'm not going until tomorrow morning. You can have too much of a good thing, you know! No. It's a quiet night in front of the telly for me tonight."

Dances with wolves

The club was filling up quickly and Anna had to move to keep an eye on the door. It was years since she had been out on Christmas Eve and she hadn't realised it was going to be so packed. But it wasn't long before Roz appeared in the room. Standing in a pool of light, she looked like a contestant in a glamorous gameshow. Her blue jeans were moulded perfectly to the shape of her body, as was her black fitted shirt. Her shoulder-length hair looked less tamed than usual and her deep brown eyes glinted as the light made its way through her whipped lashes. The total effect made Anna's heart jump – once again, her breath had been taken away. Judging by the number of heads that had turned to enjoy Roz's entrance, Anna wasn't alone in her assessment, so she left her booth and went over to stake her claim.

Roz was striding across the dance floor when Anna brushed her hand across her waist. "You look amazing," she shouted in her ear.

"So do you," Roz replied, kissing her lightly on the lips. "Shall I get some drinks?"

"I've got a bottle of wine. It takes ages to get served at the bar."

Roz followed her to the booth in the corner and sat down.

"So, this is my Christmas treat?" said Roz, leaning in close to her lover so her voice could be heard over the booming music.

"It's as near to the day as I could get. It's okay, isn't it?" asked Anna nervously, waiting for Roz's approval.

"I can't quite believe it. I've had my head stuck in my work for so long, I'd forgotten this kind of life existed." She looked around her. "I like the sound of the music, being close to you –"

"Do you want to dance?'

"In a minute. There's something we need to talk about."

Madame X

Kat was angry with herself for having mistaken a stranger for Maddie. Close up, she could see that whereas Mads was short, this woman was tall; Mads was Olivia Newton-John blonde, she was strawberry blonde; Mads had tits, this woman had arse. In fact, Maddie looked more like Ivana Trump than this woman. It was an all too painful reminder of Kat's absurd keenness to see her – which was hardly surprising, given that Miro was being such a killjoy tonight. At least Maddie knew how to have some fun.

Kat peeled the label off her bottle of beer as she contemplated her options. "If you don't want to dance here, what about somewhere else?" she asked. The bartender's selection of tinny 70s disco was pissing her off anyway.

"It's not the place... I'm just really tired. It's been a long term, I'm not up to speed with this new course I'm teaching next year... We could just go home and have an early night."

"But it's Christmas Eve!" moaned Kat.

"It would be romantic, just the two of us."

This was exasperating enough, but it was the arpeggio calm before the vocal storm of 'I Will Survive' that drove Kat out of her chair to the loo.

"I'll see you outside in a minute." She'd take her time. A short wait in the cold wasn't going to do the ice maiden any harm.

Heartburn

"I can't accept this," gasped Anna as she turned the heavy platinum ring over in her hands.

"Of course you can," said Roz. It took a little manoeuvring to get it over her knuckle but then the ring looked like it had found its natural home. The third finger of Anna Foster's right hand.

Anna couldn't believe it. She had never been given something so expensive before. She ran her fingers over the plain band which had a single, inlaid white stone. She didn't ask what it was, but the overall effect was understated extravagance. Roz was smiling at her enjoyment of the gift and Anna kissed her gently on the cheek. But she was in a turmoil. Was it just a present? Was it a signifier of their relationship's changing course? Was it just that Roz really liked buying people stuff? Anna felt the initial ripples of panic start to pulse out from her body's centre. The atmosphere suddenly became oppressive, squeezing the coarse white wine back out of her stomach so that it burned the back of her throat.

"I think I'm going to be sick," said Anna, trying to sound as composed as possible.

Bananas

Malcolm was upstairs wrapping his presents for the morning, Tom was in the loft looking through his old university books and Maddie was taking a bath, so Sheila thought she'd sit down in the living room and have a mince pie. After all, even though she said it herself, she did make a darn good one. The secret was in the pastry-to-filling ratio. There had to be enough filling to moisten the pastry (short crust, of course) to stop it clamping itself to the roof of your mouth for the duration of the Christmas holidays. Five chews, a soft bolus and an easy swallow. Perfect.

Sheila turned her attention to her children. She hadn't seen either of them for ages. Tom was looking well, if a tad porky. At least that meant he was eating properly. But then again, beer was fattening, wasn't it? Perhaps he was just living on Scotch eggs and beer. He'd always had a thing about Scotch eggs, ever since that holiday to Scarborough – and that was over twenty years ago. Think of all the cholesterol he must have consumed since then. She would confront him about it sometime. Not now, though.

She listened for stirrings from upstairs. Apart from the faraway hum of Maddie's radio in the bathroom, all was quiet. The candles on the fairy mobile needed lighting, but maybe there was time for another mince pie...

Maddie, on the other hand, was looking slimmer than she'd been in ages. She was never going to be whippet-thin, but the fact that Sheila could see less bust and more definition around the waist was enough of a signal that weight had been lost. She was looking more pensive than usual and Sheila was thankful that the articles she'd been sending her had hit the mark. She congratulated herself on the subtlety of her campaign and went to peel some potatoes.

Her freezing cold, red hands were covered in starch when Maddie came into the kitchen. She pulled herself up onto the counter and watched her mother work.

"Mum, I thought I'd show you some information about a computer course I'm starting next year," she said.

Sheila plopped the half-peeled spud back into the saucepan of water and dried her hands. She took the leaflet and looked at the course details, wondering how much it cost.

"This looks wonderful, Maddie," said Sheila. "I wouldn't mind doing something like this myself."

"You should, Mum."

Usually Sheila would dismiss the idea out of hand but instead she put the idea on the back burner, next to the intention to start going to aerobic classes, which had been bubbling there for some years.

"Sounds like this should be right up your street, darling. And it'll help you become more secure financially."

"That's the plan."

"It would be so much better if you were financially independent." Maddie didn't groan or moan or protest. "Is there something else, pet?" Her daughter's eyes fell to the floor. For a long time she didn't say anything.

"It's me and Anna," replied Maddie. "I think we're growing apart."

"Come here, my darling." She rocked her daughter in her hug and told her everything would be all right. She knew it would, because she'd planned for this moment.

"It doesn't surprise me, darling." Sheila stroked Maddie's hair. "I knew you weren't happy."

Maddie pulled away from her mother and smiled. "I do appreciate the effort you've been making." Maddie's smile was comforting, maybe this process wasn't going to be as hard as Sheila had imagined. "All the stuff you've been sending me. It's really nice that you've been taking such an interest."

"It's the least I could do. I knew it was only a matter of time before you saw sense."

Maddie frowned. "Saw sense?"

"I was sure it wouldn't take much for you to see the disadvantages of the kind of lifestyle you had with Anna." Sheila glowed with pride at the role she'd played in her daughter's decision. "I knew it was only a phase, Maddie. The sooner you're out of that flat, the better. You can come and live with us for a while if you like, that way you can rebuild your life. Needless to say, I haven't told anyone around here about your..." Sheila picked her words carefully. "The nature of your relationship with Anna, so you'd be able to start afresh. There's a young man who's moved in next door, who I can introduce you to. I'm sure you'll hit it off. He's such a nice man. Professional – real husband material –"

"Hold on a minute," said Maddie gingerly. "I think you've got the wrong end of the stick. I'm only talking about my feelings for Anna, not my 'lifestyle', as you so delicately put it. Nothing's –"

"But it's so obvious," Sheila raised her voice to cut her off. "It's just not right for you! Any fool can see –"

"Mum!" shouted Maddie. Her cheeks were flushed and she was pacing around the kitchen. "I thought I'd explained it to you. I'm gay and there's nothing –"

"No, Maddie!" argued Sheila. She wrung the sodden tea towel in her hands and yelled back at her daughter. "I will not have you shout at me in my own house! I gave birth to you! Give me a little credit, for heaven's sake. I know exactly what you are and what you're not and you are definitely not one of those... people." Sheila was beside herself with frustration and anger. "Why can't you understand I'm only trying to help you!"

"You can't say things like that, Mum," screamed Maddie. "I thought we'd gone over all this!"

"There's no shame in changing your mind! That's what you've got to understand."

"For fuck's sake, this is the last thing I need right now."

"I'm not going to talk to you if you start swearing! You stupid girl! Get up to your room and only come down when you can speak civilly and talk sense!"

"What on earth is going on in here?" Malcolm bellowed from the doorway, his voice cutting through the cacophony.

"Mum's gone absolutely freaking bananas!"

Maddie pushed past her father and stomped out of the house.

If these walls could talk

Kat hovered over the urine-splattered loo seat and relaxed the muscles that had been squeezing her urethra shut. The liquid thundered into the bowl and Kat heaved a sigh of relief. There was nothing more satisfying than having a good old horse piss, she thought, as she scoured the cubicle for some toilet paper. Why was there never any loo roll? You didn't have to be Nostradamus to predict that, in a dyke bar, a fair amount of loo roll was going to be needed in the women's loo. She tutted and hitched up her trousers, ready to shuffle round into the neighbouring stall and continue her search. She had her hand on the lock when she heard the main door open. It was too early in the evening to bare her arse to complete strangers, so she set about ripping off some of the cardboard loo-roll inner. It looked absorbent enough to do the job.

The sound of a familiar voice stopped her in her tracks.

"It's nothing to worry about. I just needed to get out of there for a second."

Kat smiled. It sounded like Anna. They must have changed their plans after all. She was about to call for their help with her predicament when she heard the second voice.

"Anna, darling. I didn't mean to upset you. It was a gift to show you how much I care about you. That's all," said a slightly Spanishy, Americany, Londony voice.

Kat's inflated lungs held onto the air that was about to produce her friend's name. That wasn't Maddie. She listened, motionless, as the foreigner spoke.

"I have been feeling this way for a long time now. I think about you all the time when I'm not with you. I can't bear it when you leave me and I just seem to wait for the next time I'll see you. I love everything about you, Anna –"

"I don't understand. Why are you telling me this now?"

"I will be going away early next year. The company wants to transfer me to the office in New York and I have accepted. I'd like you to come with me. Say something, Anna, please."

"What can I say?" Anna's voice was shaking but excited. "That is probably the most exciting thing anyone has ever said to me! There's nothing I would like more –"

Kat let out a high-pitched, involuntary scream.

"This isn't the place. Let's go back out." Anna's voice tailed off as the door swung shut.

Kat sat on the loo, bewildered and motionless, her trousers round her ankles.

Spy hard

"It's nice to see Barbara and Graham getting on so well but I thought they were never going to go," said Betty, as Doris handed round nibbles and schooners of dry sherry. "So, come on, Doris. What's all this about Anna? Did you get her to say anything?"

"We are having sausage rolls, aren't we?" Vi had wandered in from the kitchen. "We always have sausage rolls on Boxing Day."

"They're in the freezer," said Doris. "Barbara said she'd pop them in the microwave when they get back from the pub." Having confirmed that a break in routine wasn't about to occur, she hoped Vi would settle so they could get down to the business end of the conversation.

"Vi! For pity's sake, I'm trying to talk to Doris!" said an exasperated Betty. "So did you or didn't you?"

"Oh, shut up, you daft old bird!" muttered Vi as she pottered off in the direction of the garage, for it was there that the freezer was kept.

"I didn't get much out of her," Doris admitted. When she'd sat up with Anna into the early hours of Boxing Day morning, Doris had hoped to create the perfect environment for her granddaughter to open up to her. She'd laid the ground work with noises to denote respect and love for her as an individual and a woman, but Doris's best attempt at getting to the bottom of Anna's strange, distant behaviour had failed. "But there's definitely been some kind of rapprochement between Anna and Graham –"

"At least Barbara's sojourn in London had some effect, then," said Betty.

The pings and dings of the microwave and the clattering of plates being taken from the dishwasher provided a lively soundtrack to Doris's recollection of her late-night conversation with Anna. The more detail she went into, however, the less sure she became of her interpretation of events. "All she really said to me was that an opportunity had presented itself at work and there was a big decision she had to make," concluded Doris.

Finally Vi emerged from the kitchen, flakes of puff pastry stuck to her polyester safari-style jacket. "Who's got a decision to make?" she asked as she tried valiantly to post the remainder of a sausage roll in between her grinding mandibles.

"It's Anna," explained Betty. "She's really not herself and we were trying to work out what on earth could have happened to make her look so sad."

"I think *you'd* be pretty buggery confused if your lover had just invited you to move to New York with her!" said Vi, as she lowered herself into her chair with a groaning sigh.

"What in heaven's name are you talking about?" asked Doris. Where did she get this information? Why had Anna confided in Vi and not her? Was she a bad grandmother? Was this one of Vi's 'jokes'? Doris didn't know what to think.

"I heard her talking to her on the phone yesterday."

Doris couldn't believe Vi's nonchalance.

"How could you have heard all that?" challenged Betty.

"Oh, all right! I picked up an extension while Anna was on the phone and happened to overhear their conversation. Does it really matter?" said Vi.

"Vi!" Doris was too shocked and too interested to chastise her friend with more vigour.

"What were they talking about?" asked Betty.

"Well, it looks like Anna's been having a bit of a ding-dong with a foreign type at work. Spanish, I think. Nice voice –"

"Get on with it!" chivvied Doris.

"It all fits now, you see. The mystery woman who used to call at the house to pick Anna up when they were with us at the Grove; the new – and might I say, very expensive-looking – ring that has appeared on her finger; the slight glow of someone who is indulging in new and regular –"

"Vi, please!" Betty looked indignant, but Doris had to admit there had been something about Anna over the last few months that looked a little like a glow.

"Well, it would seem that Anna's fancy woman has taken a job in America and told Anna there's the opportunity to go with her if she'd like," continued Vi.

"Oh, poor Maddie!" Betty whipped out the hanky that was tucked under her expanding watch strap and mopped up the tears that had forced their way into the corners of her eyes.

"And what did Anna say?" Doris was more concerned about her granddaughter moving to the other side of the world.

"Well, I have to say, she seemed quite keen on the idea. Sausage roll, anyone?"

Baby steps

Julia's legs felt heavy as they swung over the precipice. She looked down and all she could see were the tops of thousands of heads, wedged in and milling around like the magnified bacteria of a dense disease. It was surprising that there weren't even more people, but then, arriving at the river at half past ten for a firework display that wouldn't start until midnight was a little excessive.

Tower Bridge was glowing against the flat black sky. It looked like the plastic, dome-encased bibelot that her French exchange partner had once bought on a day-trip to London, rather than a functional structure.

"Why won't they let us on the bridge?"

Her question was directed at Ed, but he was too busy marking their territory with carrier bags and rucksacks to take any notice. Maybe they were going to raise the bridge and a giant, waving effigy of the Queen or Charles or even some minor royal would come floating down the Thames as a New Year's Eve treat. It was occasions like this that made you realise the true value of a monarchy. She looked across at the Tower of London and thought how Henry VIII would have been perfect fodder for *Hello!* magazine. 'Henry and Catherine share their joy about their forthcoming marriage and show us round their lovely home...' Imagine, six weddings, multiple births and all that mourning... talking of which, what was Ed up to now? She twisted with the anatomy-defying flexibility of a Barbie doll to see where he had got to.

Although she didn't manage to locate him, she did make eye contact with Andy. She had been waiting all evening to have a quiet chat with him. She mouthed the words, "Where's Anna?" Andy mimed a squatting motion and Julia guessed she'd gone to the loo. He squeezed his narrow arse into the space next to her, reserved by Ed's rucksack.

Julia hadn't been absolutely sure whether Anna had spoken to Andy about the extent of her affair with this Roz woman. Confiding in a work colleague might be too risky. The look on his face, however, made it obvious Anna had spilt the beans pretty much everywhere, except for on her own front door, of course. Andy was about fit to burst by the time he opened his mouth.

She let the tidal wave of words wash over her as she suddenly felt really, really sad and very, very guilty.

"Do you think we should tell Madge what's going on?" asked Julia.

"I don't know," said Andy, shaking his head. "I really don't. Sometimes I look at that poor woman – did you know she's got a job, by the way?"

"No!" Julia was shocked. How did she not know something as important as that? Had she subconsciously been avoiding talking to them?

"Shop assistant in a camera shop in Waterloo," continued Andy.

"That's nice."

"Very." He pulled the corner of his mouth over to one side and raised one eyebrow. Julia had seen this face before and hated that he was mocking her friend. "I don't think we can say anything. We should let Anna work herself out..."

"Yeah. She said that to me too."

"It'll resolve itself soon, one way or another," blustered Andy. "Come on, Jules. Cheer up. This is New Year's Eve, 1999!" Andy put his arm round Julia and gave her a hug, as if he were trying to squeeze all the bad feelings out of her body.

It didn't work though. It wasn't like she was a carbuncle or even a spot. There were only hours left of the old millennium and nothing was ever going to be the same again. Anna was going to live in New York, Maddie would be devastated, there would be no more spur of the moment trips to Brighton, no more nights eating and drinking into the small hours, no more after-work spontaneous partying. You can't do that sort of thing when you're pregnant anyway. Her hand automatically dropped to stroke her belly.

There was a loud bang from the mass below and a scream. Some tosser had thrown a firecracker. Maybe she shouldn't tell Ed about the baby until she'd absolutely made up her mind what she wanted to do.

The parallax view

"Cheers Ed!" said Maddie as more pre-mixed gin and tonic was poured into her plastic picnic cup. "What's the time?"

"Quarter to eleven."

"Not long to go now." Maddie jiggled up and down to try and generate some warmth in her fleece-covered body. "You would have thought they'd put some music on or something, wouldn't you?"

"That would have been a good idea," agreed Ed. "How on earth are Kat and Miro going to find us in this lot? You did tell them where we were going to be?"

"Kat's gone AWOL," explained Maddie.

"They're not coming?" Ed sounded disappointed.

"She left some nutty message on my voicemail. I don't know what the bollocks is going on with her but she 'wants to be alone'. She'll have snapped out of it by lunchtime tomorrow, I'm sure."

"Shame," said Ed. "I was getting quite excited about meeting Miro."

"Me too!"

Maddie scanned the crowd, which was swelling by the second. All that man-made fibre brushing up together must be a fire hazard. She wondered what her parents were doing but tried to push the thought from her mind. There was no way she was giving her mother mind-space until she admitted how awful she'd been and apologised – and if that took forever, then so be it. Maddie had more important things to think about.

From their platform over the Embankment, she could see the weave of the throng getting more and more tightly knit. It seemed to be pressing down towards the Tower and the river so as to avoid getting stuck behind the tall buildings lining that stretch of water. She knew it was only a matter of time before it started creeping up the steps that led to their elevated section. How would she get to the loo? Would she ever find her way back again? Knowing her luck, she'd be hovering over some vile mass of chemically degrading shit at the stroke of midnight and miss the whole shebang. She put her drink down. What doesn't go in, won't have to come out, she reasoned.

Maddie listened to Ed rattle off statistics about the height and speed of the river of fire, the number and cost of the fireworks and the precise capacity of the Millennium Dome. She wondered why boys – even boys as lovely and entertaining as Ed – were so obsessed with numbers. She addressed the conundrum while Ed rambled on – numbers mean facts, facts equal science, science is the bedrock of patriarchal power and knowledge, power and knowledge are essential ingredients of supremacy, and supremacy facilitates absolute domination. Phew! She was glad she'd got to the bottom of that little sociometric teaser.

"So how's it going with you and Jules?" asked Maddie as she grabbed at the conversation's handbrake and spun them into a U-turn.

"It's great, Madge." A huge grin appeared on his face.

"This moving-in thing looks like being permanent, then?"

"Completely. It's like we've been made for each other."

"Yeah, yeah. You wait until you've been together as long as we have..." Maddie didn't want to sound like a bitter old cynic, so she didn't bother finishing the sentence.

"Still having a hard time?"

"You could say that. I just wish Anna would speak to me about whatever's on her mind. If she's going to leave me, I'd rather have a three-minute warning."

"She's not going to do that, is she?"

"Who knows? Sometimes she's really normal, like good old Anna, and other times she's totally unrecognisable."

"She'll get over it. I'm sure. Give her time, Madge."

"She hasn't said anything to you or Jules, has she?"

"Not as far as I know."

"I guess Jules would have said something if she had..."

Maddie suddenly found the whole business far too tiring to contemplate. She tried to divert her own thoughts to the computer course she would be starting in a couple of days. When that didn't work, she decided there was only one thing dull enough to numb her brain entirely. Turning to Ed, she asked: "Did you say there are forty thousand fireworks on sixteen barges, or sixteen thousand fireworks on forty barges?"

Can't hardly wait

What with genning up to teach a new subject, and spending time with Kat, Miro hadn't done many Friday nights down the pub with her colleagues recently. Jackie's New Year party was the perfect opportunity to catch up with them, but when she saw Brian heading straight for her, she dipped into the Pringles and braced herself.

"Joanie, how are you?" he asked. "Or should we all be calling you 'Miro' now?"

"I'm very well, Brian, and you?" As much as she hated the fact that he had met Kat and was privy to details about her personal life, she was totally mesmerised by how different he looked without his tank-top. Was that a Ted Baker logo winking at her from the seam of his shirt pocket? Surely not.

"Ditto." Miro watched him make a show of looking round the room. "Where is that gorgeous partner of yours tonight then?"

She hated the way his voice pawed at the word 'partner'.

"Kat's not feeling too good actually, but she insisted I shouldn't miss out on the party, so here I am."

"Her loss is our gain," smarmed Brian. "I hear Jackie has persuaded you to teach computer design at her evening school next term. Maybe you could pop over to the science department and use your new skills to touch up my schemes of work..." Brian's words faded as Miro slipped out of his clutches.

She hadn't sat on the stairs at a house party for more years than she cared to remember, but at least she wasn't drowning her sorrows with a litre of cider and a Nilsson tune. She swirled her wine round her glass and watched tiny bits of Pringle get flung to the sides. Backwash was a disgusting phenomenon.

She still couldn't work out why Kat had suddenly cooled their relationship down. So Miro hadn't felt like going clubbing that night – so what? Kat knew she'd been busy. Maybe if Miro had come clean about the nature of the new course and all the work it entailed, things might have turned out differently. It was ironic that she'd only hidden the truth because she thought it wouldn't fit with Kat's image of her. If pandering to Kat's artistic principles hadn't helped keep hold of her, she had no idea what would.

In spite of the fact that Kat was far too unpredictable to be worth worrying about, the thought of never seeing her again made Miro feel like all the air had been sucked from her body.

Kat had said: "I just need some time to try and understand what's going on." This implied that the situation was temporary, didn't it? She adored Kat. She didn't want to leave her. But she didn't want to get hurt. Not again.

"Joanie! It's nearly midnight!" shouted Jackie from the living room. "You're going to miss the fireworks!"

Miro heard voices working themselves up into an obligatory frenzy of anticipation. Finally the rhubarb faded and gave way to a deep, resonant clang as Big Ben's donger marked the beginning of a new era. Fireworks started to pop and oohs and ahhs, congratulations and celebrations rippled round the living room.

Maybe moving on was her only option.

A cry in the dark

The light from the fireworks was being refracted by the tears in Kat's eyes. Her studio window multiplied and the shards of light split into a starburst as she tried to blink them away. She pulled her knees into her chest and, without its anchor, the hanging chair started to swing comfortingly from side to side.

Another boom was followed by a flash of white light that penetrated and withdrew from her darkness as quickly as a finger entering scalding water. A fug of gunpowder started to roll in off the river and float away to feed on what little ozone was left in the atmosphere.

Kat imagined Maddie down at the Embankment. Was she having a good time with the others, or had Anna told her she was leaving? Ever since overhearing that damn conversation, Kat had been tearing herself apart. She couldn't possibly have gone out with Maddie and Anna. If she told Maddie what she knew, she'd look like a complete bitch.

And telling had other repercussions. Maddie might talk things through with Anna, who might then change her mind about going. Kat didn't want that, did she? On the other hand, if she didn't tell Maddie what she knew, she might deny her best friend the chance to save the relationship. Then, if they did get together, Maddie might always look upon Kat as second best.

Either way, she was going to come out as the shit-stirring baddie. There was no way of being a winner in this situation. Sitting tight and avoiding contact was the only thing she could do. She didn't even want to *think* about what she was putting Miro through. She had to find out what was happening with Anna and Maddie – what Anna was doing, whether Maddie had feelings for Kat – and then she would finish it properly with Miro.

"Happy cunting New Year," she said to herself as she swung from a chain in the blackness of her studio.

End of a millennium

"Was that it?" asked Maddie as she pulled on Anna's sleeve.

"Mads, for fuck's sake, watch the fireworks!" replied Anna. This was an historic, moving occasion, a real 'once in a lifetime', and it was just so typical of Maddie to spoil it with her fixation about this river of fire.

"But have we had it yet?" Anna didn't shift the 120 degree angle of her chin to respond to Maddie's question, which was then repeated to Phil.

"Did you see the river of fire, Phil?"

Anna didn't hear Phil's answer, but Maddie had obviously succeeded in engaging him in conversation, as she continued: "It's just that I was told that there was going to be a two hundred foot wall of flame that was going to be travelling down the river at six hundred and fifty miles per hour. Maybe we haven't had it yet..."

Anna looked round and saw Maddie in a New Year's clinch with an elfin blonde woman. How did she manage to find the only homosexual in this sea of straightness? Anna felt a surge of jealousy – not because someone else was kissing Maddie, but because they hadn't chosen *her*. She winced guiltily. What the bollocks was she going to do? Roz was putting pressure on her to end it with Maddie and make some commitment to going to the States. When they were together, making plans was exciting. It was exciting, but it was also surreal. Did Anna go along with it because she thought it was never going to happen, or did she really want to up sticks and go?

All around her, people were dancing, singing, snogging and jostling. The battle for personal space had turned into an indiscriminate sharing of passion. She stared up at the exploding sky and remembered what Roz had said to her earlier that day. "When I watch the fireworks at midnight, I won't feel sad because even though I can't be with you I know we will be under the same sky, looking up at the same spectacle. I will watch them and think of you."

As the last echo of the last word faded away in Anna's mind, she felt the crowd take a collective in-breath. After the relentless spurting of colour there was a split-second hiatus that signalled the impending climax. Like sixteen ultra-violet jets of ejaculate, the final missiles launched themselves into the air and, with a penetrating boom, sent their seeds of fire wriggling into the cold, night air. The gang-bang was over. It was 2000.

The Big Picture

She was totally focused on the job in hand. Slowly, she dabbed paint over the last offending splatter. Calm. Steady. She salvaged the best bits of her work. The large swathes of dark green were honed down, trimmed back, clipped to conform to a more acceptable aesthetic. Finer, more see-able, more contained.

Maddie luxuriated in the feeling of inevitability that had engulfed her. Time would always march on and she would always be taken with it, either actively or limply. But the new year was a fresh start, anything could happen. She was surprised that, for once, it was with anticipation rather than foreboding that she embraced this concept. She pulled open a drawer and rummaged around for a long fine-tipped brush. She ran the soft bristles over her lips and looked at her notes. The journey from her original idea to the stage she was at now was difficult to pick out. She lowered herself into her chair and closed her eyes to picture how best to link the elements that had appeared on the canvas. Individually, they were strong. Did they need to be connected? Did they need to be physically joined to be related? Maybe it was the space itself that was holding them together.

Car wash

Anna turned up outside the studio at two o'clock as arranged. They were going shopping to buy Maddie something new to wear to work the next day and some stationery for her course. A vacant jetwash in a garage on a Bank Holiday was too good an opportunity to pass up, though, so they decided to stop off en route.

Anna hooted with laughter as she watched Maddie trying to train the spurting water onto the car.

"It's got a mind of its own!" squealed Maddie. The lance was thrashing around like a writhing snake in her hands. Everything was getting covered in water except the filthy car which was serenely awaiting attention.

"Take your finger off the trigger!"

"I have! It's fucking jammed!"

"Hold on! You've got the lead tangled!" Weak with laughing, Anna tried to fight through the jet to help. Beaten back by the heat of the water, she approached from the rear. She reached over Maddie to get at the pole, pushing Maddie's hat over her eyes in the process.

"Anna, help! I can't see!"

The machine thundered to a halt and the lance died in Maddie's hands. The weight of Anna's body leaning over her sent them both careering to the ground. Anna pushed Maddie's woolly hat back out of her eyes and they surveyed the car from their puddle of watery foam.

"Got enough change for another token?" giggled Maddie.

Back in the comfort and warmth of her own home, Anna couldn't remember the last time they'd laughed together so hard. It was times like these which made her situation so difficult. Maddie brought her a cup of tea and settled down next to her on the sofa.

Anna had promised Roz she would talk to Maddie today, but how could she now? That would be too cruel.

"Fancy watching the video?" asked Maddie, poised, remote in hand.

"Okay." She'd take Maddie out for a meal tomorrow and confront the issue then. But it was her first day at work tomorrow. That would be even crueller.

Maddie whizzed through the adverts, until they got to the main feature. Anna wished Maddie hadn't chosen to watch *Manhattan*. How was she meant to watch and not imagine herself there? When Maddie relaxed against her, Anna shifted forward to pick up her mug. She couldn't bear such close contact. Maddie flicked a questioning glance across at her and moved down to the other end of the sofa.

"Shame we didn't get to go shopping after all," said Maddie.

"Yeah."

"I really wanted to buy a torch."

"There's one in the car you can have," replied Anna before she'd considered the statement. "Why do you need a torch?"

"It's my first day with Glen and Pete tomorrow. I want to be prepared."

Anna smiled and was suddenly consumed by a warm glowing love for her partner. Only Maddie would consider a torch an essential item for a first day at work. She hadn't made her feel that tingly in a long time. Was it a feeling of love, habit or regret?

The day the earth stood still

"Glen and I have got to be away by four today 'cos we've got a gig in Neasden, so I won't give you a go on the Beast today."

Maddie looked at the huge 'feed 'em in, spit 'em out' machine and was quite relieved. It had been weird enough getting up and coming into work without being bombarded with information.

"You can have a read of the manual out the back if you like," Pete added. "That should keep you busy."

She hadn't sat on the grimy sofa-chair for long before thinking the time looked ripe to go and flash her Maglite around the makeshift lab in the basement to see what equipment was down there. Glen was poring over one of his lists at the counter and Pete had gone 'down the road', so it was easy for her to sneak away unnoticed.

An unfortunate by-product of not announcing her intention to visit the basement was that Pete locked her in.

It had been quite scary when her torch battery suddenly gave out, but she focused her mind on her favourite things and eventually, when the two brothers had stopped arguing about the folly of leaving the door to the basement open so 'any old tea leaf could come in and half-inch their gear', Glen heard her hammering and cries and came to free her.

"What the fuck – excuse my French – were you doing down there?" shouted Pete.

"I just wanted to have a look around." Given Pete's demeanour, she thought it best to come clean. "I do a bit of photography myself and was interested to see what kind of equipment you've got." Maddie bit at a fingernail nervously as she waited for his response.

"Really."

Maddie nodded.

"What kind of photography?"

Guessing that talking was the best form of defence, Maddie blathered on about the techniques she'd learned at college and the product shoots she'd done till Glen poked his head round the door.

"The van's loaded up, Pete. We'd better get going."

Pete had been eager to hear more about her experience of composite contour prints, but time and gigs in Neasden would, apparently, wait for no man, so, instead of sacking her, they agreed to resume the conversation the next day.

Maddie had plenty of time to contemplate her first day at work as she made her way to the college that would be her Tuesday- and Thursday-night home for the next ten weeks. Ultimately, she concluded that, tempered by the opportunities the Creative Computing course would afford her, work wasn't going to be so bad.

It made her sad to think that the kind of experiences she would usually share with Anna – like the getting locked in the basement on your first day thing – wouldn't figure in their conversation these days. Anna was somewhere else entirely. Maybe it was just her work, but it was hard to avoid concluding that Anna was probably having an affair. Maddie didn't know for sure and had been so immersed in her own life changes that she had been deliberately trying not to find out.

Now, she realised the five-year lock-in period on their mortgage was the only thing keeping them together. Their home and the mechanics of running it were the umbilical cord sustaining their relationship. She just needed to get over this last hurdle, then she would be able to give it some attention. It wasn't as if they had stopped loving each other. Things couldn't be that bad. They just needed to start appreciating each other again.

As she approached her destination, she suddenly felt quite nervous. It was odd, starting a course in the winter. The darkness and the rain didn't engender the same security and confidence as a September Indian summer. Feeling soggy and a little shabby, Maddie slunk into the reception area of the low-level modern building.

She was leaning on the high counter waiting for the administrator to tell her which classroom to go to when it happened. Out of the corner of her eye she saw a door open and turned to glance at the person backing into the room, arms full of papers. The casualness of the action meant Maddie's head was already turning away by the time her brain and body had started to react to the image she'd seen. That was when everything started to slow down. Maddie had experienced a double take before, but never a slow-motion one. Her widened eyes travelled back to the woman, who was now walking towards her. Her pupils pinged back to meet the edge of her irises and she felt dizzy with the sudden influx of light. She looked at the woman's face.

Dark brown hair, longish, pulled back.

– Her palms started to sweat –

Mouth slightly open, moist lips.

– Her breath became shallow –

Nose refined, elegant.

– Her temples pounded –

Eyes aqua-marine.

– Her heart leapt. For an unidentifiable period of time, the woman looked back at her and their eyes locked. The woman smiled and Maddie was attempting to smile back when the administrator's voice brought her back in sync with the rest of the world.

"It's always the same when you start a new subject but it'll get easier as you get to know the routine," she called out to the Vision. "Have you got everything you need now?"

"Just about!" replied the woman. "I'll give you these back, then." She dumped the papers on the counter.

"Could you take this student with you? She's one of yours."

"Of course. Follow me."

"Do you need a hand?" asked Maddie, as she lurched out of the door after her. The most stunning woman she had ever seen stopped and let Maddie catch up with her. The woman's eyes were laughing, even if she was biting her lip to stop any noise escaping. Maddie replayed the words in her mind. She had only asked her if she needed a hand, hadn't she? She hadn't *thought* her words and *said* her thoughts, had she? If she had, it would certainly account for the embarrassment, but the woman wasn't running away, so maybe Maddie hadn't actually asked her if she believed in love at first sight.

"You can carry my bag if you like, but I think I can manage."

Maddie took the bag, which had been offered as a joke, and cringed. Hadn't she been carrying some papers just now? The proximity of the woman, the smell, the touch, the everything of her washed all other thoughts from her brain, making her stumble down the hallway with ovine obedience.

They walked in silence. When they arrived at room G12, Maddie had finally worked out what she was going to say.

"I guess you can manage from here."

"Yes. Thank you..." The woman raised her eyebrows questioningly as Maddie handed back her bag. Instead of answering, Maddie found herself echoing her facial expression. "Your name? What's your name?" her tutor prompted gently. "I'm Joanie."

"I guess that makes me Chachi!"

Joanie's look made Maddie shrivel like an Immac-coated hair.

8 FEBRUARY 2000

Ultimatum

"You've been saying that for months, Anna."

Anna continued to stare out of her office window. The builders, who had only just started cleaning the block opposite when she'd first moved into the office, had nearly finished their work, that's how long she had been putting off making a decision. However agonising it was, Roz was right to demand some action.

"I promise, Roz. This time I'll do it. But I can't tell her tonight because she's going to college."

"Tomorrow then. Make her have the morning off. She only works in a shop, for heaven's sake, I'm sure the country's economy can manage without her for a couple of hours."

"Okay. Tomorrow." She hated it when Roz talked about Maddie like that. It was fine for Anna to criticise Maddie for having such low expectations, but it sounded so much harsher coming out of Roz's mouth.

"And we'll go to the embassy about the visa on Thursday."

It was presented as a *fait accompli*, but Anna went over to her computer to check she was free. The phone rang and Roz groaned.

"Anna, hi, it's me."

"Julia! I've been meaning to call you for ages."

On hearing Julia's name, Roz tapped her watch impatiently.

"Yeah, me too," continued Julia. "I really need to speak to you. Can we get together for lunch, coffee, tea – anything?"

Roz had come up behind Anna while she was talking and was busy moving an appointment Anna had scheduled for Thursday lunch to three o'clock. The words 'US Embassy, meet Roz' were appearing in her electronic diary as she spoke to Julia.

"How about next week sometime?"

Anna put her hand over Roz's and tried to guide the mouse towards a different time slot.

"Can't you do anything sooner? It's really important. I need your advice."

Roz had clicked on the following month. Weak from protesting, Anna watched as she typed 'Move to New York to begin new life with Roz'.

"Let's say next week for definite and I'll give you a call if something comes free sooner."

"Oh. Okay."

Julia hung up.

Clueless

The college pub was an old-fashioned, dyed-in-the-wood male establishment complete with old geezer and dog in the corner and collection of bank notes from 'foreign lands' above the bar. Maddie usually would have avoided it like the washing-up, but who was she to try and challenge the supremacy of the designated gathering place?

She took her pint and Joanie's glass of wine over to the table. The group had thinned out a bit. Tigi, the Iranian warehouse manager, had engaged Sinead, the Irish cocktail waitress, in an in-depth discussion about stock management, which left Joanie on the sidelines. This is my moment, thought Maddie, as she slipped into her seat quietly, trying to draw an invisible cordon around her and her teacher. Every week she'd rooted out a really interesting exhibition to invite Joanie along to, just in case an opportunity to ask her presented itself, but neither the Serpentine, the Hayward nor the Photographers' Gallery had been called into action as yet.

Maddie took a swig of beer to steady her nerves. "I've heard there's a really interesting exhibition on at White Cube² at the moment. Would you like to go and see it with me?"

"Sounds nice. I haven't been over there for ages. What's on?"

Joanie smiled and nodded as Maddie regurgitated the article she'd read in *Time Out*.

As soon as Maddie left the pub, she called Kat. The first time it rang and clicked into voicemail; the next time it went straight to voicemail without ringing. Maddie was beside herself. She needed to tell someone about her 'date' with Joanie, and Kat was still holed up somewhere going through her 'I want to be alone' phase.

"Where are you when I need you?" Maddie shouted at her mobile as she walked home.

Joanie had said yes! Her stomach flipped over again. She started to dream about what she would say to her when she saw her, what Joanie might be wearing, whether she had any idea how strong her feelings were for her.

She called Kat's number again. This time it was engaged. At least it signified life at the end of the handset, which was good for someone who had gone into a self-imposed reclusion. When she got through to the voicemail again, she did leave a message. "Oy, Rip Van Winkle! When are you planning on re-integrating yourself into normal society, you freak! Call me. I miss you."

Look who's talking

Anna couldn't compete with the feel-good banter of the morning radio presenter so she turned the noise off.

"Maddie!" She tried to stop Maddie's morning flit around the flat, gathering her things for work.

"What?" she replied. "I'm late, Anna, make it quick."

Anna followed her into the hall. She had her coat on with her lapels half in, half out, and was opening the front door. Anna had to resist the urge to make her look presentable.

"We need to talk. Can't you be late for once?"

"Of course I can't!" she scoffed. "If you've got something to say, say it now. And quickly." Maddie continued stuffing her things into her bag.

"No, I mean properly. Talk properly. Can I meet you after work? We could go out somewhere."

"I'm busy today."

Anna's heart sank. What was she going to tell Roz when she met her at the embassy that afternoon?

"Friday's good though. Let's do something then?"

"Okay."

Maddie slammed the door and was gone. Overwhelmed by a wave of nausea, Anna rushed into the bathroom.

The great escape

Miro poked her head round the door to check the coast was clear. It was coming to the end of lesson five, so she'd have to make a quick dash for it if she didn't want to get caught leaving school early. She didn't feel too guilty about it. Brian had agreed to stand in for her period six in return for some computer training, so it looked like she'd covered every eventuality. She'd nearly made it into her car when a voice stopped her as she was turning the key in the lock.

"Playing hooky are we, Ms Petrowski?" challenged Jackie as she walked over to Miro.

"Would you believe me if I said I had a doctor's appointment?"

"Looking like that? I don't think so! So, where are you off to?"

"I'm going to meet a friend."

"Must be a pretty special friend if you're taking a sickie." The statement hung in the air, demanding a response.

"I think you're jumping the gun a little there," said Miro, although her obvious desire to get on the road suggested Jackie was perfectly in sync with the gun.

"I'm sorry, Joanie," said Jackie. "That was insensitive of me." She moved in closer to Miro and lowered her voice to make her next question more intimate. "So how is Kat? Did everything work out in that department?"

"We've decided to take a break. Just for a while. Just to make sure it's what we both want."

Jackie patted her arm gently. "That's nice, dear. That's nice."

Miro got in her car and sped off in the direction of the East End gallery. She couldn't remember how easy it was to park in Hoxton Square and didn't want to be late.

Dangerous liaisons

After pacing around in the cold, deserted square, Anna plonked herself down on the bench to wait for Ed to turn up. He'd sounded desperate on the phone, too desperate to brush off, so she had arranged to meet him at Grosvenor Square. She only had a half-hour window between a lunch meeting in Mayfair and meeting Roz, and hoped it was something she could deal with quickly. His request to see her alone was unusual – unprecedented, in fact – but this was still a really bad time.

In half an hour, Roz would arrive and they would go into the embassy to get Anna a work visa. Her first real steps towards a totally new way of life. The entire scenery of her world would change. She would feel like a dinosaur waking up after the meteor hit earth. The idea made her panic. Andy had said it was a wonderful opportunity, Julia had just cried, and Anna was vacillating between the two extremes like an oversensitive bubble in a spirit level.

She looked at her watch. The last thing she wanted was for Ed and Roz to meet.

Finally, she saw him appear at the corner of the square. Hands stuffed in his pockets, Anna marvelled at how he managed to wear nothing thicker than his denim jacket all year round. They hugged and kissed and he apologised for being late.

"So what's up, Eddie?" she asked, eager to move things along.

"Jeez, Anna. I know this is all a bit odd, but I really had to talk to someone."

"Are you okay?" Anna was suddenly concerned for him. He looked pale and had lost weight. "You're not ill, are you?"

"No, I'm fine. Well, not fine, but I'm okay."

Anna let him sit and gather his thoughts. The calm, laid-back, un-flappable Ed had turned into some shivering, nervy impostor.

"It's about Jules," he said finally.

"What about her? Is she okay?" Anna's blood pressure cranked up a notch.

"It's about the pregnancy –"

"The what?" She had no idea. Her best friend was pregnant and she didn't know. How fucking self-absorbed was that?

"She hasn't told you?"

"No, she hasn't mentioned a thing."

"Jesus! I can't believe it!" Ed pushed the heel of his hand into his forehead.

"What?" asked Anna. Her friend's emotions were so blurred, she couldn't make out what he was feeling.

"I was sure she must have told you. I need to know what she's going to do."

"Hold on a second, Ed – Jules is pregnant and you're asking *me* what she's going to do? Haven't you discussed it with her?"

"No. She doesn't know I know."

"Why don't you just talk to her?"

He shook his head.

"What do you want me to do?" she asked.

"Find out how she feels. I don't want to lose her, Anna, so I need to know how to react when she tells me."

"It'll be okay, Ed, really. I'll talk to her." Anna tried her best to calm him down.

"Now?"

Anna would miss her appointment with Roz if she went to help Ed that minute. Julia would be at work. She could hardly barge in and confront her there. Nevertheless, Ed needed her. Julia needed her. They got up off the bench and headed towards Bond Street.

"Come on," said Anna as she took hold of his arm. "You look like you could do with a stiff drink."

Ed didn't protest. They had been walking for a couple of minutes before he spoke. "What about your meeting?"

"It doesn't matter. It wasn't anything important."

True romance

It was six o'clock when Anna finally arrived at Roz's flat. The tall, thin townhouse had become almost like a second home; her toothbrush was in the bathroom, a clean pair of knickers in her drawer in the bedroom. She took the glass that was passed to her, surprised that Roz wasn't more annoyed about their aborted meeting. Anna had been ready for a lecture about commitment and how irresponsible it had been for her to go dashing off to the pub with her friend on a whim, but it didn't come. Instead Roz was clucking around, talking about how difficult it was to reschedule meetings at the embassy, but said she'd try and fast track them another appointment.

Anna was knackered and a bit pissed but at least she'd managed to calm Ed down and reassure him that she'd talk to Jules. Now, the last thing she wanted to do was talk about The Future.

"Why don't we go to the movies?" she suggested.

Roz stopped in her tracks as if she'd never been to the pictures in her life before. "Okay," she said, tentatively. "What do you fancy seeing?"

"*Being John Malkovich* is on. I'd quite like to see that again."

"Oh my God, no! Sitting through that nonsense once was more than enough for me."

Anna was shocked by Roz's response. She'd been to see the movie with Maddie at a film festival and it had immediately become her favourite film of all time. "You didn't enjoy it?"

"I saw it back home, Anna. It was ridiculous, like all those

American 'independent' films. The story was completely farcical and that woman, what's her name...?"

"Cameron Diaz?"

"No, the other one..."

"Catherine Keener?"

"The dark one, yes. I just think she was rather trite."

Roz's words made Anna open her eyes for the first time in months. How could she possibly even consider going to another continent to share her life with a woman who thought Catherine Keener was 'trite'? Trite? That was absurd! She was one of the most fascinating actresses in modern-day Hollywood, how could anyone ever think she was 'trite'?

The promise of glamour, twenty-four-hour opening and authentic pretzels had sucked her into the idea of moving to New York, but what she felt for Roz wasn't love. She fancied her and found it hard to resist her like she would always fancy and find it hard to turn her back on a cream horn if she saw one in a baker's window. She enjoyed spending finite moments with her, but what would it be like waking up with someone when the chips were down, knowing that they hated all US independent movies? *Chasing Amy*, *Clerks*, *Hairspray*, probably even *Desperately Seeking Susan*, would all become non-shared experiences. What common ground would there be to fall back on when it was cold outside and she didn't want to go to work? When the washing machine broke down, when she ran out of Marmite, when she had dreadful PMT and needed someone not to mind that she was snapping at them... What would it be like if, all along, she knew they believed *Being John Malkovich* was a crap movie?

"Maybe it would be better if we just stayed in," said Anna. All she wanted to do was go home and make amends. Her relief at finally having made a decision was palpable. Her body relaxed like a distorted telephone flex that was finally being untwisted after months of being wound into unnatural shapes. Her head was the appliance on the end of the flex, spinning maniacally as its weight teased out the kinks.

She had so much ground to make up with Maddie. She'd been a worse person than she'd ever thought herself capable of. Her best friend was thinking of having a baby, her girlfriend's best friend hated her, her best male friend didn't know what he could say to whom. It was time for the madness to stop. It was time to tell Maddie how much she loved and cared for her. She reached out for Roz's hand and guided her onto the sofa next to her.

"Roz, there's something I have to tell you..."

Truth or dare

"I thought you were meant to be doing something with Madge tonight," remarked Julia as she wrenched a load out of the washing machine and stuffed her smalls into the empty drum.

"We were going to, but something came up. Suddenly some bint called 'Joanie' calls up and all of a sudden plans get changed, partners get fobbed off."

Julia didn't have to look at Anna to know that her face had drooped into a deep sulk, that she would be sitting on the kitchen worktop with a pout plumper than Jean Shrimpton's.

"I can't believe you have the audacity to say that, Anna!" She saw her friend flinch as she cracked a tea towel like a cat o'nine tails.

"What do you mean?"

"You have spent the last God knows how long having some torrid affair and were that close –" Julia held her fingers up to denote a measurement of about an inch "– from leaving your partner, friends, family and everything to go and live in the States. Now suddenly, after months of behaving like a complete dullard, just because you've come to your senses at last, you expect everything to immediately slot back into place. You only dumped this Roz woman a few days ago –"

"But I –"

"Ah, ah, ah, ah, ah! I haven't finished yet! While you were out gallivanting around with your lady friend, Madge has had to make a different life for herself and she's done a fucking brilliant job. Where were you when she was distraught about not being able to pay the mortgage? Where were you when her business was going down the pan? Where were you when Pete offered her the job at the shop? Having it away with some fancy piece, that's where! So now she's made a new friend – so what? It's something you've got to live with, Anna. She's still got her head in the sand about all this. You have to wait for her to realise you've come back to her."

By the end of Julia's diatribe, she was surrounded by a pile of very neatly, very precisely folded washing. She leaned on the sink and sighed. A hellish day at work and this thing growing inside her, sapping all her energy, meant a good rant had been exactly what she needed. It was Anna's laughter that broke the silence.

"So, I take it you're still having trouble embracing your pregnancy?"

Shopping

Maddie was pushing the trolley around the supermarket, trailing after Joanie like a puppy on wheels. She'd done her Supergirl impression by the time they got to the exotic fruits, so she hadn't really left herself anywhere to go trolley-trick wise. Instead she marvelled at how intimate food shopping could be. Especially with someone you didn't know that well but had huge, heart-stopping feelings for. For a start, the very idea that Joanie did something as functional as eat made her seem like less of a goddess and more touchable, more fallible, more human. Although Maddie was enormously attracted to this woman, she was totally in awe of her presence, so to see her eyes light up at the sight of a BOGOF was a revelation.

"Would you like some, Maddie?" Joanie was holding up two packets of biscuits, one apple flavour, one orange. Maddie just shrugged in wonderment and watched as she tossed the packets into the trolley. The whole experience was giving away more about her friend than anything they'd ever done together.

She liked sun-dried tomatoes and Star Wars spaghetti shapes. She bought half-fat paté but full-fat mayo. She was a wholegrain Ryvita woman who liked cottage cheese with salmon and dill. She chose anchovies, granary bread, malt loaf, cheese strings, British steak, New Zealand lamb, French apples and a huge jar of Nutella.

The way she picked a can of thick vegetable soup up off the shelf and rolled it around in her hands as she scanned the label for the nutrient information was so sensual. The way she reached for the melon right at the back of the display and pushed her thumb into the dent at the end to see how ripe it was...

"You could come and have dinner at mine if you like."

Joanie's invitation came out of the blue as they walked back to the car. Maddie hadn't banked on being asked to eat the food her friend had just bought.

"Unless you've got other plans..." continued Joanie.

"No. Yes. That would be really nice. Thanks." Maddie smiled and waited as Joanie stretched across the passenger seat to open the door for her. She saw Joanie's fingers grip hold of the pokey-out thing that unlocked the door. Those hands. She had such beautiful hands.

Joanie's flat was comfortable and spacious. How could someone so meticulous have such shabby paintwork? Maddie wondered as she looked around surreptitiously at the photos on the walls of the open-plan living room, searching for some clue that would tell her how Joanie lived her life, either in the past or the present.

Maddie had been quite open about her relationship with Anna but Joanie never spoke about anyone of either sex in terms of a relationship or even attraction, and the photos weren't giving away much information. There were a few old-fashioned ones, in frames, of what looked like a group of east European farmers waving at the camera, but the rest of the stuff on the walls was just common or garden art. She had a Joan Miró print hanging over the fireplace. 'The lark's wing ringed in the blue of gold meets the heart of the poppy asleep on the field adorned with diamonds' – Kat's favourite, thought Maddie. Kat loved Miró. She'd love that picture. When was Kat going to pull herself together? Maddie would give her a ring tomorrow.

With a couple of glasses of white wine down her and the end of the evening drawing near, Maddie finally stopped trying to tease information out of Joanie and decided, if she was to complete her mission and leave with a definite understanding of her sexual orientation, the direct approach was her only option. They were sitting on the sofa drinking strong Turkish coffee when Maddie finally stuck her head over the parapet.

"... With me and Anna, it feels like our relationship has just run its course. It's just kind of fizzled out, so I think she's going to be moving out when she's got time to find somewhere," Maddie explained. Move out? She chastised herself for over-embellishing the story – how was the idea of Anna moving out going to help her cause? "So what about you?" she asked with an intense lack of interest. "Are you seeing anyone at the moment?"

"No," said Joanie, whose hand went up immediately to brush some non-existent 'thing' out of her eye. "There was this woman, but, oh God... you know!"

Even though Joanie was obviously floundering, wanting Maddie to say something to cover the end of the sentence she was struggling to finish, all she could do was stare. When she did come to her senses, they skirted round the subject instead of ploughing right through it.

They talked about love and the different kinds they had experienced; monogamy and whether it was necessarily natural for humans to have one life-partner; and sex and how different it was sleeping with a man as opposed to a woman.

"It's quarter to twelve," declared Maddie. "The last tube goes at eight minutes past, so I guess I'd better be going."

"I'd offer you a lift but I think I've had too much to drink..."

"The walk will do me good." Maddie struggled into her coat. Joanie walked with her to the door. "Thank you for a lovely evening," Maddie said politely.

"My pleasure."

They hugged for a second. Maddie could feel her friend's hands running over her back. Joanie kissed Maddie on the cheek. They always did that. Two kisses. One on either cheek. Then they pulled away. This time the whole ritual was executed with far more care and deliberation so, even when they pulled away from each other, there wasn't much space between them. Maddie looked into Joanie's eyes. The clear blue was warm and smiling. They looked inviting. They looked like they were saying yes, so Maddie couldn't stop herself. She bent in and kissed Joanie lightly, lingeringly on the lips. She waited for a sign, a reaction, some response.

"I can't, Maddie. I'm really flattered. Really. It's just... Not now."

High society

Kat couldn't remember the last time she'd said anything to anyone that didn't involve some sort of financial transaction. The owner of the local newsagent had become her best friend. Even Stewart – one of the few people she could talk to who wasn't embroiled in her sordid emotional drama – hadn't bothered to come back from Bolivia yet, so Miro's phone call caught her off guard.

"I need to see you," declared Miro, after weeks of innocuous text messaging. "Let's go out to dinner so we can talk."

Kat didn't know whether she was just anxious about seeing Miro or whether her nerves were linked to a creeping form of agoraphobia. Just in case it was the latter, she agreed to meet her.

"Okay," she croaked. "How about a curry?" It was automatic for her to suggest Brick Lane. It was close, cheap and tasty. Kat's culinary horizons didn't stretch far beyond these criteria.

"Let's meet in Soho. Somewhere nice."

Kat paused before replying. That would mean getting on a bus, wouldn't it? She remembered Soho, the crowds, the traffic, the stench, and sighed fondly. She hadn't been there for ages. Maybe it would be good to make the effort.

"Okay," she squeaked.

"Good. I'll see you tomorrow. Seven o'clock by the ticket barrier at Leicester Square tube."

It had been months since the whole Christmas debacle – Kat's life had floated by in a haze of varnish and paint fumes, memories of Miro and fantasies about Maddie. It wouldn't be out of the question for Miro to suggest that 'the break' should be turned into 'a split' but Kat was nowhere nearer making any sort of decision than she had been when she'd first gone to ground. She'd been waiting around for Maddie's call to say Anna had left her, but it hadn't come. She should have been more proactive. She shouldn't have distanced herself totally from her friends. There was no way she could get in touch with Maddie, tell her about Anna's plan to leave, declare her undying love and ask her to decide if she felt the same, all in the twenty-four hours before seeing Miro.

Miro's voice. It wasn't as if she hadn't been thinking about her. Miro's face. She had deep, sincere feelings for her. Miro's touch. She didn't want to lose her. Miro's smile. But she also didn't want to hurt her.

Stand by me

Miro frowned as she arranged the stripped bones from her rack of lamb on the edge of her plate in the most appropriate order that her knowledge of anatomy would allow and concentrated on positioning her knife and fork in exactly the half past six position.

Kat was still eating her fish. The clatter of the room concealed their silence and gave Miro the space to wonder why she hated the way Kat held her knife so much. The handle should be obscured by the palm of the hand, forefinger on top for vertical steering, with thumb and third finger looking after the lateral plane. It shouldn't poke up in between the thumb and forefinger like a pencil. Or a dart. Maybe that was why it was so unpleasant. It would only take a ninety degree elevation of the forearm to turn an inoffensive item of cutlery into an offensive piece of weaponry. Maddie didn't hold her knife that way.

Kat pushed her plate away from her slightly when she finished. The white-bellied waiter swooped in to clear the table and Miro watched her follow his movements. Anything to avoid the real issue that had been brought to the table.

"I need to know where I stand, Kat," said Miro. "And I'm worried about you." There was neither a reply nor a direct look. "It's not good for you to shut yourself away like this. If there's something I can help you with, I wish you'd just say." Another gap with no filler. "What I'd like most of all is for us to get back to normal. How it used to be. I miss you so much, Kat, but you have to tell me if you don't feel the same. It's not fair to keep me hanging on for something I don't even know is going to happen."

"Is there someone else?"

Miro hesitated. Should she tell her she'd met someone, that this person was obviously keen, and that it was only the possibility of salvaging her relationship with Kat that was preventing her from getting involved? In the end, she didn't think that knowledge would provoke an honest, rational answer, so she kept the information to herself.

"No, but..."

"I don't want to lose you..."

Miro was aware that her hesitation had done the damage.

"Well, you'd better pull yourself together, then!" she said.

"When I get back, everything will have been sorted. I promise."

"Get back from where?

"I'm going on a kind of holiday," said Kat.

"When?"

"Soon."

Unforgiven

The river was so mashed up by boats and currents that, as the swell hurled itself against the concrete wall, small isolated drops of water kept jumping up over the top. Anna watched them as they hung in the air for a second before disappearing back into the murk. There was something mischievous about the process that made her want to laugh. But she had to bite her tongue. Maddie didn't like laughing at off-beat observations any more. So they sat on the bench, side by side, not talking, not touching, just staring.

Anna guessed the others would be nearly at the end of the second film by now. It had been a bizarre double bill, even for the middle Sunday of a Sean Bean season. She had just about struggled through *Caravaggio* – Andy's choice – but left after that, suggesting she would meet the others outside later. Even the presence of Anne Archer hadn't made a second helping of *Patriot Games* very appealing. She had been surprised when Maddie followed her into the foyer. These days Maddie usually took any opportunity to avoid her but this time she had chosen to be with her. She could have just gone to sleep in the theatre and waited for the shooting to end but she hadn't. She'd trailed after Anna into the shoplettes at Gabriel's Wharf, shown a passing interest in some hand-dyed chunky knitwear and then followed her to her bench by the river. That was a good sign, wasn't it?

"It's quite warm for the time of year, don't you think?" said Anna, turning to look at Maddie.

"Yes. It is warm, isn't it?"

The response had been lively, upbeat even. Maddie certainly wasn't depressed any more. She had a sparkle in her eye Anna hadn't seen for a long time. A very long time. Anna was surprised to find tears pushing through her eyes. She knew it wasn't her who had turned Maddie's mood around. At best it was the excitement of her new job, which she seemed to enjoy, and the course, which she was really flinging herself into. At worst, the source of her contentment was another woman.

Boy, had she fucked up big time. She hated herself for having been so shallow. So naive. So impressionable. If only she hadn't met Roz, if only she had paid Maddie more attention, if only she'd valued her more. If only, if only, if only.

They might be sitting fifteen inches apart, but the size of the bridge needed to repair their relationship meant that space might as well have been the River Kwai. She had tried flowers, she had tried kindnesses like doing the washing-up and always making sure the loo paper stack had nine rolls in it. She had tried small gifts, loving notes in the lunchbox, not complaining when Maddie wanted to watch some obscure documentary on Channel 4 even though Anna knew *Vets in Practice* was on the other side.

She reached out to touch Maddie's hand which was resting on her thigh. The thigh tightened and the hand withdrew. Anna strained her eye muscles to try and suck back the tears. She needed something to focus on. She concentrated on Maddie's outfit as she tried to regain control of her emotions. She knew the history to every single garment her girlfriend was wearing. In her mind she chanted the items like a rosary. Bootleg cords, brown: Gap, January 2000 – cheap, fitted better on the hips than the black ones. Black jumper: M&S, October 1999 – roll neck as she fancied a departure from her usual turtle. Underneath, there was a faded, burgundy Stanford University T-shirt her brother had bought her during his tour of the States. A favourite, a staple. Faded black socks that Anna had been trying to throw out for ages from Kilburn market circa '98. Black leather boots from Carnaby Street she'd bought last year and had hardly taken off since. Black bra: M&S 36B; black knickers, size 12 – both Christmas presents from Anna last year.

She wondered if anyone else had become acquainted with the kind of pants Maddie liked to wear. She had to do something to reach out to her. Maybe this could be the moment to bring up the tickets.

"Hey Mads," said Anna after a sharp in-breath, "my assistant was saying she had some spare tickets to see Texas on Friday – I kind of said I'd have them. Do you fancy it?" Surely nothing or no one had the power to stop Maddie accepting tickets to see Texas...

"Sorry. I can't. I'm meeting Kat on Friday."

"Kat?" Kat bleedin' schmat, thought Anna. This was serious. "She's finally come out of hiding, has she?" She couldn't disguise the bitterness and disappointment in her voice.

"Yes. She called and said she needed to see me."

Good God, thought Anna. We're going through a relationship-threatening nadir and all she can worry about is tending to the whimsies of Captain Whimsy herself! Anna's shock at being turned down was exacerbated by the appearance of a running, screaming Ed, attempting to recreate the speedboat duel that had just rounded off the film.

Meet the parents

"Maybe Julia would like to go with you instead," suggested Maddie as she moved her bag off the bench so Ed could join them.

"Go where?" he asked.

"To see Texas in concert."

"Really? I didn't think they were playing until the summer."

"I'm sure Dinah said the tickets were for Texas," said Anna.

Ed wondered why she sounded so upset. It was only a gig, for Christ's sake. There'd be others. "No. I'm pretty sure it can't be." Ed looked over his shoulder for Julia and Andy. The film had got him a bit over-excited, and he was nervous about making their announcement. Not that he should have been. Anna had no doubt already told both Maddie and Andy about the baby.

"Oh, well. I've got tickets to see *some* band, *somewhere* on Friday..." Anna's voice wafted over him as he kept his eyes on the door to the cafe through which Julia would appear.

"Where are the others?" asked Maddie.

"Just coming. Julia needed cake and Andy needed something to drink." Suddenly he saw the door glint as it opened and Julia and Andy emerged. "Here they are!" He ran over to greet Julia. He realised it was a little excessive, seeing as they'd only been apart for a matter of minutes, but he was still hurt by the way Julia brushed him off. Andy passed Ed the bottle of fizzy water and five paper cups and went on ahead.

"Are you sure you're happy about this?" asked Ed one last time.

"Of course I am," said Julia, "aren't you?"

Ed swallowed hard. "Of course." Ever since he'd found out about the baby he'd been trying to come to terms with the idea of being a father. He was still trying to change a few entries in his life planner. The trip to South Africa would be moved to the 'retirement' section and 'think about promotion prospects' would have to be brought forward. When they arrived at the bench, he lined the cups up on the wall and opened the bottle of water.

"Everybody," he said. "Julia and I have an announcement to make." He watched four sets of eyes looking at him. Irises of brown, blue, green and a weird kind of grey were all boring into him. "As you may or may not know..." For some weird reason his throat had suddenly become dry and tight. He coughed and pulled at the neck of his sweatshirt.

"Spit it out, Ed!" said Julia.

"Jules and I are going to have a baby." He passed the cups of water round. "So will you join me in a toast to Julia and Tobias."

It was Andy's words that stood out from all the other exclamations of congratulations.

"That's fantastic, Ed. You're going to make a great dad. I know you're only a whipper-snapper, but you've got 'daddy' written all over you. Don't you think, girls?"

Ed's brow furrowed as he realised how 'steady' his friends thought he was. Am I really that boring? Do I really have so little about me? So little gumption?

"Who the bleedin' hell is 'Tobias'?" asked Julia.

Ed consoled himself with the fact that at least his family name was controversial as he mustered enough strength to reply.

The Big Picture

It was seeing the Joan Miró print in Joanie's living room that had given Maddie the idea. What her picture needed was a horizon of some kind. A line dividing the space in two. If she worked it in carefully, she could probably make the yellow sphere look as if it were sinking into the thick black line that was going to bisect the canvas. Or rising from it. One of the two. She pulled out her test pad and, for once, practised her technique instead of flinging the paint straight at the canvas. No pressure, just experimentation.

She relaxed her mind and let her thoughts float through her as she painted. She hadn't seen Joanie since that night at her flat, but they had been conversing via text messages and phone calls. She remembered the words Joanie had said to her after they kissed: "Not now." That definitely implied that at some point, there would be a right time. Joanie's messages had been short, intimate missives, sent late at night or on weekday mornings; times when you wouldn't expect the sender to be thinking of someone they considered to be just a friend.

If it turned out Joanie did feel the same way about her, she would have to leave Anna. She stopped painting and stood up straight. The thought of saying those words to Anna was horrible. Really horrible. It wasn't as if she had set out to hurt her. It wasn't as if she didn't have good times with Anna – take Sunday with Julia and the boys for example – but how could she continue living with her when she was full of thoughts and desires for someone else? It was crazy. She ran her fingers through her hair and sighed. Anna had had her 'weird period' as she called it, and now was over it and paying Maddie more attention than ever, just when she had met someone else. Typical. It would be silly not to go ahead and finish the painting, though. It would be something for Anna to remember her by.

Maddie looked at the clock. Kat, the crepuscular creature she was, had said she'd be over around seven. Should she strike while the iron was hot, transfer her idea to the big picture and risk hearing Kat's critique of the unfinished piece, or should she pack up now and get herself out of the line of judgement?

"Ehhh, what the hell," she said to herself. "Let's plough on."

True grit

Kat stopped and listened. She could hear water running down the pipes and the sound of Maddie singing. Not full voice singing but soft, fragmented singing that was dipping in and out of a soundtrack playing in her head. It made Kat's heart quiver to hear her. She wished the pipes would stop rattling so she could make out the words. It would give her some sort of clue as to the mood Maddie was in.

She couldn't believe she was going into this situation so unprepared. She had no idea what had happened in her friends' lives over the months since New Year; Anna could be living in New York by now, but she doubted it. She'd been picking up Maddie's messages and none of them had mentioned such a life-changing development. The best she could hope for was that Maddie had found out about Anna's affair and a huge irreconcilable rift had opened up between them. That was the scenario she was going to go in with.

Kat took a deep breath and closed her fingers round the smooth, rounded wood of the bannister. She lifted her right leg and put it on the next stair. Her left leg should have followed but it didn't. A feeling of utter hopelessness pinned her to the floor. How do you go in and tell your best friend whom you haven't seen for weeks on end that you're in love with her and want to share your life with her? The bannister creaked as Kat's weight leaned into it. She hauled herself up to the top floor.

It was her own studio, so she didn't know why she felt compelled to knock.

The Texas chainsaw massacre

"Sharleen looks very different in the flesh, don't you think?" yelled Julia in her friend's ear.

Anna had explained the concept of tribute bands to Julia earlier that evening, but she wasn't altogether sure she had grasped the idea.

"It's not really her, Jules," shouted Anna patiently. "They're a cover band. They just try to look and sound like the real thing." It wasn't worth going through the whole deconstruction of the name again. Anna shook her head incredulously. The difference between 'Texas' and 'TexUs' wasn't huge but she was sure Dinah had wilfully misrepresented the facts when she'd snatched the pristine twenty-pound notes out of her hand.

TexUs, my arse, thought Anna. She hoped Dinah was looking forward to photocopying all the files she had put on her desk with instructions to make three copies of each, making sure all the original documents and the copies are correctly stapled in their original groupings. Following that, maybe a mail-merge might be on the cards...

"Oh, come on, Anna, I love this one!" screamed Julia as she dragged her towards the front of the group of swaying people. Anna hung her head and let herself be led.

A few steps into their journey to the front of the stage, Julia's strutting surge slowed to a wincing mince. She looked over her shoulder at

Anna, pulled a face and pointed at her swollen stomach. Anna got the message and led her to the side of the auditorium.

"Are you okay?" she asked anxiously.

"Yeah. Just a twinge, that's all."

"Why don't we go upstairs and watch the rest of it from there?" Julia looked disappointed.

"There are seats..."

As she followed her friend up the stairs, Anna wondered how much longer Julia would be able to squeeze herself into her already straining Moschino jeans. She wondered also why Kat had wanted to see Maddie so urgently tonight. She wasn't going to tell her about Roz. Was she?

Confessions of a bigamist

Maddie'd had her hair cut since Kat had last seen her. She looked more worldly, more sophisticated, which, in turn, made Kat feel a bit gauche. Immediately Kat realised *she* should have been the one waiting in the studio for *Maddie* to arrive. The momentum was pushing her in the wrong direction. Maddie was the one who was comfortable and in control of the space and that wasn't at all how Kat had envisaged this meeting. Had she learned nothing from her self-help binge?

"I brought some wine," said Maddie after they'd hugged and appreciated each other's appearance. "Unless you want to go out?"

"Stopping in's fine," said Kat. She wondered whether she'd made the right choice opting for the hanging chair. She didn't feel very grounded but there again she probably wouldn't stay sitting when she told Maddie she was... when she told Maddie she was in love with her.

"Thanks Mads." Kat took the glass that was handed to her. It was then that she realised it wasn't just her friend's hair that had changed, something else was different, too.

"So where have you been hiding out, you old slacker?" teased Maddie as they clinked glasses. "I thought I'd lost you for good!"

"Nah! You can't get rid of me that easily," said Kat as she took a gulp of wine. It was cold but rough and made her throat smart as she swallowed. "I needed some time to sort a few things out, you know."

Maddie nodded seriously. "So have you?"

"What?"

"Sorted things out."

"Yeah. Kind of. In my head. I just need to convert thoughts into actions…" Kat was staring at Maddie. What was it that was so odd about her?

"So aren't you going to tell me about it?" Maddie probed.

"Yeah. That's why I wanted to see you, Maddie. There's something I've been meaning to tell you for a long time and I… I…" She ground to a halt.

"What is it, Kat?" Maddie leaned forward and her voice was full of concern. She put her hand on Kat's knee and asked again.

Kat continued to stare at her friend. She was transfixed and obsessed by the change she could feel but not see.

"This is really hard for me to say, so you must promise –" Kat stopped herself abruptly. "What is it about you, Mads?" she said, changing tack. "There's something different. Something's changed."

"I don't know what you mean." Maddie's smile burst open into a laugh.

It was one of those stupid, nonsensical laughs that just comes out when you're thinking about something obscene or some illicit lover.

"Jesus! That's it! You're happy, aren't you! You've met someone, haven't you?"

Edge of sanity

Friday nights for Miro meant her last evening class of the week. It was the duller of her three days at the college because her classes didn't coincide with Maddie's. She had just finished teaching a group of adults (with more enthusiasm than technological nous) how to import images into Quark documents. A drink and a neck, back and ego massage from a besotted admirer was just what she needed but Maddie wasn't free – a friend in need, according to her text message.

Miro stopped to look at next semester's timetable on the board. Only two classes. Shame about that. She'd have to ask about doing some more. She scanned over the usual dog-eared adverts that clung tenaciously to the cork noticeboard. The ubiquitous pleas for someone to buy second-hand camera equipment of no specific origin were present and correct.

She wished again that Maddie had been free. It would be really nice to get to know her better...

The picture of the eighteen-year-old woman looking for a job as an au pair was still there. Still grinning, still looking.

Maybe when this girlfriend of Maddie's finally moved out, Miro would be able to go round. Find out where she lived, how she lived...

The council house exchange – Camden for anywhere in Wandsworth – and the pensioner who was willing to pay five shillings for an hour's gardening were persisting with their quests.

Kat had made it quite clear she wasn't interested. 'Going away.' She wasn't going anywhere. That was bullshit.

Ohh, fluorescent pink paper, eh? thought Miro as she spied a newcomer to the noticeboard. That was a cut above the ripped-off strips of A4...

Holiday Apartment in Sitges!
Luxury two-person apartment in privately owned block available for one week. Last-minute booking due to cancellation.
Relaxation, nightlife, water sports, an hour from Barcelona...
... it's got everything you need!
For dates and info call Juanita

A ridiculous thought popped into Miro's head. What better way to get an old lover out of your mind than take a new one to a beautiful town on the Mediterranean? Miro glanced up and down the corridor. No one was around so she tore the glowing piece of hope from its place and stuffed it in her pocket. She walked quickly along the corridor towards the car park. Head down, she concentrated on punching a message into her phone.

Desperate remedies

"Wales? You can't take Maddie to Wales."

"Why not? A cottage in the country would be nice. Romantic," insisted Anna.

"A cottage in the country in Wales says comfy, it says cosy, it says five-hour drive through hideous traffic on the M4."

Anna played with the gold nylon fringe of the burgundy shade of the miniature lamp in their booth. Her jowls were practically flapping round her knees, she was so despondent. She waited for Julia to provide a better idea. For a moment, TexUs had gone quiet on stage. The lights had gone down and Anna wondered if they were just teasing or if it really was the end.

"Well? What would you do?"

Julia leaned back in the booth and ran her hands over her child-bump as she thought. "Think bigger, Anna. You want to sweep her off her feet. Take her somewhere where it'll be just the two of you, so she'll have to talk to you. Somewhere luxurious, somewhere sophisticated. Somewhere with decent shops, for Christ's sake."

Anna mulled this over. "Do you reckon Kat has already told her about Roz and that's why she's ignoring me, to get back at me?"

"I don't think so, keeping her feelings to herself isn't really Maddie's style –" Julia cut herself off and looked towards the stage where the lights had come up and a strange sound was filling the auditorium. "Good God – is she all right?"

Anna followed her gaze. There was a bit of flailing going on downstage left, but 'Sharleen' didn't seem in distress.

"It sounds like she's having an asthma attack," observed Julia as she peered down into the light. "Why isn't anyone helping her?"

Anna shook her head and listened. They were too far away to be of any help so they slid down to the end of their booth, draped themselves over the railing and watched with concern from their perch in the balcony.

Then the music kicked in and everything fell into place. "Oh! I don't think it's a medical emergency," said Anna confidently. "They're having a stab at 'Say What You Want'."

When their laughter and the performance had died a natural death, they went to collect their coats and play 'spot the illegal mini-cab'. Julia sighted and snared a Nissan Bluebird within seconds. They squeezed into the back seat and crossed their fingers.

"After tonight, there's only one place I can possibly take Maddie," said Anna.

"Oh my God, where? Please don't say Paris, Texas!"

"Nope. Paris, France."

Great expectations

Maddie heard her phone beep to say she had received a text message, but she was in full flow and not stopping for anything. Not that Kat was putting up any resistance. She looked a bit stunned, really. But who could blame her? It had been a long time since Maddie'd had anything to write home about.

"… I mean, she hasn't actually said anything explicit, but when we kissed, she didn't say 'no' outright," explained Maddie. "And she's been sending me all these messages ever since, so I think she must be at least a little bit interested. I just can't stop thinking about her, Kat. It's crazy. Even at work, Glen asked what the –"

"So you met her at your computer course?" butted in Kat.

"Yeah."

"Sounds a bit boring, Mads." Kat was definitely scoffing.

"It's not like you think –"

"Shame though. If she's a computer nerd, there's no way Miro would know her."

Maddie was relieved. The thought of outsiders getting involved in her private liaison would complicate things unnecessarily.

"What does she look like?"

"I'm not going to tell you if you're going to take the piss." Maddie wasn't sure she was liking Kat's tone.

"I'm sorry. It's just a bit of a shock, that's all."

"So where does Anna fit in?"

"Well, I know it's wrong, but I kind of gave her the impression that Anna and I were over. I might have said something about Anna moving out…"

"You did what?" Kat sounded genuinely taken aback.

"I thought it might put her off if she thought I was still with some-one," explained Maddie. "Anyway, it's true. The way I feel about her, it's like, if she said she felt the same, I'd leave Anna. It's not a crush, Kat." For a second, she was too self-conscious to complete her sentence. "I'm in love with her."

Maddie couldn't understand why Kat was crying. Sobbing. She tried to reach out to her, make her sit down and talk about it, but she brushed her off as she searched for her jacket.

"It'll be okay, Kat," said Maddie as she tried to calm her friend down. "It won't make any difference to us."

Kat shook her friend's hands from her shoulders and looked her straight in the eye. "What's her name?"

"Joanie."

"What kind of stupid fuck-arse name is that?"

The slam of the door made the paint pots on the shelf jump.

Kat's exit left Maddie dazed. Confused, she wandered aimlessly around the studio and tried to make some sense of her friend's reaction. It dawned on her that it had been Kat who had requested they meet. It had been Kat who said she had something to tell her; it was Kat who had distanced herself from her friends for so long... and Maddie had just ploughed on with her own news, regardless. She reached for her phone. Maybe Kat would take her call, at least. She picked it up with the intention of calling her friend, but the envelope icon reminded her she had a new message.

Heavenly pursuits

Miro was sitting at the bar, waiting. She looked over at the door as it swung open. It wasn't Maddie who stepped in, though, so she turned back to her drink. When she'd told her she wanted to talk to her, she hadn't expected her to say she'd be there within the hour.

Friday nighters were steadily filling up the bar and Miro wondered how long she could hold onto the stool next to her. She'd turned away several requests for it already, even though there was still no sign of her friend. She pulled the pink holiday advert out of her pocket and read it over again. Wouldn't it be fantastic if Maddie was free, if the apartment was still available? Lying on the beach all day, a trip to Barcelona, a bit of shopping, a bit of art, a little sun, a lot of –

"Sorry I'm late, Joanie," said Maddie, as she touched her shoulder and squeezed into the space next to her. Maddie kissed her hello and ordered more drinks.

"Glad you could make it." Even though they had been in contact a lot, Miro felt first-date shy about seeing her in the flesh.

"So am I." Maddie smiled. Their thighs brushed as someone used Maddie's back as leverage to get to the bar. Maddie blushed. Miro smiled coyly as she enjoyed the sensation the contact caused.

"Your friend didn't show up tonight, then?" Miro had to ask the question twice as the music was turned up a notch.

"Yeah. But it all got a bit crazy. I don't know why, but we were just talking and suddenly she started getting all emotional and got up and left."

"Christ! Was it something you said?"

"I don't think so. I don't know. I don't really want to talk about it. Do you mind?"

"Of course not." After her last meeting with Kat, crazy friends were the last thing she wanted to hear about.

"How was college? Busy?"

"Actually, college was quite interesting," said Miro.

Again, someone lurched into Maddie's stool and the flow of their conversation was broken as drops of drink were brushed off her jacket and apologies responded to. With so much going on around them, it was an effort to keep Maddie's attention.

Instinctively, Miro took hold of her friend's hand. "Maddie, this is kind of hard for me to say –"

"Jeez, not you too!"

Miro was going to ask Maddie what she meant when her phone rang. She looked at the name on the display. It was Kat.

"Aren't you going to answer it?" asked Maddie.

Miro looked into Maddie's eyes and felt something twirl inside her stomach. Her finger, which had been hovering over the 'answer' button, turned the phone off. There and then she made the decision to get rid of Kat and concentrate on letting things happen with Maddie. She placed her hands on Maddie's thighs and enjoyed the look of bewilderment and pleasure in her eyes. Full-on touching hadn't been in the rules before. People didn't bat an eyelid when she got off her stool, stood in between Maddie's legs and kissed her firmly on the lips.

She held her close as she asked: "Maddie, would you like to go on holiday with me?"

Breathless

Maddie heard the bedroom door open. The light from the hallway wormed its way into the room. Anna's long, thin silhouette made its way towards the bed. It was late. Obviously the concert had been better – or longer – than she had expected.

Maddie felt the duvet rise and then settle as Anna crept underneath. The warmth of her body oozed into the bed.

"Mads, are you awake?"

Maddie didn't answer. Her wide, staring eyes looked straight ahead and she hoped Anna wouldn't try and wake her up. It wasn't hard to play dead, though. Joanie's idea to go on holiday together had left her in a state of shock. Joanie had wanted to call the number there and then, but it was too late at night and they didn't want to piss the proprietor off. The piece of pink paper was lying next to the phone in the spare room to remind Maddie to call and book it in the morning. As if she would forget.

She felt Anna's arm creep round her shoulder and wished it were Joanie's. Should she tell Anna the truth before going away, or wait until after the holiday?

The big sleep

Thoughts, plans and a high-pitched ringing in her ears kept Anna awake. She was pleased Julia had talked her out of the Wales idea. Paris was altogether more appropriate. Tomorrow she would phone Eurostar and book some tickets. Or should she buy a guidebook first, book a hotel and then book the tickets? Or should she go into Maddie's work first, check with Pete that it would be all right for Maddie to have the time off and then call Eurostar? Fuck it. If they wouldn't let her have the time, she could just leave the job. It wouldn't be the end of the world. Anna was earning enough money to support both of them now. At least for a little while. What was more important, eh? A stupid job or fixing your relationship?

An image of life with Roz in New York floated across her mind. She quashed her flagellant alter-ego by turning her attention back to planning their trip. There was no doubt in her mind that she'd made the right decision.

She closed her eyes to get a clearer picture of how it was going to be. Maddie was going to have the surprise of her life.

Lost in transit

Maddie was running round the flat with a piece of toast hanging out of her mouth.

"Anna!" she yelled as she went from spare room to hallway to living room, scouring the floor and cursing her stupidity.

Anna glided out of the bathroom serenely. Did she do that to try and piss her off or was she just naturally irritating? Like thrush. The smirk on her face made Maddie want to smear natural yoghurt all over her smug expression.

"What's up with you? You're acting like you've lost your marbles." Anna said as she ran a comb through her freshly washed hair.

"I've lost a piece of paper, actually. I left it by the phone. Have you seen it?"

"What kind of paper?"

"Paper fucking paper! What do you think?" That got rid of the smirk from her face. "It was bright pink and had a telephone number on it."

What would she do if she couldn't find it? Maybe the receptionist at college would remember who put it on the noticeboard.

"No, I don't remember seeing it. Maybe you left it in your jacket pocket or your wallet or somewhere."

Maddie felt awful. She shouldn't have snapped. Anna was only trying to help.

"I've checked everywhere, it's freaking disappeared and I've got to go."

"Sounds like it was important," said Anna as Maddie turned her bag upside down for the second time.

"Believe me, it was." How was she going to tell Joanie she'd lost it?

"Why don't you go off to work? I'll have another look round and give you a call if I find it."

"Okay. But I don't think it's here."

Dead calm

As soon as Maddie left, it was as if a poltergeist had been miraculously exorcised from the flat. Anna finished drying her hair, put her shoes on and a fresh apple in her briefcase, before sitting down to drink the coffee she'd made earlier.

She waited for exactly five minutes before pulling the crumpled piece of fluorescent pink paper from her pocket and smoothing it out on the table. She smiled. She hoped Maddie wouldn't be too cross with her for booking it without asking. But there again, Maddie had obviously meant it to be a surprise for *her*, so the only difference was that the surprise would be coming from the other direction.

It was clear how much Maddie wanted to go. Anna picked up the phone and dialled the number. It would all work out perfectly. Although Paris would have been nice, Sitges was a much better idea. They could go sailing and diving and soak up the sun on the beach. They would have more time to talk. Everything always looked better when the sun was shining.

She listened to the long, even sound of a European telecom giant stirring into action. The line crackled as the person at the other end picked up clumsily.

"Dígame."

"Hola," said Anna. Her knuckles whitened as she gripped the phone even tighter. She'd exhausted her knowledge of Spanish with that one brief opener.

Women on the verge of a nervous breakdown

Maddie put the phone down just as Pete came back in the shop. He pushed Maddie's doughnut along the counter towards her and called for Glen to hurry up with the tea.

"Jesus, girl, are you all right?" asked Pete. Glen backed into the room with the tray of mugs. "You haven't been playing her your demo tape again have you, Glennie-boy? What have I told you about upsetting the staff!"

Glen tossed his hair out of his eyes, shrugged and grinned hopelessly, like a seasoned joke-butt.

They looked at her, expecting an explanation for her red nose and the damp processing forms. This put Maddie in something of a spot. If she told them what was up, she would have to admit to using the phone to call overseas, but if she didn't, they'd harp on about it all day and probably the next. She decided to come clean.

"I really wanted to go on holiday and I'd found this perfect place and it was all going to be wonderful, but I just spoke to Juanita –"

"Juanita?"

"The woman who owns the apartment I wanted to book –"

"I used to know a bird called Juanita," said Pete as he raised his Led Zeppelin mug to his lips and inhaled the liquid loudly.

"Pete!" Glen reprimanded him. "What did she say?"

"She said the apartment had been taken. Someone had phoned up this morning and booked it then and there. If only I hadn't lost that freaking piece of paper with the number on, I would have got in first and everything would have been fine."

Glen pushed the doughnut on its paper bag further towards her. He nodded and smiled encouragingly as if the bun was the answer to all her problems. "There'll be other apartments," he reassured her.

"Not like that, there won't. Anyway, what am I going to tell her? She gave me one thing to do and now I've gone and ruined everything."

"I tell you what Maddie, why don't we go down the Elephant at lunchtime and see if we can't pick up a couple of brochures for you and your bird. I'm sure we'll find something. She'll never know the difference."

Maddie looked at Glen's smooth, angelic face. How could she refuse such an offer?

"Okay," she sniffed. She needed to go out and buy tampons anyway.

Pack up your troubles

Anna told Dinah she had an urgent meeting and scooted out of the office at three o'clock. She stopped to pick up some fresh flowers and made her way over Southwark Bridge. She decided to walk along the river and turn off at Blackfriars Road and onto The Cut instead of taking Union Street. It was more atmospheric and longer, therefore giving her more time to think about what she would do when she arrived at Snap Happy. She'd only met Glen and Pete once, briefly, and wasn't sure if it was appropriate to tell Maddie about the holiday in front of them. They might make a fuss if Maddie hadn't booked time off in advance and there was no way she wanted anything to scupper her plan. Unless she could entice Maddie out of the shop, there was no way of controlling whether they were there or not. She'd have to play it by ear.

Left luggage

Miro was dealing with a kid who had glued her forearm to the desk while trying to mend her false nails when her mobile started vibrating in her pocket. Although the cutting implement did look quite vicious and the kid quite startled, she retreated to the corridor and let the firemen get on with their job.

The men – in full firefighting regalia – attacked the desk to which the child's arm was stuck, as she spoke to Maddie. She watched the trail of dust from their saw make a tidy pile on the floor while she listened to Maddie explain that the apartment had been taken already, that it was the only one available, and how it had been suggested that if they really wanted to go to Sitges at the start of the season, it would be best to book a little further ahead. She heard Maddie talk about some brochures she'd been out to get with Glen.

Through the reinforced glass window, she saw the child stand up and back off as the last piece of desk was cut away. It looked like she had an extra limb coming out of her elbow. Miro opened the door and gestured to the disorientated child to follow her. They walked down the corridor to the sick bay: Miro, the student and Maddie, who was still talking on the phone. She told Maddie that Greece sounded good but they would have to talk about it later. The child's wooden appendage was dragging along the floor and the noise was driving her insane.

"Pick your arm up, Letitia," she snapped.

The child looked at her and pulled a face. "It was an accident, Miss," she whined.

Finally they got to the sick bay and Miro had to say goodbye. As they sat and waited for the ambulance to arrive, she thought what a shame it was. Jackie and a couple of the other tutors at the night school had booked apartments in the same block, as it turned out, and Miro had briefly thought of the advert as fate. It certainly would have been fun.

Kiss me goodbye

"Mads, there's a woman outside the shop," said Glen as he peered through the window display. "She looks like she's staring at the pit bull, but she keeps cupping her hands round her eyes and wedging her face up against the window like she's trying to see inside."

"That pit bull terrier is a crowd-puller," replied Maddie without taking her eye off the machine. "She'll go away when she gets bored."

Glen wasn't so sure, however. She looked a little sinister to him. He shut his *Guinness Book of Hit Singles* and put his pen down. Slowly he made as if to go to the common room out the back. If she was on the rob, a seemingly empty shop was exactly what was needed to entice her in and catch her in the act. He moved into the doorway and waited. Sure enough, the cupped hands went up and the eyes shone through the glass. He watched her as she came towards the door and pushed it open. The electronic bell rang as she trod on the mat and Glen slid out of the shadows. His narrowed, suspicious eyes and the woman's, wide and surprised, locked. She froze in the doorway, one hand behind her back.

"Can I help you?" he asked tentatively. She could have anything in her hand. A knife, a gun, a roll of film. Anything. He had to proceed with caution. Suddenly he heard Maddie pipe up from the back of the shop.

"Will whoever is standing on the doormat please get off? That bell is sending me off my –" Maddie had come towards the door. "Anna! What are you doing here?"

Glen relaxed as he realised the person offering Maddie a large bouquet of flowers was the infamous Anna. He hadn't met many lesbians before so he took the opportunity of extending his knowledge while they stared at each other. Nice clothes, quite smart. But then all gay people were loaded, weren't they? He'd read an article about the pink pound only last Sunday, so he knew all about that. Short hair – that was no surprise. She was tall, but not masculine. Not the harridan Maddie made her out to be. She was actually a bit of all right. Okay, so she had looked a little stern when she first came in, but when she saw Maddie, her face had lit up. In fact, that was the only giveaway. When Maddie had come in the room she'd looked straight through him. Not a whiff of interest. He might as well not have been there.

He watched as Maddie guided her over to a corner where she thought he wouldn't be able to hear what they were saying. He put some transparencies on the lightbox and pretended to scrutinise them as he eavesdropped.

"Maddie, I'm sorry. I didn't mean to embarrass you, but I was so excited, I had to tell you."

"Tell me what?" Maddie's voice sounded impatient and annoyed, but her partner continued.

"I've got a surprise for you and I thought I'd tell you about it here because you might have to ask Pete or Glen about it."

Glen looked up at the sound of his name and smiled at Anna but Maddie's glare meant he was soon nose to nose with the lightbox once again.

"What do you mean? What sort of surprise?"

Glen couldn't believe how ungrateful Maddie was. Blimey, if *he* had a girlfriend and she came into the shop offering flowers and a surprise, he'd be a bit more bloody excited than she was.

"Maddie – I know you'll have to check it out with these guys, but I hope it'll all work out okay, because I've gone and booked us a holiday."

"You've done what?" She almost shouted the words.

Glen felt all warm inside. How bleedin' romantic was that?

"It's going to be fantastic, Maddie. You and I are going to be travelling to Barcelona where we will be collected and taken to our luxury holiday apartment in Sitges."

"Sitges?"

"I know! For a whole week."

Glen didn't know where Sitges was but he'd been to Barcelona for a European Cup tie a couple of years back and it seemed like an okay kind of place.

"There's no way I can go, Anna. How did you...?"

"Of course you can. I'm sure your boss will let you have the time off, won't you?" It was the first time Anna had spoken directly to him. He smiled and nodded.

"No. It's just not fair –"

"Of course it's fair, Maddie," said Glen as he lolloped over to lean on the counter. "She's been banging on about missing out on some holiday all day." He lifted his chin and rolled his eyes conspiratorially. "We even went out to get some brochures to see if there wasn't something else for the both of you."

"I guess you won't be needing those now," said Anna as she put her arm round Maddie, who looked pale with the shock of it all.

"I can't go, Anna."

"Don't talk rot!" replied Glen. She'd been so upset earlier on; he realised how much this trip meant to her, so he was going to make sure she went if it was the last thing he did. "When are your flights?"

"Next Saturday."

He made a play of thinking about whether it would be convenient but both he and Maddie knew one week was very much like the next at Snap Happy. "I don't see why that would be a problem."

"But Glen, that gives you no notice at all," said Maddie.

"Jesus, girl, anyone would think you didn't want to go!" said Glen, who was distracted by the sound of Pete heaving his Marshall amp in through the door.

"Go where?" asked his brother.

"On holiday," answered Glen.

"It would only be for a week," explained Anna, looking at them both expectantly. Pete's breath was still laboured from the weight of his amp. Glen waited for his brother to speak. It could go either way with him. It all depended on his amp. If the repair shop had been able to mend it, he'd probably say yes. If not, things could be very different.

"The way she's been moping around here this morning," said Pete, "you can have her for a fortnight, darling!"

Big up to the repair dude! thought Glen, as he nodded his head with excitement. Everything was going to be fine, fine, fine.

"But –" Maddie tried to say something but Pete shouted her down. It was going to be odd in the shop without her, thought Glen, but stuff like this was important. She'd better not put up too much of a fight though, or he'd change his mind.

"Ah, ah, ah. I'm not going to take any lip from you! Even though I know you can't bear to be parted from us, you, my darling, and your lovely ladyfriend here are off to... Where are you taking our little ray of sunshine, sweetheart?"

"Spain," said Anna quietly.

"You are going on your holidays to Spain and that's the end of it."

The Big Picture

Maddie stood back from her work to take in the overall effect. It was always going to be hard to know when it was finished, but finally she knew there wasn't much left to be done. Gone were the manic dives of colour that had been fighting for air. Now the look was clean, simple, primary. Controlled even. She couldn't help smiling at the irony of it all. The picture had started out as a present for Anna, to reflect and celebrate their commitment, but now that it was finished, so were they. She would probably still give it to Anna – if she still wanted it – as a thank you for the last seven years. Something to remember her by. Not now, though. She would break the news on holiday and drop it round when she picked up her things. It would be the Saturday morning after they got back. It would be quite sunny and warm and calm. Anna would be out, probably with Andy or Julia who would be consoling her, while Maddie and Joanie went round to pack the last of her things. She would leave it propped up against the sofa, maybe with a note, just to explain. Maddie put the dust sheet back over the frame, overwhelmed by a feeling of catharsis.

Airplane

That was it. The moment when the climb started to level off and the engine sound changed from a roar to a whine. She hated that bit. Below them Luton was disappearing into the distance. The cars lining the tarmac at the factory looked more like tiny beetles than Vauxhalls and then like nothing at all. She felt the pressure of Anna's arm as she leaned over to see out of the window.

"Exciting isn't it?" said Anna, peeling Maddie's fingers from the arm rest to hold her hand.

Maddie nodded. It was exciting. And nerve-racking and frightening. She'd never thought it would end like this, but then that was probably because she never really thought it would end. Trying to tell Anna that she didn't want to go away had been a disaster. Anna's insistence had been greater than her own resistance so she ended up going along with it. At least when she got round to telling Anna she was leaving her, neither of them would be able to storm off. They'd be stuck together and have to talk it through. They would be more likely to remain friends afterwards if they had that time to discuss things. Maybe they would meet up and go bowling once a month, or something like that, now that Anna had become a convert. She squeezed Anna's hand and felt sad to the bone.

House of smiles

The noise of wood being dragged over tiles made Anna's spine vibrate but she was determined the beds would be joined so she persisted with the task. Breathless, she lay down and studied her surroundings. She reached up to the switch next to the bed. Maddie had turned the bedside lights on before getting in the shower, from a switch in the 'kitchenette'. As a result of Anna's experiment with her switch next to the bed, they were now off. The lurid prints in gilded plastic frames that hung on the wall, the arse-worn sheets and the mop and bucket in the corner suggested it could only be this feature – the one-gang, two-way lighting system – that put the 'luxury' in 'luxury apartment'. Still, it was comfortable, clean and their home for the next week.

Anna heard the shower being turned off and got off the bed. The towel she had twisted round her waist dropped to the floor as she opened the bag in search of something to wear. They were going out for a meal so she wanted to make an effort. It was important to make the first night as easy, as intimate and as romantic as possible. Although she couldn't see them, her own experience and Maddie's behaviour told her that vultures were already circling over the carrion that was their relationship. The odour of putrefying love and rotting commitment hung in the air between them and if she could smell it, it was bound to be obvious to others. Usurpers were being attracted by the odour of a bleeding heart. It wasn't the kind of stench that would be chased away by superficial plug-in-the-wall-air-freshener tactics. Only the sweet smell of honesty could neutralise the bitterness and resentment causing the pong – Anna braced herself and hoped she would be up to the job.

Maybe she'd pop down and ask Juanita's advice about which restaurant to go to. For that, however, she would need clothes. While searching for the shirt that went with her best black trousers, she discovered her mask and snorkel. She hadn't used it since Fuerteventura '98 and wondered if the rubber had perished. She pulled on the strap. It seemed okay, but it was the fit round the face and nose that was most important. Brushing her wet hair out of her eyes, she pulled the mask on and positioned the snorkel in her mouth. It felt okay and it wasn't steaming up too much, which was probably a good sign. She tapped on the glass and made herself flinch. It was weird how the world slowed down when it was seen through a diving mask. The sound of her breath was so obvious, so regular, it dictated the tempo of her movements like a metronome. She put her hand over the top of the snorkel and blew. No air escaped, so it hadn't been punctured.

Where were her flippers? She remembered putting them in a Sainsbury's carrier bag and leaving them out in the hallway, ready to go. She hadn't left them at home, had she? Maybe Maddie had stashed them somewhere already. As she stopped rummaging in the bag, she noticed Maddie standing in the corner of the room, her towel limp in her hand, staring at her and looking slightly shocked. Obviously, wandering round the room in nothing but a snorkel and mask wasn't the way to go about rekindling the romance. She wrenched off the contraption, pulled on some clothes and muttered something about going to find Juanita as she bolted for the door.

It's love I'm after

Juanita had given good culinary advice. The restaurant was perfect, small but bubbling, and well off the track beaten by men with accordions, miniature guitars and shrink-wrapped roses. It had just gone midnight by the time they left the flower-edged *hosteria* and sauntered down the winding street towards their apartment. The air was gentle and warm and London felt like a lifetime away.

The meal had gone well. They'd amused themselves by monitoring the waiter's inept attempts at flirting with the men on the neighbouring table. Maddie looked more relaxed than Anna had seen her in ages.

"Why don't we go down to the beach," said Anna. Then, remembering Maddie's comment about her getting too intense, she added: "We could suss out where we'd like to head for in the morning."

The nearer they got to the sea, the noisier and more crowded the town became. There were gay men bulging, bumping, staring and grinding everywhere, swaying to the music that poured out of the bars to form an indiscriminate Euro thud in the middle of the narrow pedestrian street. The tans, the clothes, the tightly packed, bulbous crotches were second to none. Anna chuckled as she imagined what Andy's reaction to the spectacle would be. She turned to Maddie, who looked as intrigued as she was by such an unprecedented concentration of vanity and beauty. Anna spotted a side street and caught hold of Maddie's hand to lead her out of the mêlée.

The sand was finer than Anna had expected and it flushed out the last tenacious flakes of London that were still lodged between her toes. After locating the loos – proper, flushing ones as opposed to the chemical cesspits at the back of the beach – at Maddie's insistence (she didn't like to be too far from a convenience), they sat down at the water's edge.

"So you fancy coming here tomorrow?" asked Anna.

"Yes. Looks good." Although not effusive, there was enthusiasm in Maddie's reply.

"We should make a note of the name of the sunbed man on the way back."

"I think it's Carlos or Fernando, or something."

Anna pushed her feet into the sand and dug trenches with her toes which were immediately washed away by the sea like a drawing on a magic slate. Although they were far from alone on the beach, it felt quiet and private. It was the right moment to 'say something'.

"Maddie?" she started nervously.

"Ummm." Maddie had stretched out on the sand and was looking up at the sky.

"We've been going through a hard time recently, haven't we?"

Anna waited for an answer but Maddie kept on staring up at the sky, so she lay down next to her and leant up on her elbow, almost hovering over her. She let handfuls of sand slip through her curled fist. It was such a big subject, such a long period of time to dissect, she wasn't sure where to start.

"I know I wasn't the kindest, easiest person to live with for a while but I want you to know, Maddie, I realise now that things got... They got out of hand. I lost track for a while." A high-pitched scream diverted her attention as a naked, drunk couple went charging into the water. She smiled and turned back to look at Maddie, who wasn't reacting. She would have to plough on, unencouraged.

"Everything was so confusing, there were so many decisions to make. The flat, my job. There was so much pressure at work to do the right thing, I think I lost my grip on what is important. I forgot that, if it weren't for you, none of it would mean anything." Anna broke off but again Maddie didn't stir. "I just want you to know that I'm sorry I wasn't there for you when you needed me. Did you know Jules had a real go at me?"

Maddie shook her head slowly.

"She really laid into me about what a shit I was being. All that stuff about your job and the money... it makes me hurt to think about it..."

Maddie glanced at Anna, who was struggling to find the words.

"I don't know if you can understand, Mads, but it was like I got swept along by this huge corporate machine. I started believing it when people said I should be doing more, aiming higher, taking responsibility, earning more money. I wanted to do it for us. I never meant for it to come between us."

The sand in between them was pitted with dents made by the weight of Anna's falling tears. Still Maddie was silent.

"I know that, in effect, I've been driving you away. I don't know exactly how far you've been pushed or what into, but you have to understand, Maddie, I want things to be like they were before. I'll do anything you want me to. Honestly, I will. I've been so stupid and I want to make things right. Just tell me what you want me to do. We're so right together, I don't know what I'd do without you. I love you so much." The blood that had rushed to Anna's damp nose was making it throb. "Please say something, sweetheart." Anna watched Maddie and waited, but her expression wasn't giving anything away.

"You can't just turn back time, Anna."

Your friends and neighbours

Maddie felt better for a day on the beach. Her cheeks and nose were the colour of a Victoria plum, but other than that slight oversight, the base for an even tan had been laid. With the layer of suncream, sweat and sand having been shed in the shower, she strode onto the balcony feeling fresh and invigorated. She fancied a drink, some olives, crisps and chorizo, and hoped Anna would soon be back from the shop.

The day had been spent churning Anna's words over and over in her mind and even now, they wouldn't leave her in peace. She didn't believe the 'corporate machine' crap. It was obvious now that Anna had been having an affair and Maddie was shocked at how much it hurt her to acknowledge the fact. It was so typical of Anna to make it look as if she was being honest and open without actually coming out and 'calling a spade a spade' as Vi would say. Maybe, in her head, she'd justified the whole thing as some sort of pre-mid-life crisis linked with her job, but it was a pretty gutless way of asking for forgiveness.

Maddie folded a towel and spread it over the plastic chair before sitting down and stretching out. She loved this time of day, when the blue of the sky started to get deeper. She watched the seagulls competing for space on the roof opposite, listened to the stereos cranking up the volume in preparation for the night ahead, and set about picking out her favourite beach towel from the selection draped over the balconies of the building opposite.

She wondered who had turned Anna's head. What did the woman look like? Was she anything like Maddie? She shut her eyes and gave the matter her full attention.

"Excuse me." The voice startled Maddie, who jumped up, stretching her T-shirt down to cover her knickers as she did so. She saw a woman's head poking round the piece of frosted glass that divided each balcony. "Sorry. I didn't mean to scare you."

"That's okay. I was miles away."

"I just wanted to ask if you had any Coke we could pilfer? Got fucking shed-loads of Bacardi, but no bleedin' mixers – I'll do you a deal if you like." The woman smiled hopefully.

"I've got a bottle of Diet, but it's a bit flat," said Maddie, responding to the friendly tone of the woman's voice.

"Don't you worry about that."

"I'll pass it over. Hold on." Maddie got up to go inside.

"That's okay, doll," replied the woman. "I can come round."

Maddie had only just reached the fridge when she heard a knock on the door. The woman was standing there in a long, tie-dye T-shirt with tassels flapping around her scorched thighs, and came in without being invited.

"Lena," she said and held out her hand. Maddie debated whether she was meant to pass her the Coke or shake the outstretched hand.

"Hello," said Maddie, trying to smooth down her unbrushed hair and wipe the smudged mascara from underneath her eyes. She offered her the bottle.

"I can't take the whole thing," said Lena as her eyes scoured the room. "Nice gaff, isn't it?"

"Take it, really, it's okay," replied Maddie. "Anna has just gone to the shops, so we'll have plenty. Honestly."

"Cheers love! How long are you here for, then?"

"A week."

"We've got a week, too. Never long enough though, is it?" chattered Lena. "When I say we, I mean me and my mates, Tasha, Susie and Jackie. They're all teachers, but me, I'm a nurse. Just as well though, given the scrapes they get into! I suppose I'm no angel. We just came over here to have a good time, a few bevvies and get a tan. The locals are quite friendly, if you know what I mean. But we're lucky, you see, 'cos Susie is a Spanish teacher, so she does all the par-laying. Do you speak the lingo?" Lena pulled up a chair and seemed to have forgotten about the urgent need for Coke that had brought her round in the first place.

"No." Maddie became fascinated by Lena's elongated London vow-els and her ability to have a conversation with practically no input from any other party.

"Oh. You'll be all right, most of the locals know English. Bleedin' hot though, innit? Juanita said it was 'unseasonably warm'. Get her, eh, and her fancy phrases! I might laugh, but it's a bit bad for Susie. She gets this prickly heat rash, you see, and has to sit under the tent business at the back of the beach. We go back and sit with her at lunch, but I'll be buggered if I'm missing any rays! No, but we all have a good laugh. But you're a bit lucky getting this place."

"Really?"

"Yeah. There were going to be six of us, but two of our mates had to cancel at the last minute – pet death in the family or something. I know some people get a bit stupid over their pets 'n' all, but welching on a holiday we'd had booked for ages is a bit much, don't you think?"

"I –"

"And then, another mate – this other supply teacher friend of Jackie's – was going to take the spare apartment. She was going to come out with this bird who had been sniffing around her, like. We were getting excited 'cos she'd been going on about her for ages, but nobody'd met her, so we all thought we were going to get a butcher's at last – but that went pear-shaped 'n' all. Looks like we'll have to put up with you as neighbours instead! So, where are you from?"

Maddie laughed politely and paid no attention to the question. So they were Joanie's friends! That was incredible. It looked like loads more information to be coaxed out of Lena if she were led down the right path.

"Shame they couldn't come," said Maddie, softly, as if she was talking to an unpredictable animal. "Sorry about messing up your plans." She edged nearer with her hand outstretched. "Your friend must have been disappointed to have missed –"

She was cut off by the sound of the door. She and Lena both turned round. Damn. There was no way Maddie could go on with her interrogation, so she herded Lena towards the door. Anna's arrival had turned Lena into an uncontrollable beast capable of lumbering off in an inappropriate conversational direction if she wasn't banished.

Anna looked surprised to see that Maddie had company. She'd be even more surprised if she found out it was a friend of the woman Maddie was planning on leaving her for.

"Hello," said Anna brightly, as she put the bags of groceries in the kitchenette.

"Our neighbour, Lena, just popped round to borrow some Coke," explained Maddie, trying her hardest to imply the task had been completed and the visit was now over.

"Cheers for that!" said Lena, waving the bottle in the air.

Maddie shepherded her further towards the door but Lena stopped and turned suddenly.

"Why don't you two come down the beach with us tomorrow? We have a right laugh – Tasha's got one of them crocodile-shaped lilos. It's a fucking riot when the wind gets up."

"Oh, okay." Anna smiled, nodded and looked over at Maddie.

"I thought we were going to take that boat trip tomorrow." There was no way she could let Anna spend time with Lena, who would soon realise this was Maddie, as in Joanie and Maddie. She didn't want Anna to find out like that.

"Shame," said Lena.

"Yeah. There's a beach down the coast that's really good for snorkelling and stuff, so we thought we'd go down there," continued Maddie.

Anna looked at her questioningly. "But you hate diving..."

"But you don't, sweetheart. I thought we'd agreed it'd be nice to have a boat trip and then I can lie on the beach and you can have a float round the rocks."

Anna looked mighty confused. "That's very considerate of you, honey," she said with a cheesy, false smile.

"Come and have a drink with us then, yeah?" suggested Lena. "You could bring that bottle of tonic I can see poking out of your bag!" They all laughed at her brass neck.

As Lena turned to give Anna a slap on the back, Maddie shook her head and mouthed 'no' at her partner.

"Okay," said Anna, still laughing.

Careless talk

The first thing Anna noticed when they went into their neighbour's apartment was Tasha. She was a tall, thin Liverpudlian with an accent as deep as the Mersey and as thick as an old pan of scouse. Feet up, fag on, she lounged on the balcony and flung her words over her shoulder towards her friend.

"What kind of waifs and strays have you gone and rounded up now, Leen?" she shouted as they came in the door.

"It's our neighbours, Tash. You know, the ones who got the apartment Joanie wanted," explained Lena. "They've just popped round for a bevvy."

Anna watched as Tasha twisted round in her chair to get a better look. "Well, come in then, girl! Pull up a chair!"

"Thanks," said Anna, moving into the room. She looked over at Maddie who seemed equally intimidated by the confidence of these two women.

"Jackie's gonna get a gob on her when she hears we've been entertaining without her!" said Tasha and she lowered her legs from the balcony and pushed her white linen blouse further off her shoulders. "Hurry up with them drinks, Leen – I'm spitting feathers here."

"Sorry about spoiling your friend's plans," said Anna. It was the only common ground she could think of to tread on, so she struck out. She smiled at Maddie and couldn't understand why she was giving her the evil eye.

"Nice places though," Maddie butted in. "Have you been here before?"

"Loads of times," said Tasha as she lit a fresh cigarette from the burning embers of the old one.

"No need to be sorry, mate," chipped in Lena as she clinked in with two large gin and tonics and two Bacardi and Cokes. She eased herself into a chair with a groan. "I think it was probably for the best really, wasn't it, Tash?"

"Yeah." Tasha nodded knowingly. "It was a bit of a queer old do, if you ask me."

"Really? Why?" Anna ploughed on. If this conversation turned out to be a dead end, she had already lined up 'women's bars in Sitges' and 'the pros and cons of buying your own parasol while on holiday' as possible topics of conversation.

"This Joanie, she'd been going out with this one bird for ages, but then she – the bird – went all peculiar and it was like, fizzling out," explained Tasha.

"Even though Joanie said she was okay with it being over, everyone could see she wasn't ready to move on," added Lena. "She had a real thing for this last woman, so coming away with this new bit of skirt wasn't going to do anyone any favours."

"Didn't she like her, then?" asked Maddie. She had been so quiet, the strength of her voice took Anna by surprise.

"Oh yeah, she liked her all right, but it was never going to be anything serious."

"A bit of fun to take her mind off things?" questioned Anna, taking a keen interest in these people, as if they were old friends.

"Exactly. And what's more, this new bird was starting to get really heavy. You know, commitment, moving in, love –" continued Lena while Tasha smoked and nodded.

"And she doesn't feel the same?" asked Anna.

"Does she, arseholes! She's still well into this first bird – the one who went all peculiar."

Anna frowned as she watched Maddie suddenly turn white and run out of the room. The door slammed behind her.

"I mean, she might say that she's over her, but I still think she's kidding herself." Lena took a swig of Bacardi. "But then, that's only my view. None of us can really know what's going on in someone else's head, can we, doll?"

"No," the other women agreed.

They sat pondering the facts before Lena broke the silence: "Don't you think you'd better go and see if your mate's all right?"

Like a schoolgirl dismissed from class, Anna jumped out of her chair and rushed for the door.

Tunnel vision

Why did people wave to people travelling on boats? It was ridiculous. If two buses passed each other on Liverpool Street you wouldn't get the passengers standing up and waving at each other; you didn't get people in cars waving at each other as they carved one another up on the M25 or cyclists giving each other high fives while they waited on the green cycle zones at the traffic lights. So why did people feel compelled to do it the minute they saw a person on a boat?

Another horn from the approaching cruise ship signalled its arrival and up went the hands again. It was so *nice*, it was nauseating. The boat humped over the ripples created by the other vessel – that was nauseating, too. What with the information she'd been harbouring since the night before, everything was conspiring to make her feel as sick as a woman in the first throes of pregnancy. So, Joanie hadn't meant anything she'd said about wanting to make a go of things when Maddie got back. All that stuff about going on holiday together, how she was so attracted to her, how she loved being with her, how much fun they had together… Was Maddie really just some kind of stop-gap?

"Not long now, honey," said Anna. "We get off at the next stop."

Her niceness was just adding to Maddie's queasiness. Once they'd found a couple of sunbeds on the beach, she would send Anna on a snorkelling mission in search of 'some coral that could remind them forever of their holiday in Sitges', find a phone and get in touch with Joanie. Waiting to sort out this mess was simply not an option.

It was still quite early in the day when they arrived and lots of sunbeds in prime positions – equidistant from the loos, the sea and the lifeguard – were still available. Instead of putting out her towel and reaching straight for her snorkel, Anna picked up her book.

"Aren't you going in the sea, sweetheart?" asked Maddie, trying to control the frustration in her voice.

"I thought I'd stick around here with you, Mads. I don't want to leave you on your own when you're not feeling well."

"But I feel fine now."

"Well, you don't look it."

Maddie flopped back onto her sunbed. Her spine crushed against the hard plastic supports at the back. "I don't want you to miss out though, just because of me."

Anna put her book down and looked out at the bay. Maddie followed her gaze. It was a bit choppy but there seemed to be lots of people skimming along under the surface like mini submarines.

"Are you sure you don't mind?"

"Of course not. You go off and enjoy yourself."

Maddie waited for Anna to turn back and wave, then headed up to the restaurant at the back of the beach. It was hot and sweaty inside and the sand on the floor made it feel like she was walking on terracotta. She spotted the phone in the corner, by the swing doors to the kitchen. Wedging herself into the space, she shovelled in all the coins she had with her. It was coming up for midday which meant it was only eleven o'clock back home. She chanted "please let her be in" as she dialled the number. She could feel her heart thumping in her chest as the ringing went on and on.

When she finally heard Joanie's voice, it was only the message on her answerphone. What could she say? What message could possibly convey how she was feeling? She couldn't ask her to call her back because she'd forgotten to pack the charger for her phone, which had already run out of juice. She was well and truly fucked. A couple of coins spewed out of the payphone as she slammed the receiver down, but not enough to call Joanie on her mobile. She caught the waiter's eye. She handed him a fistful of notes and he came back with a pile of coins and a Maxibon ice-cream. Again she started jamming coins in the phone. There was no way she could leave this place without talking to Joanie – asking her why she had lied. She took a deep breath and placed her finger over the '0'. 00 44 79...

The accidental tourist

Anna's lungs were bursting as she kicked her way to the surface, the water swirling around her legs. She looked down to see the sea floor moving further away from her and her fingers tightened around the piece of stone she'd found on the bottom. It crossed her mind that she could have it cut and polished and made into rings for herself and Maddie. How romantic was that? She looked up, one last push and she would be back in the sunshine and able to breathe. It was then that she heard the throb of an engine.

She looked towards the surface; it was thick with bubbles but she could make out a dark shape heading towards her. She tried to twist her body to alter her course, but it was too late. She burst through the surface and took a gulp of air before feeling a pain in her shoulder. As she lost consciousness, the stone slipped out of her hand and spiralled back towards its place on the sea floor. Anna followed.

The message

It took three attempts before Maddie heard Joanie's phone ring. She cursed the waiters who were suddenly behaving like crazy people, dashing in and out with jugs of water and armfuls of tablecloths. Surely there was no need to shout quite so loudly – she could hardly hear herself think. She jabbed a finger in her free ear to try and create a cocoon of calm. She went through the whole process of waiting for Joanie to pick up – heart thumping, blood pressure soaring. Finally it clicked into her voicemail and Maddie watched the machine swallow her credit in one go.

"I know everything – I can't believe you would lead me on like that. Joanie, why did you lie to me?" Maddie shouted into the mouthpiece. The line had gone dead by the time she hung up. Some of the message might have been recorded but she wasn't sure how much.

She was in a daze as she left the restaurant and at first she didn't register the group of people gathered on the promenade at the back of the beach. It was the ambulance's siren that attracted her attention.

She moved to one side to let it pass and wondered what had happened. The lifeguard was leaning over someone who was lying on the ground. Maddie's pace slowed as she drew nearer to the crowd. She wasn't usually this morbid, but she did like to know what was going on. Looked like a swimmer had been hurt, poor sod.

As she got nearer, she saw that the lifeguard was giving the person mouth to mouth – her wet hair covered the victim's face as she blew air into the lungs. The ambulance crew flung open the doors of their truck and pushed the crowd to one side as they wheeled the gurney through. Their movements were economical and precise. The lifeguard moved back to let the ambulance crew do their job. Maddie's pace quickened as they lifted the woman onto the stretcher. Her head was flopping from side to side as they manoeuvred her into position. Maddie broke into a jog. The lifeguard brushed the woman's hair from her face before the paramedic put a respirator over her mouth and loaded her into the vehicle. Maddie's muscles were tense and she was finding it difficult to breathe as she sped up.

"ANNA!" The cry came from the core of Maddie's being. She ran after the ambulance, faster than she ever knew she could, as it sped off, away from the beach, away from her.

Letters to an unknown lover

For hours Maddie sat at Anna's bedside. There was one nurse who spoke English who'd tried to tell her what was going on, but Maddie felt alone and helpless and wished Barbara would hurry up and get there.

Anna had had surgery on her shoulder, which had been shattered by the jet ski, and it was thanks to the lifeguard and the quick reactions of a woman on a nearby pedalo that Maddie was sitting next to her sleeping body and not her corpse. Maddie had called Barbara, Julia, Andy, Glen, her brother, Kat – everyone really. As soon as Anna was strong enough they would fly home, but Barbara had insisted on coming out in the meantime. At least it would be someone to wait with.

Maddie looked up with a start when the door opened. "Barbara! Thank God you're here." She rushed over to hug her.

"How is she?" Barbara guided Maddie over to the side of the bed.

"The doctor said she's responded well, but she hasn't opened her eyes yet."

Barbara rubbed Maddie's back reassuringly, but wasn't able to hold back her own tears. They sat in silence for a moment; the beeping of the machine Anna was hooked up to filled the room.

"I've brought someone to see you," Barbara said gently. Turning to the door, she called out: "Sheila."

"Mum!" Maddie walked on jelly legs into her mother's open arms. Her anxiety flooded out as they hugged in the middle of the room.

"I'm so sorry, my darling." Sheila's voice was warm in Maddie's ear and her tears dripped onto their cheeks. "I've been such a fool. I understand that now. Seeing you here, like this… I hope you can forgive me."

"It's okay."

"The thought of losing you –"

"We don't have to talk about it."

"But we do."

Maddie turned to see Barbara walking out of the room. "I'll go and get us some tea."

"I know now how much you love Anna," continued Sheila. "It's obvious that you're devoted to one another, and I want to help you through this. I can't believe I didn't see before that you're perfect for one another."

Sheila handed Maddie a paper towel to wipe away her tears. "I'll go and give Barbara a hand."

Her whirlwind entrance and declaration left Maddie feeling limp.

The paper towel hung loosely in her hand, but instead of drying her eyes she spread it on the table at the end of Anna's bed. She picked up the pen the nurse had left behind. It wasn't guilt that made her write to Joanie saying her circumstances had changed. It wasn't Barbara or Sheila's expectations or her conversation with Lena and Tasha that made her tell Joanie she didn't want to see her any more.

14 JULY 2000

Hang 'em high

"Mind the frame!" shouted Maddie as she and Kat tried to heave Anna's picture off Stewart's skateboard and into the lobby of Maddie's building.

"I'm trying!" replied Kat, "but it's really fucking heavy!" Huffing and puffing, they manoeuvred the bubble-wrapped canvas to the bottom of the stairs.

"There's no way we're going to do this in one go," said Kat, slumping into a heap on the floor.

"We'll take it slowly then," said Maddie, "one level at a time."

"When did you say Anna was coming home?"

"She's got physio until four o'clock, so that gives us about an hour and a half."

"Time for a fag then." Kat reached into her pocket for her packet and a lighter.

Maddie joined her on the floor and took the cigarette that was offered. She tried to picture Anna's face when she led her into the living room to see the picture – her very own big picture – hanging there, finally complete. The grand unveiling was scheduled for later that evening when the others had arrived. Maddie felt a sudden rush of excitement, firstly because she'd completed the thing after all this time and secondly in anticipation of Anna's reaction. She hoped she liked it, but even if she didn't, Maddie knew Anna would lie anyway.

That was how things had been since the accident – peachy. They'd been treating each other with evangelical kindness: it was if they were pussyfooting around a happy-clappy, egg-shell-covered, rose-tinted garden, wearing kid gloves. That kind of politeness was quite nice in a way. It had allowed them to get to know one another again and she did like what she was rediscovering. She didn't regret choosing Anna over Joanie. A voice at the back of her mind nagged her over this choice of words – with the combination of Joanie's friends and Anna's accident, Maddie had hardly been in control of events. Still, there was nothing quite like a near-death experience to help you prioritise.

"Anna's told Julia, Ed, Andy and Phil to be round for about eight o'clock – you won't be late, will you?"

"'Course not!"

"This is really important to us."

"I know," drawled Kat. "There's no need to say it like that!"

"Are you sure you don't want to bring anyone?" asked Maddie.

Persuasion

… Kat shifted awkwardly in her place on the stairs and considered Maddie's question.

There hadn't been 'anyone' since Miro and although she'd tried to make up with her, it was becoming obvious that the relationship was going to need more than an iron-on, star-spangled peace gesture to patch it up. The potential had always been there for things to go monumentally wrong and that was certainly what had happened. But there must be something she could do to persuade Miro to see her.

"Well?" asked Maddie. "Are you going to bring someone tonight?"

"I doubt it."

The big picture

Julia jabbed her finger at the intercom's button and announced her and Ed's arrival. Feet splayed, she waddled up the stairs like an *It's a Knockout* contestant in an outsize foam baker's outfit. Ed trailed behind, laden with crisps, flowers and bottles of every non-alcoholic drink Sainsbury's had ever stocked. He smiled at her as they rounded the dog-leg in the stairs.

"Why are you wearing that god-awful shirt, for fuck's sake?" snapped Julia.

"Sorry, sweetheart, I didn't know you weren't keen. I'll get rid of it when we get home."

The door was open when they got to the top floor and Maddie was there to greet them. She led them through into the living room where the picture was waiting to be seen.

"So, this is the infamous Big Picture," said Julia. "Can't I just have a sneak preview, Madge? Just a little peek?"

"No way, Jules. Kat's the only one who has seen it and that's the way it's going to stay until she arrives. I want everyone to see it together. I'm not going through it in dribs and drabs."

Ed returned from putting the drinks in the kitchen. "I'm so glad you and Anna worked things out," he said softly as he kissed her hello.

"Cheers, Ed."

"Edward. Looking as radiant as ever." Andy's voice summoned Ed over, so Julia followed Maddie into the kitchen.

"It's a shame you have to do all the work for your own unveiling party," said Julia.

"It wasn't that much work." Maddie handed Julia a glass of cranberry juice. "It's not as if Anna wasn't able to put in her twopenny worth from her place on the sofa, so it was as good as a joint effort. Apparently, her physio said her shoulder still hasn't fully healed and any strain on it now might put her back months. I don't mind really... Is everything okay, Jules? You seem a bit –"

"Pissed off?" finished Julia. "You can say that again. I wish the little parasite would just come out. I'm fed up with it already. I wonder how much I could get for it if I sold it over the internet..."

Maddie's forced laughter faded quickly.

"Nibbles?"

"Oh, yes please. I'm starving." Julia took a handful and stuffed them in her mouth. "Honestly. I wish I could stick a pin in it and watch it deflate like a bad joke." She jabbed a finger at her stomach in frustration. "When your mother tells you that having children is the only thing that makes a woman truly feel complete, don't believe her, Madge. It's all a huge great scam."

Maddie smiled at Julia's rant and got the chopping board out.

"And Ed's chirpy little Mr Happy face isn't helping."

"He's just excited, that's all," pacified Maddie.

"That's as may be, but he's annoying the tits off me. Anyway, enough of my whingeing. What's up with Kat? Are we going to meet Miro this time or what?" Julia watched Maddie as she started slicing tomatoes and layering them on a plate.

"Maybe yes, maybe no."

"Oh dear God, that girl!"

"It's all her own fault," declared Maddie. "If she hadn't gone into one of her moods over New Year, Miro wouldn't have found someone else."

"So she's not interested in Kat any more?"

"Well, it seems that Miro was really into this new woman she'd met and was getting on really well with her," explained Maddie. "Apparently Miro even told Kat she was in love with this other woman –"

"No."

"Yes. But then Miro's new girlfriend went and dumped her."

"Just like that?"

"In a letter – no phone call, no nothing. Which is absolutely dreadful, callous and hard-hearted of course, but from Kat's point of view, it means there's an opening for her to wheedle her way back into Miro's affections."

"Hence her uncertainty about whether Miro will come tonight."

"Exactly. Pass me the dishcloth, would you, Jules?"

Anna poked her head round the door. "Finished with those crisps, Jules?" Julia passed Maddie the bowl and Anna the dishcloth and watched as they swapped them over. "When are we going to eat, Mads?"

"When Kat arrives. It shouldn't be long. She promised she wouldn't be late."

Anna smiled and took the crisps over to Ed and Andy who were chatting in the living room. Phil was sitting on the sofa looking at the pictures in the Ministry of Sound CD booklet. The music stopped and Ed went to put something new on.

"You know, Anna, if someone had asked me to predict this situation eight months ago, I would have said no way," whispered Andy, as he turned his back on Ed. "Julia not only getting pregnant but choosing to have the baby. With Ed! How amazing is that, after all you've told me about her ex-husband?"

"Yeah. It was a bit shocking, wasn't it?" agreed Anna.

"It's obvious she's regretting it now, though."

"You think?"

"The signs are there for all to see. The 'jokes' about the child, the snipping at Ed. She makes out she doesn't mean it, but she is shitting herself." Andy's voice was emphatic. He guided Anna around again as Julia walked into the room. "Her body language gives it away."

Anna raised her glass to her lips and glanced in Julia's direction. She watched her friend sigh as she bit into an olive.

"You can't help feeling sorry for Ed, though, can you?" continued

Andy. "He, on the other hand, is so looking forward to the whole family/ baby/ father thing, it's obscene. As long as we are all there for him when his world comes crashing in."

"I suppose," said Anna hesitantly. They watched as Maddie went up to the picture and adjusted the sheeting that was covering it.

"So how are you two getting on these days?" asked Andy.

"Pretty good, actually." Anna rubbed her chin thoughtfully. "Nice and easy, respectful of each other's feelings, polite almost."

"Sounds sickening."

"It's helped us get to know each other again."

"Still no regrets about Roz?"

"Absolutely not. I hardly even think of her these days."

"So you don't reply to her emails then?" Andy smiled slyly and dug his elbow in Anna's ribs.

"How do you know about that?" Anna moved in closer and put her hand on his arm.

"If you *will* leave your office door open and your inbox centre-screen, for all to see..."

"It's not what you think, Andy. It's just work stuff, that's all."

He raised an eyebrow. "So the one called 'Re: Great tits' was in relation to –" Without missing a beat, he reacted to Maddie's sudden appearance at his right shoulder: "Maddie – how are you doing?"

"I wish Kat would hurry up and get her arse round here, the salmon steaks are going to be as dry as buggery."

"It'll be worth the wait if Miro does come with her, though," enthused Anna.

"Yeah. Anyway, what are you two gossiping about?"

"We were just saying how brave you are, showing off your work like this. You must be really nervous," Andy improvised.

"I'm going to get a top-up. You two okay?" asked Anna. They nodded and continued chatting while she went to get the bottle from the kitchen. She looked in the fridge. The cheese in Maddie's mozzarella, basil and tomato starter was beginning to crust around the edges. She picked a little off the plate and dipped it in the olive oil. The bread was waiting to be heated on the side and fishy smells were coming from the oven. She picked off a little more cheese.

"Oy! Caught you!" booed Ed.

Anna spun round and slammed the fridge shut. "You!" She laughed and punched him playfully in the stomach.

"I've just been talking to Phil about fuel-injection engines," groaned Ed. "Any more red in that bottle? It's my intention to get absolutely blasted today."

"Like that, is it?" Anna glugged the wine into Ed's glass, started to uncork another bottle and winced in pain before passing it to him to open.

"It seems an age ago since our chat in Grosvenor Square..." he said.

"Just under eight months, I suppose."

"I was stupid to try and second guess what Jules wanted me to say about the baby," confessed Ed.

"You're just feeling nervous. It's a life-changing experience, becoming a parent."

"It's not that. I'm too young for all this."

The pop of the cork coming out of the Rioja punctuated the end of Ed's declaration.

"What are you saying?" asked Anna.

"If I'd told her at the time I wasn't ready, it would have been a good test of our relationship. She might have said piss off and I'd have known it wasn't meant to be. Now the whole thing feels like one big charade. Especially as Julia is so obviously smitten with the idea."

"You think?"

"All those cruel jokes? Come on! That's just her putting on an act." Ed gulped at his wine and drew a sleeve across his mouth. He turned his back as Phil wandered into the kitchen to pour himself a glass of water. Ed picked up the bottle and flicked his head towards the door.

"Let's go and join the others," prompted Anna.

Back in the living room, Ed sought out Maddie and gave her a nudge. "Taking it easy tonight, are we?" he joked.

"Sometimes it's best to avoid getting drunk if it's going to make you dwell on things you're trying to forget." Maddie's reply was earnest but that didn't put Ed off.

"It wasn't your fault, Madge. How many times do we have to say it? You can't blame yourself for suggesting that beach. If it hadn't been there, it might have been somewhere else and it might have been worse."

"I will always feel guilty, but I'm not talking about that –"

"Sometimes you've just got to make the best of what you've got."

"I'll drink to that!" shouted Andy from across the room. He walked over to them. "Do we *have* to wait for Kat to arrive to see the picture, Mads? Phil and I are practically wetting ourselves with anticipation."

"Let's just give her another couple of minutes."

"Hey, everyone," announced Andy. "Mads said she's going to show us the big picture in 'a couple of minutes'!"

"Yea! Get it off, get it off." Julia started her own little chant.

"Look, the sheet's nearly falling off anyway," added Andy cheekily.

The intercom's buzzer interrupted the mounting protests and Anna ran to answer it.

"Kat is in the building," declared Anna from the hallway, and there was a slight cheer.

Maddie laughed nervously. D-time had arrived. She hurried into the kitchen to get the champagne out of the fridge. High-pitched voices floated in from the hallway followed by whoops of excitement.

"Mads, hurry up!" shouted Anna above the music and the hub-bub. "Kat's got someone she wants to introduce you to."

Maddie pushed the fridge door shut with her hip and carried the cold, slimy bottles into the living room. She saw Kat and gave her a kiss. Everyone was milling around and she couldn't see anyone new in their midst. She had half an eye on Andy, who was goading her by pretending to yank at the sheet.

"Mads, I've got someone I'd like you to meet," said Kat.

"Jesus – she's not here, is she?" shouted Maddie excitedly. "What are you waiting for? Bring her in!"

Stepping aside, Kat said proudly: "Maddie, I'd like you to meet Miro."

The champagne bottles slipped out of Maddie's limp hands and careered towards the laminate flooring. As they exploded, the ear-splitting noise made Andy stagger backwards in terror. His fingers searched for something to steady himself with and closed around the dust sheet. The tape that held it in place was no match for Andy's body weight. Floundering to regain control, he stepped on an upturned plug, squealed again and plunged to the floor, taking the cover with him.

The cacophony of shattering glass and screams of pain and excitement as the big picture was finally revealed meant that no one really noticed the look of horror on Maddie's face.

More new fiction from Diva Books

The Ropemaker's Daughter
Virginia Smith

A gripping debut about truth, lies and pretenders

Rebecca habitually questions the people she meets and steals the
stories they tell her, claiming them for her own. But then she meets
a man whose story is already familiar, a man who says he knows her.
The real Adam threw himself off a cliff ten months earlier – so who
is this imposter, and what does he want? Enter Paige, who wants to
help Rebecca discover the truth about herself, about Adam – and
about love between women. But even she
may not be what she seems.

"A novel for the new millennium: passionate, compassionate,
intelligent, insightful, full of unexpected twists. I loved it. Smith
manages to sustain an aura of constant threat while exploring
the complex interplay between truth and deception. I read it in
one sitting. I defy you to do otherwise"
Manda Scott (author of *No Good Deed*)

RRP £8.99 ISBN 1-873741-70-7

Smother
Linda Innes

A dark comedy about the harm we cause each other

Mary has an obsession: to prove her devotion to Tanya, no matter what abuse she gets in return. But why are the two of them locked in conflict over the very nature of love? And what would it take to push Mary over the edge? As the story unfolds, memories and events show how each woman's relationship with her own mother has affected her adult love affairs. And now, it seems, someone will have to pay.

"A hugely enjoyable debut novel; a passionate journey through a landscape of damaged relationships. Innes writes beautifully with a divine eye for detail. This is a powerful new voice, exploring difficult and important territory, and it's immensely readable, too" Julia Darling (author, *Crocodile Soup*)

"A damned good read... Dialogue is the usual slangy mix of insult and humour but it's the narrative that drives this novel, sketching in terse, punning sentences the outlines of very dark secrets... Read it and weep" Rainbow Network

RRP £8.95 ISBN 1-873741-61-8

The Touch Typist
Helen Sandler

A tale of sanity, secrets and cybersex

Joss is going bonkers. She's being terrorised by her neighbour,
ignored by her girlfriend, marginalised by the boss and besieged
by mice. It's time to log on.

The Touch Typist is the first 'proper' novel from the author of the
highly improper *Big Deal*. In it, she explores what happens when
one woman's life begins to fall apart.

"Funny, witty, moving"
Ali Smith, author of *Hotel World*

**"A delight to read... light like a soap opera, but also moving and
thought-provoking" Rainbow Network**

**"This is one of those novels I wish I'd written myself. It's
unputdownable" *Kenric* magazine**

"Utterly readable" *Out Front Colorado*

RRP £8.95 ISBN 1-873741-65-0

*The first of the stunning new Red Hot Diva series:
wild sex for modern girls*

Cherry
Charlotte Cooper

Which lucky girl will pick Ramona's cherry?

Ramona is feisty and philosophical, flawed but sensitive, fierce and
funny and cute. *Cherry* is the super-sharp story of her
sexual adventures as she steps out in queer London, following her
fast-track progression from baby-dyke to scene face.

Desperate to pop her lesbian cherry, Ramona soon finds that shagging
women in real life bears little resemblance to the dirty books she's
been reading under the covers. Every dyke has to ditch the theory and
put herself out there if she wants to get some action and *Cherry* goes
all the way... Ramona pursues and is pursued by the coolest, hottest,
richest, wildest – and sometimes the saddest – girls around.

It's sexy. It's sassy. It's so, so slutty.

**"Modern, mucky, memorable, masturbatory dirt that delivers.
As Ramona would say, 'Lap it up!'" Babe of Rock Bitch**

RRP £8.99 ISBN 1-873741-73-1

How to order your new Diva Books

Diva Books are available from bookshops including Silver Moon at Foyles and Libertas! or direct from Diva's mail order service:
www.divamag.co.uk or freephone 0800 45 45 66
(international: +44 20 8340 8644).

When ordering direct, please add P&P (single item £1.75, two or more £3.45, all overseas £5) and quote the following codes:
Maddie & Anna's Big Picture MAD715, The Ropemaker's Daughter ROP707, Smother SMO618, The Touch Typist TOU650, Cherry CHE731